an anthology of cold horror

ABSOLUTE ZERO

Anne Woods • Bryan Holm • David Rider
E.J. Bramble • Frederick Street • G.M. Garner
Jay T. Dane • L.W. Young • Marcel Feldmar
Marzia La Barbera • Matt Dodge
Neil Williamson • William Jensen

DEATH'S HEAD PRESS

Published by Death's Head Press, an imprint of Dead Sky Publishing, LLC

Miami Beach, Florida

www.deadskypublishing.com

Cover by Anthony Galatis

Formatting and Design by Apparatus Revolution, LLC.

Edited by Anna Kubik, Megan Yundt, and Kristy Baptist

Copyedited by Megan Yundt & Jorja Jackson

ISBN 9781639512133 (paperback)

ISBN 9781639512317 (ebook)

It's antarctication.
Cryopreservation.
Icy annihilation — now you're blast frozen.
Winterized asphyxiation — now you're blast frozen.
Benumbed extermination — now you're blast frozen.
Nitrogen pure liquidation — now you're blast frozen.

A glacier on two legs,
Brumal bones and blood,
Numb and dead in frore freeze,
Accept your boreal demise.
Blast frozen. Blast frozen.

*Lyrics for BLAST FROZEN from the BROKEN HOPE album
"MUTILATED AND ASSIMILATED" 2017

CONTENTS

WATCH 'EM FREEZE
L.W. YOUNG

E ven though it had been snowing outside continuously for the last 10 years, it was the first time Henley felt truly cold.

"How..." Henley breathed smoke as he pointed a shivering finger towards the monitor, still not quite believing what he'd just watched, "how did you get this footage?"

But Woods was already going over to the other side of their small room, thumbing her frigid fingers against the touchscreen and disengaging the life support for the shelter below.

"Stop!" Henley cried, getting up so fast his chair fell over, "they'll all freeze if you do that!"

"These options must only be triggered in extreme circumstances, such as a full-scale invasion from IS05," flickering green letters on the humming monitor read, "are you sure you want to proceed?"

Henley gasped as Woods pushed 'Yes' right in front of him.

"Woods, we can't..."

She then spun around to face him, fire in her eyes.

"Stop standing up for them!" she jabbed a gloved finger at him, "Have you already forgotten what we just saw?"

Henley bit his tongue. He certainly hadn't forgotten, the canned laughter was still ringing in his ears.

"We need to think about this first," he attempted, "what if…"

"There's nothing to think about," Woods grunted, moving aside for him, "now, all you need to do is put your override password in too."

"Woods…"

"They deserve to die, Henley!" Woods almost screamed at him, smoke rising off her breath, "what kind of civilization would leave their own people to die in the freezing cold and treat it as entertainment!?"

Ignoring the howl that battered the encasing glass windows, Henley tried to think of some kind of rationale that could explain what they'd just watched. It had been a programme, under the guise of a 'family friendly' entertainment show, which had featured drone footage of poor, starving, innocent people trapped out in the icy cold for the purposes of the audience simply watching them slowly freeze to death. Meanwhile, a dapper host had boasted about the show's high ratings while an audience sat there and laughed from the comfort of a warm studio.

"Listen, perhaps it was faked," Henley said, trying to convince himself as much as her, "Before the Second Ice Age, society had come a long way with AI generated videos…"

"What difference does it make?" Woods cut him off, now on her feet, "Fake or not, this is what they get off on!"

Henley didn't want to believe it. Ten years ago, this place had seemed like a haven for him and his family. He had been able to sleep easy at night in this job knowing that his family were spared from certain death from the freezing wastes within the shelter of ISO343, even if it meant he didn't get to see them.

"There must be some mistake," Henley said as the life support consoles seemed to blink in thoughtful sympathy with him, "ISO343 is a shelter full of decent people, *exemplary* people of the old world. They wouldn't do something like this."

"But neither of us have any idea of what it's actually like down there, do we?" Woods scoffed, kicking an empty tin across the floor, "All we have is the propaganda they feed us 24/7."

Propaganda? Henley reeled, slightly offended that his vision of a pristine, white walled utopia below might only be a fantasy.

"How did you get that footage in the first place, Woods?" he asked, deflecting the topic.

Woods groaned, knocking her head against the terminal as if caught red handed.

"It's not important," Woods sighed, looking at the floor.

"This is serious, Woods! You need to tell me everything, understand?" he asserted, "Otherwise, we can't have a constructive dialogue about this."

Turning her head, still pressing it against the large screen, Woods chuckled at him.

"You're always acting like my dad, you know?" she sighed, rubbing her tired cheeks, "In a way, that might be what led to this whole mess in the first place."

Henley stepped back. Woods was giving him the same amused and knowing smile that she always defaulted too whenever having an argument with him. Sometimes, when work got tough, they'd argue over the last quarter's numbers, or perhaps some forgotten memory of the politics of the old world. However, every time it got heated, she'd always switch on this grin, and it would suddenly be over. 'You know, you're right' she'd sometimes just say like it only mattered to him and not her. It often felt like she was laughing at him.

"What are you talking about?" Henley asked patiently.

Woods grunted, pushed herself off the console and crashed back into her swivel chair, turning away from him.

"I have a secret to tell you, Henley," Woods sniffed, keeping the chair's back to him, "and you might not like it."

Woods and Henley had survived many a cold night in this God-forsaken control room with only a plug-in heater and a nostalgic story to keep them company. They were a team, especially after 10 years, and he doubted there was anything Woods could say that would change that at this point.

"I'm listening," Henley said, "just say what you have to say."

Woods took a deep breath.

"I have a personal contact inside the shelter, inside ISO343, okay?" she confessed, nodding to herself, "It's how I received the footage of that... show."

"What?" Henley leant in towards her, "You knew about this all along?"

"No! No, but only because I'd been asking for *other* kinds of media," she panicked, eyes darting away in embarrassment, "I... I was lonely, you see... so I used him to get me certain... adult media."

"Adult media?" Henley shimmied into view.

"You know the kind of stuff I mean," Woods groaned miserably, pushing away, "before the Ice Age, we used to call it 'porn'."

Henley immediately stood up and backed away from her, cheeks red.

"Oh," Henley blushed, "I... see."

There was a round of awkward silence as Henley felt his cheeks glowing hot despite the cold.

"So, exactly what kind of stuff did this 'contact' send you?" Henley sniffed, trying to sound casual, "was it anything like what we just watched?"

"Of course not!" Woods shook her head, "but there was still, well... it's... embarrassing to talk about..."

Henley put his hands on the woman's shoulders, forcing her to look up at him.

"Woods, a few seconds ago you were seriously talking about killing everyone down there," Henley's eyes bore into her, "I need to know!"

Woods inhaled a shuddery breath. The woman was close to tears.

"Okay, well, there was a lot of... debauchery, hedonism, and masochistic stuff on some of the tapes I received," she clenched, wiping her eyes, "and I'm not certain all of it was consensual..."

Henley took a second to process the information.

"But you still watched it?" he asked.

Woods hugged her jacket tighter around her fading blue boiler suit and hid her freckled face behind a dangling fringe of drab, brown hair.

"I wanted to stop but, I... I kept getting lonely," she gulped, rocking back and forth, "I kept relapsing."

Henley said nothing. After studying her in silence for a moment, Henley took a deep breath and went over to the emergency phone which was holstered in a cream white receiver by the emergency exit elevator. There was only one button on the phone which would link Henley to his superiors down in the shelter. Henley's hand hovered over it.

"Don't, Henley," Woods chased after him, getting up from her chair, "please don't rat me out!"

"I'm sorry Woods, but you should have told me about this sooner," Henley told her as softly as he could, his finger still trembling, unable to go any lower, "I'm sorry for you, but I can't compromise my job over this."

"Please," she grabbed his arm, tugging the receiver away, "I don't want to get in trouble!"

Henley tried to fight back but was caught off guard as Wood's swatted the phone from his hand, leaving it dangling against the wall.

"Why would your contact send something like this?" he asked, honestly looking for an excuse to stall.

"I... I don't know," Woods stepped back, "Maybe he's been trying to influence me this whole time. Maybe he's against ISO343 too."

"But why now?"

"I just told you..."

"No, I'm not talking about that, I mean why should *we punish* ISO343 now?" Henley jolted himself back into motion, pacing back to the viewing port and looking out into the cold oblivion beyond it.

"What do you mean?" Woods asked.

"After years of living up here together, sharing the same toilet, and eating the same food every day," Henley addressed, stalking the room, "meanwhile, the people of ISO343 have running water, hot meals, and God knows what else to do at their leisure thanks to us, what gives us the right to judge them *now*?"

Henley stopped travelling and faced her dead on, expecting an answer. Between them, the distance was the widest it had been since this nightmare evening had started. Woods tittered.

"Come on Henley, we've shared many stories of what the Earth used to be like before all this snow," she sighed, her eyes glassy with nostalgia, "Green grass, summer breeze, bird song..."

Henley honestly didn't remember, and he didn't care to.

"We used to have all of that," she continued, inhaling a heavy sigh of the cold air before casting a new, vengeful stare towards the ground, "and *they* took it from us!"

Uneasily, Henley's eyes scanned the room for an answer from one of these infernal, beeping machines. He'd gotten used to the sounds over the years, but tonight they were proving intolerable.

"The inhabitants of ISO343 were appointed by the last governments of the old world," he recited soberly, not able to look at her, "they're the best of humanity."

"Or so we've been told," Woods countered, "But what if they're actually spoiled, rich psychos, no different from the other shelters who attack us every week? What if this tape proves it?!"

Henley shut his eyes, almost wishing he could fall asleep and escape from this discussion entirely.

"Even so," Henley said instead, a sad smile floating to his face, "they aren't to blame for what happened to our planet, are they?"

"Not to blame? The Epsteins, Rockefellers, and Trumps of the world all *paid* for their spot in these shelters after the second ice age," Woods crossed her arms indignantly at him, "Meanwhile, the innocent majority with no say were left to fend for themselves, and most of them died in the process..."

"Exactly."

The one-word utterance caught Woods off guard.

"What!?" she choked, "What do you mean 'exactly'?"

With his muscles loosening again, Henley clapped his hands decisively, locking eyes with Woods.

"Woods, blaming the remnants of humanity means blaming the *majority* of humanity at this point. It's our duty as guardsmen to preserve these people, even if they don't deserve it," he stated flatly.

Silence.

The distance between Woods and Henley was now wider than it had ever been.

"You're really happy to remain a bootlicker for these psychopaths?" she crossed her arms at him, surprised and disappointed, "You're happy to serve the people who would gladly watch you freeze to death for their own amusement, and call it a privilege?"

"It *is* a privilege," Henley shrugged, "You may have accepted this job out of mere desperation, Woods, but I did it to protect my family. They're safe inside the walls of ISO343."

"Safe?"

"Yes."

There was a second or two more of silence, except the howling wind and beeping consoles, before Woods walked up closer to him.

"You never thought it was strange that they don't let you see them in person?" she hushed seriously, "Not even through a video call?"

Henley grimaced. Weirdly, it felt like it was getting even *colder* in here.

"Henley, I hate to be the one to break this to you," Wood's tone was oddly soft, "but if these tapes show what the culture is really like down there, your family is probably long dead."

Then, Woods had her hands on him, caressing his shoulders. The feeling of her hands on him sent a distressingly pleasant shiver down Henley's spine.

"Woods," Henley trembled under her grip, "please, don't..."

"Listen, Henley, I've been playing all the same points in my own head over and over again for all these years," she hushed in his ear, "but all it did was prevent me from acting sooner."

With that last line, her fingernails grabbed him, digging into the knots in his muscles. Henley winced.

"Deep down, we've always sensed something was wrong with this place, haven't we?" she breathed, sounding excited, "let's finally do something about it."

She slid a hand around his waist, dangerously close to his buttock, and pulled him close to her.

"How..." Henley trembled, his lips dangerously close to hers, "how would we even survive out there?"

"We won't need to leave. I've been stashing my protein pills, enough for us to last a year, maybe even longer," Woods's breath tickled his ear, "then, when the colony eventually thaws out again, we'll have the place all to ourselves."

Henley bit off a gasp.

"No..."

"Henley, I can't take this anymore," Woods now pinned him against the wall, her words turning into primal growls that warmed his face, "We must exterminate those *fuckers* downstairs. We have the power!"

Henley fought to keep his eyes away from her as he stared off. Instead, he looked out through the frost covered glass of the nearest window. It was so dark out there; he could mainly see his own reflection with tears brewing in his eyes as Woods writhed against him hungrily.

'I can't deny my life's work,' he thought, shaking his head, 'I can't deny my family!'

"Just let me think..." he said instead trying to struggle out of her grasp.

"I'm done thinking," Woods howled like a wolf under a full moon as she threw him back against the wall, "it's time to act!"

With that, Woods grabbed Henley's hand and tried to pull him back towards the control room's main terminal.

"Come on," she purred, her eyes full of a primal hunger, "let's just DO IT!"

Henley was scared. This was exactly the kind of encounter that he'd spent the last ten years trying to avoid. He wasn't going to give into his temptations now, he had to resist. He still had a family; he couldn't betray them!

Henley shoved her away. She toppled over.

"Oh shit!" Henley realised, "Woods, I'm sorry!"

Flailing her arms for support, Woods lost her balance and went down.

"Hang on Woods," Henley finally came back to his senses, making a dive to catch her, "I've got you!"

But it was too late. Woods yelped as, halfway down, she hit her head on the sharp edge of the bulky monitor. There was a dull thump as her woolly hat went flying off. She landed in a heap on the floor with her hair splayed out.

"Woods!" Henley raced over to her.

Henley crouched down beside her. At first, she didn't seem to be breathing.

"Woods?" Henley hushed as he started shaking her by the shoulders, "*Woods*?"

Henley jumped up backwards, almost tripping over his feet. He thought he could see blood.

'What have I done?' he thought with his hand over his mouth, 'what in God's name have I done!?'

"Woods!" he panicked, "speak to me!"

Henley flipped her over. She wasn't moving. The gash was hidden beneath her hairline. Blood matted her hair like paint. Henley wrung her limp hand in his as his eyes flitted around the room for a first aid kit. It had been almost a *decade* since he'd received first aid training...

Then, she stirred.

"Woods?" he looked down, "oh, thank GOD!"

Grabbing her arm in both of his hands, Henley realised that Woods was twitching, and soft breath was still whistling through her lips. She was alive.

"Thank God," Henley repeated, collapsing onto his backside, "thank God..."

However, he didn't have a second to lose. Swiftly remembering the conflict which had led to this moment, Henley realised that he only had a short time to resolve this before she woke up fully. Setting her down gently, Henley made his way over to the phone and pushed the button to be connected to his supervisor, all the way in the depths of the city. He needed to tell them what was happening. Woods was clearly under a lot of stress, and it was making her act irrational, tape or no tape. Maybe, if he did this now, he could get her the help she needed without getting into an argument over it.

"Please hold," the emotionless female voice requested again as Henley heard the hold music.

Henley waited there for almost five minutes as the twinkling, chiming hold music taunted him. This just wouldn't do. Henley slammed the phone back in the receiver. He now had no choice but to use the emergency elevator and try to get medical assistance from the city directly. Henley sure as hell hoped it still worked.

"I'm sorry Woods," Henley told her as he stepped over her twitching body and grabbed the elevator's key from his desk, not even sure if she could hear him, "but this is for your own good..."

The elevator down had been a hellish ride, grinding and groaning, as the gears and cables battled the environmental damage done by the extreme cold from many years of disuse. Eventually, Henley made it to the bottom floor.

He found himself in a long, empty hanger. He'd been walking in a straight line for 15 minutes and was just starting to see the main colony gates looming up ahead. The black walls around him, glistening like freshly cut marble, were coated in a reflective resin which bounced his lonely footfalls back at him.

'Temperature resistant coating,' Henley knew, 'after the tricks ISO5 have tried using over the years, we owe it our lives.'

Henley pondered his use of that word as he travelled. We. Would the people inside the colony think the same of him? After all, they had set up plenty of distance between his and Woods's control room and the place where ISO343's *real* citizens ate, slept, worked, researched, made love, and made sick televised programmes...

He shook his head, 'let me just focus on getting help for Woods, Jesus.'

The gate itself was more like a chrome wall, reaching about a mile upwards towards the roof of the tunnel, with little in the way of defining features save for a thin parting line down the centre.

From the little time he'd spent in the ISO343 interior city, he knew their architecture consisted of austere, brutalist minimalism just like this. Beneath him was a length of train tracks embedded in the floor, extending from underneath the gate towards where Henley was approaching from. There was a solid red light hanging from above showing that nothing was currently permitted to pass.

"Hello!" he called, his words echoing around him, "I need to talk to someone, is anyone there?"

From one of the control spires, a black clad figure instantly popped out with his rifle raised. Henley froze as he saw multiple green targeting lasers shoot out from unseen hiding spots and aim at his forehead and chest.

"I'm a friend!" Henley gulped, raising his arms, "I'm Facilities Operations Officer David Henley, I'm from the control room..."

Before Henley could speak further, a team of armed guards had swarmed out of their hiding spots and were upon him.

"On the ground!" a fierce voice to his left commanded, "Face down!"

"Okay," Henley obliged, trying to sound polite, "I'm doing it..."

Attempting to do what he was told was the last thing Henley recalled before being struck on the back of his head and knocked out cold.

Henley awoke to see a single overhead lamp blazing down, hurting his eyes. In the corners of his vision, there were shadows roaming about the darkened room, circling him. Henley's arms, legs, and head were strapped to a slab underneath him, he couldn't move.

"W... what's going on?" he slurred, "Where am I?"

The shapes in the room ignored him. All he could hear was the slow, thoughtful beeping of his heart rate being monitored and the hum of the room's central heating. Punctuating this was the soft tinkling of medical equipment at the other side of the room. Was he in a medical station? Why was he strapped down so tightly?

A door whooshed open. The thick stomp of heavy stormtrooper boots entered the room.

"Report," a cold, bored voice requested.

"We found his partner up in that messy control room," the guard's voice crackled through the speaker on his helmet, "looks like he killed her."

Strapped to the table, Henley's heart seized up.

Killed her?

"Is that so?" the disinterested voice replied, muffled by his medical mask, "Pity, we'll need two more Facilities Operations Officers after this."

"I doubt any of our own stock would be willing, that job stinks," the guard returned, "Besides, I was under the impression there was too much work to be done down here."

"Don't worry," the medical officer responded, "I'm sure we can farm some poor soul from the surface desperate for a lifestyle upgrade."

The guard chuckled.

"Woods was breathing when I left her, are you sure she was really dead?" Henley struggled against his restraints, "please, I'm not a murderer!"

"He needs another sedative shot," the guard commented, walking over to them.

"Why waste it?" the doctor replied, "I'll be done with him shortly."

A shadow passed over him, and Henley found himself staring up at the black outline of a man in medical scrubs.

"Station Officer No. 02 has clearly suffered a severe mental lapse, I suppose ten years in virtual isolation will do that," the medical officer asserted, not really looking at him, "regardless, he's no longer fit to operate the ISO343 control room."

"You've got it all wrong!" Henley tried his best to sound sane, "Listen, I have a family down here, they'll vouch for me!"

The shadow loomed closer, revealing a hawkish, balding man with circular spectacles, smiling at Henley piteously.

"I'm afraid you're very much mistaken, Sir. Our records show that you have no family down here. Never did," he said softly, "We only responded to your rambling messages to keep you placated."

"W... What are you talking about?" Henley muttered.

The medical officer simply walked away.

"Hey!" Henley shouted after him, "Answer me!"

"What will we do with him now?" the main guard asked from the corner of the room, "Use his body for research?"

"No," the medical officer waved his hand, "Just... *dispose* of him, would you?"

❄

Henley showed no resistance as a masked, black-clad guard wheeled his gurney from the darkened lab and through a series of upward slanting corridors and silent elevators until they reached a bulkhead door.

"Here we are, champ," the guard said, dropping the gurney so Henley was facing forward, "time for your 'disposal,'"

Still strapped to the gurney, Henley was staring. Webs of ice glistened in the corners of the door, shimmering like diamonds. Outside, he heard the familiar whisper of gale-force snowstorms battering the hull.

"Oh God," Henley gulped, a single tear falling down his face, "how can you do this to me?"

"Relax, it'll be over before you know it," the guard assured, approaching the door, "think warm thoughts."

But Henley wasn't thinking about the cold. He was thinking about what the doctor had said. Henley had never had a family after all. Were his memories all implanted or something? Was *that* the kind of research that was being done down here in ISO343?

Henley could distinctly recall his memories with vivid detail: the bitter cold of the nights his family had spent in the old slum district, hugging their bodies together to preserve heat, and the hungry days when the intense winds had stopped them from reaching the nearest food shelter. The gruelling task of teaching his wide-eyed, seven-year-old son to defend himself from raiders ("go for the eyes," Henley had told him), and his daughter once begging him to comb her hair one morning, only for the strands to be too clumped with ice for him to sift the comb through. But he also remembered the good times, huddling around a wood fire and telling stories, just as he had once done with Woods, while his kids listened with excitement. He remembered each time Henley and his wife had told them that everything was going to be alright in the end.

He *knew* those sensations. They couldn't be faked.

Woods…

The poor woman was surely the only other person on this planet he'd ever shared such a deep sense of companionship with, and he'd *killed* her. Did someone like him even deserve to live?

At the swipe of the guard's identity card on a wall panel, the bulkhead door groaned open. The sighing of pistons and the rattle of gears quickly gave way to the howl and chill of the biting wind as it rushed inside. The guard raised his arm to protect himself from the open elements. Beyond the pale light from their corridor was endless black, specked with fast-travelling snow. Henley couldn't tell if it was night or day, it was always like this whenever he looked outside.

Henley's tears froze on his face.

"I'll come back for the gurney once the cold has finished you off," the guard clapped, planting a firm grip on the gurney, and wheeling him forward, "Adios, I wish it didn't have to be like this, but I've got to follow the rules, you know? I've got a pension to worry about."

"Wait! At least tell me what happened to my family!" Henley begged as he was pushed forwards, "I have to know!"

"You don't have a family, buddy, weren't you listening to the doc?" the guard shrugged, "Never did."

"It must be some mistake; I *know* my family is down here!" Henley wailed, tugging at his restraints as he felt snow crunching under the gurney's wheels, "My name's Henley, David Henley, there should be records from when we moved into this shelter. Please just check!"

Suddenly, the wheels stopped in the snow.

"Wait a minute, did you say: 'Henley'?" the guard now asked, calling over the wind and shifting around to meet him face on, "*David* Henley?"

"T… that's right," Henley shivered, the cold of the metal gurney stinging his back.

Pacing, his boots crunching in the snow, the guard pondered.

"Why does that name sound so familiar?" the guard repeated thoughtfully.

With that, the guard suddenly pivoted the gurney back through the snow and wheeled it inside. Behind him, Henley heard the hiss of the pressurised bulkhead closing as the wind noise dipped out again. The air became mercifully warmer, and he started to regain feeling in his fingers and toes.

"What are you doing!?" Henley struggled against his gurney, "What's going on!?"

"Relax," the guard said, unclipping the straps on his helmet, "we're on the same side, Dave."

The guard unclipped Henley's restraints and removed his own helmet, revealing a slim, ginger haired young man with freckles and pronounced Adam's apple. As Henley fell forward off his gurney and rubbed his freed wrists, the young man held out his hand for Henley to shake.

"The name's Fox," he said with a plucky, buck toothed grin, "I was Woods's contact on the inside."

Henley stared into the guard's hazel eyes and cautiously accepted the handshake.

"Woods?" Henley trembled, his hand feeling very limp despite being almost twice the kid's size, "is... is she really dead?"

"Afraid so, champ," Fox winced, rubbing the nape of his neck, "You really did a number on her up there."

Henley's heart broke and he put his hand on his chest, collapsing against the wall.

"You okay, boss?" Fox laughed, "Having a heart attack or something?"

"I... I didn't mean to hurt her," Henley clenched his face, looking down shamefully. "It was an accident."

"Relax, I'm not here to judge," Fox rubbed his shoulder, "besides, I didn't know the chick too well myself, only that she was into some freaky shit. Fortunately for her, the media factories of ISO343 were *more* than able to oblige her tastes."

"So, it's true," Henley now looked him in the eyes, "this place, ISO343, the population is full of..."

"Amoral sadists with no sense of shame? Surely, you've seen that for yourself by now, haven't you?" Fox flashed him a grin, "But don't worry, Dave, I figure we can take this place down from the inside now. Together. You with me?"

Fox gripped Henley's hands in his black, padded gloves. Henley studied him in return. It seemed Woods had been right all along; her contact was working against the colony and had been trying to turn them too. Despite this, Henley found himself angry.

"My family," Henley pressed him, withdrawing his hands from Fox's grip, "You said you recognised my name; does that mean you know about them?"

The cocky expression on Fox's face slackened.

"Well, yeah, kind of," he sighed, eyes cast downwards, "but, here, listen..."

Before he could finish, Henley grabbed his shoulders and pushed him against the far wall.

"Where are they?" Henley demanded.

"Whoa, whoa, slow down buddy," Fox raised his arms with a nervous smile, "They're not here anymore, okay?"

Henley released him, heart pounding in his chest.

"I'm sorry, I just..." Henley attempted to coordinate himself, "What happened to them?"

Hesitantly, Fox took something off his belt and showed it to Henley. Henley squinted, not recognising the little device. It looked like a hand-sized, black mirror. Henley was startled when the small, flat screen sparked to life and started playing a video. No way could the video monitors in the control room fit into the palm of your hand like this.

"I have something to show you, partner," Fox began, pushing the device in Henley's face, "but you're probably not going to like it..."

❄

After taking Fox up to the control room via the emergency elevator, Fox had shown him the footage of the infamous premiere episode of Watch 'Em Freeze a second time, just to clear up any remaining doubt. Fox leaned silently against one of the consoles as Henley collapsed into Woods's swivel chair and held the thin screen in his hands, fat tears falling as the dreadful footage played out. There was no mistaking it, these 'contestants' were *his* family.

"I'm so sorry, Davey boy," Fox placed a hand on Henley's shoulder, "I'm just... so sorry."

Henley hardly heard him. The footage had shown Henley's wife, son, and daughter, beaten, and bruised, being dragged by black-clad guards through a shelter bulkhead, and then tossed out into the cold like sacks of human garbage.

The lens of a drone hovered above the shivering form of his family, cast in a spotlight. Henley's wife had held the kids close, mouthing for them not to be scared. Her words were inaudible over the laughter coming from a delighted studio audience.

"Turn it off..." Henley breathed, pawing ineffectively a the screen with his gloved mitts, "Please..."

"What?"

"TURN IT OFF!"

Hurriedly, Fox dotted his finger on his portable screen. For a while, Henley was too numb to react. Woods's body remained silent on the floor next to them where it lay wrapped in a blue tarp. They couldn't even be bothered to move her.

Behind him, Fox gripped Henley's shoulder.

"So, Dave," Fox said by his side, "are we doing this, or what?"

Sinking deeper into his chair, Henley clutched his head in his hands, immobilised by anguish.

"Listen Dave, I appreciate how difficult this is for you, but the other guards will soon be wondering why I haven't reported in," Fox insisted, gripping him tighter, "they could be up here any second, and our chance for revenge will be gone. It's now or never!"

With that, Henley raised his head. His wet eyes were burning with rage.

"Let's do it," Henley uttered, feeling oddly serene, "Let's see how *they* like it!"

"My man," Fox hushed, lifting Henley by his shoulders, and guiding him towards the room's main terminal, "now, all you've gotta do is input your code, okay?"

"Right..."

In a trance, Henley floated over to the looming, black screen and summoned the correct series of input windows, following the exact same process he'd seen Woods complete earlier.

"That's it," Fox nodded excitedly while helping Henley move his trembling fingers across the screen, "you're doing great."

Henley input his code. The computer thought about it for a few seconds before the light in its circuitry went completely dim. Then, a thunderous jolt shook the room, travelling up from the underground connecting shaft to the colony as all the shelter exits were sealed tight and the air filtration supply was severed. Inside the control room, the humming of the surrounding computer terminals went completely dead.

All lights in the room popped out and were replaced by a soft, red glow from a single emergency lamp on the ceiling. In the flat screen of the main console, Henley saw his warped reflection staring back at him in black and red. Outside, all they could hear was the wind.

"There," Henley gulped, "it's done."

"Fantastic, the entire colony should last about a month," Fox sighed in relief behind him, clapping his hands together with finality, "Anyone who doesn't freeze to death should starve."

"Right..." Henley bowed his head, already aware.

"That wasn't so hard, was it?" Fox slapped Henley on the shoulder, "Don't worry, it'll take them a while to figure out what has happened, by which point we'll be too far away to hear their screams."

Screams. Henley side-eyed Fox, disturbed by the pleasure he seemed to be taking in this.

Fox hurried over to one of the office's viewing ports and cupped both hands around the emergency exit handle.

"Right, I've arranged for an air lift via drone to carry me out of here," Fox said, checking his watch, "I can't believe it, I'm finally going home!"

"Home?" Henley asked.

Ignoring him, Fox yanked the handle of the viewing port upwards with both arms. The window blew outwards in a burst of ice and glass. Wind and slurry from outside rushed in, drenching the useless computer consoles. Henley was forced to raise his arm to protect himself from the spitting snow, like tiny razors.

"Wait!" Henley shouted over the wind, "What about me?"

"Oh yeah," Fox slapped his helmet absentmindedly, "almost forgot..."

Casually, Fox whipped a pistol out from his belt and shot Henley in the chest. The sound of the silenced handgun was barely audible over the wind. The impact caught Henley so off guard he didn't believe it had happened at first, not even when he touched his wound and saw blood sticking to his fingers.

Henley had time to look up before collapsing against the wall, leaving an imprint of red as he slipped down and landed next to Woods on the floor. It was only then, that he saw that the ice blue tarp had soaked up a lot of blood around her head area, far more than he'd initially left.

Supporting himself on one arm, Henley tried to crawl under Woods' table for shelter. However, Fox dragged him out. Blood leaving him rapidly, he pulled Henley in close for a final embrace. Fox shouted into Henley's ear over the wind.

"Watch 'Em Freeze is actually the highest rated programme in *our* colony," Fox explained, feigning sympathy, "Once I get back to ISO5, I'm looking forward to watching it live again."

"Y...you're..." Henley trembled, colder than he'd ever felt in his life, "a... plant...?"

"Yep," Fox patted him on the shoulder, "don't worry, I shot you in the gut, so you'll have plenty of time to dwell on what an idiot you've been, yeah?"

"You're..." Henley's teeth clenched, trying to make his last words impactful, "you're... just... as bad... as us..."

Surprisingly, the statement had some effect. Fox reeled, inhaling a sharp gasp.

"Come on now, ISO343 are snobby eggheads, sure, but you guys are *way* too full of your own moral pride to enjoy the suffering of lesser beings," he laughed, leaning in closer, "That's why you lost today."

Fox patted him glibly on the shoulder before walking away.

"We'll be back to take this colony in a few months once it's thawed out," Fox turned his back on Henley and offered a departing wave, "Adios, Davey boy."

Before Fox could make it back across the floor, Henley managed to wrap his freezing fingers around the man's boot. Barely using any strength, Fox shook it off and continued walking. Outside, the chop of reinforced drone blades could be heard scything through the wind towards the open window, ready to pick up its passenger.

"My... family!" Henley clawed after him, leaving a snail-trail of blood across the floor.

"We captured them during our raid nine years ago, must have been before you people updated your population records," Fox laughed while lighting a pop flare from his utility belt, and waving it out of the window, "it was the famous premier episode of the show, man! I wouldn't delete it for anything."

Henley was hardly able to hear the man anymore as he continued gloating. All he knew, as ice seemed to pump through his veins, was that Woods was lying on the floor beside him. Sleeping. Even though her body was concealed, her form was still the most beautiful thing in this cold, cold world. Henley managed to raise his shaking arm around her and pull himself close. Fox, ignoring him, leapt from the window and disappeared into the night.

Henley hugged Woods' body.

Perhaps they could finally sleep together...

THE GUEST IN THE ICE
E.J. BRAMBLE

I found you, cold and stiff and frozen, and I am taking you home. Silly thing. Hidden under that jut of ice as you were they'd probably never find you, even if they looked. I did, though. You can thank me for that later. Goodness knows what you were doing under there in the middle of winter. It's lucky I was taking a walk through the mountains and happened to see your shoe poking out of the snow and was brave enough to drag you out by your ankle, revealing the rest of you to me, perfectly preserved. Dark trousers, blue coat, cold cheeks, red hat. You would have been there till spring if I hadn't saved you. But I did. And aren't you a right beauty? Yes, you'll be just fine. Oh look, you can see the house down there now. I left the lights on so we could find our way back. Almost home now, love. Oh, I'm going to take such good care of you.

We get home safely before long, just as I promised. The door closes loudly behind us and the hot air rushes up to my cheeks, burning ferociously. I swear under my breath. I had not thought that I would find you today. I had not prepared. I must act quickly.

The rock-hard lump of you drags down the cellar steps and I shove you into the freezer, following you in, the sweat that had started building beneath my hat from the heat of the house instantly turning to tiny shards of ice that flitter to the floor as I whip it off. My ears, cold and then hot and then cold, throb.

I have other things to worry about than the pathetic mess of my own body though, like the frozen one I have curled up in my house. I look down at you for only seconds before I fall to my knees, overwhelmed with appreciation, and I take you into my arms and rock you a little, being careful not to overheat you. You do not talk, do not even move, or blink your eyes, but I do not expect anything from you. You are fine as you are, there is no pressure. I know it has been a rough few hours. Days? Weeks? How long had you been left out there? I am sorry I did not walk that way sooner. But I have you now. You are safe.

I will keep you.

I promise.

And I do.

It has been nine days now, and I have been caring for you. You can stay as long as you want, of course. For the winter, at the very least. You clearly are not safe to be left out there alone. And I promise I will never bore of you or kick you from my house.

I check on you at least once a day, my most visits so far sitting at fifty-eight.

On the first morning, I lugged you into a chair before the small wooden table, and it is there that you wait for me, each time.

I am sorry, I must say now, for leaving you so unceremoniously sprawled on the floor that first night, but you must understand that I did not have any scrap of strength left in me after bringing you home. You are heavy, and large, so wrapped up in your clothes, but even they could not keep you safe from the cold. I have let you keep them, of course, to protect you from the chill, as best they can, and they shine out from beneath the translucence that encases you. Blue and red. To match your fingertips and your cheeks.

Obediently, since that first morning, you have sat in that chair, positioned just so you can see me coming through the door. Waiting for me, like a dog. Your eyes gleam from within, a twinkle dancing in them wherever you see me, I am sure of it, and I sit opposite you, eating meals with you, and keeping an eye on the thermostat, and smoothing the ice gently with a pumice should it fall out of shape around you.

And I talk to you.

There are not many people around the mountains at this time of year, which is why I was so surprised to see you, and I am so grateful that I did, because you would have died out there, and you are such a good listener, and I can tell already that I love you exactly as you are.

I stay late with you tonight. It is so hard for me to leave you, but I cannot stay in the freezer, even though I have lived all my life in the cold. Modern amenities have made me soft. I need my sheets and my radiators and my candles, and I worry that my hot breath in the night would melt your precious little cheeks. I could not stand to hurt you so. So, I must leave now, I am afraid, only for a few hours, and you will probably enjoy the peace, I am sure. I can go on just a little bit when I am alone in this big house in the middle of nowhere surrounded by snow. So, I am sure you will enjoy the quiet, but I will make sure not to stay away too long for I don't want you to be lonely without me.

I take the plates away, mine empty and yours full but I cannot blame you for that and will not scold you or throw you out for I love you just the way you are. I take the plates away and I wash them in the sink, the hot water scalding my numbed fingers, and I leave them to dry on the side, and then I walk around the house and make sure every light is off.

I have not seen any of them yet. The ones that follow my guests, sometimes. The red coats and the yellow stripes and the white hats. The flash of their lights echoing and bouncing off the rocks and the snow. The whirring of the helicopter rotors. I have not seen them yet, but they might still appear, and it would not do for them to come knocking on my door and disturbing us, so I will hide us away in the night and nobody will get to us.

You poor thing. Isn't anybody looking for you? I looked for you. I found you. I love you. I will take care of you.

It is early afternoon now and I have been watching you all day, sitting on your chair and gazing at me lovingly, but I need to collect logs from the shed for my pathetic body. I am sorry, my love. I will try not to be long.

I make my way to the back door, and I slip out quickly, already dressed for the snow from my visit to you, but on the step, I stop, letting the cold air rush into the house. Slowly, I pull the door closed behind me and glance furtively around. Something is not right. I can see the expanse of the mountains laid out before me and they are completely deserted, but I am sure those should not be there.

The lone trail of footprints, walking up to the kitchen window and away again.

I lean towards one. Fresh. Still stinking a little of leather. I am a little disquieted, but the mountains are abandoned now, so perhaps these are just the final wanderings of a lost soul looking for somewhere else to die. It is a shame, slightly. Perhaps I would have enjoyed saving them. But don't worry. I have you and I love you and I would never replace you. You are safe where you are.

I grab a shovel from the shed, and I cover up the footprints, lest you were to get jealous, and I take the logs inside and I lock every door and every window, and I close every curtain. But do not worry. I am not scared. I will take care of everything. I just don't want anybody to pry on us. You are too special. We are safe, I promise. I am making us some dinner, and I am placing yours in front of you and making polite conversation with you. There is nothing unusual about anything.

I am eating a stew this evening, and it burns my stomach deliciously. It is a wonder you don't crack right out of the ice to eat your bowl and lick it clean with a groan. I know you would simply adore my cooking if you were to only just try it. I don't blame you for not, of course, but even so.

I move the bowl slightly closer to you, across the table we are sitting around, and I chomp down on a piece of fatty deliciousness. I moan and the sound bounces off the ice around us delightfully and I wonder if you can hear me. I wonder if you wish you could make me do that. I could make you; I am sure. Starting with my cooking.

I move the bowl a little closer again. I know you would like some. Am I teasing you? Maybe you will be able to at least smell it if I move it nearer. I could even find a screwdriver and hollow out your nostrils, so you could know of the stew and of me. I want you to be able to know me.

Once more, I inch it closer, the rich scent rushing up towards the icicles above us and I can almost imagine I see your face flicker, your chest rise and fall with a deep breath.

Excited, I climb onto the table and crawl towards you, drooling onto the wood and into your bowl. I would give anything to watch your face as you eat something I gave you, made for you, slaved over for you. I would not even be angry if you did not like it. You could spit it out, I will not be mad.

I cup the bowl in my hands, and they sizzle against the heat, and I bring it up a little higher, a little closer, but not too close, I do not want the steam to melt your precious cheeks. Can you smell it? That must be almost as good as eating it, right? Does it permeate the ice? Will you come out smelling like stew and like me?

You do not move, and I rest it once more in front of where I am kneeling on the table before you, worshipping you, taking you in. It is alright. I understand that you do not want to eat my food. It is just simple mountain food. And I am not sure that you trust me yet, despite me saving you and dragging you home and keeping you safe. Because you are safe. So safe. As safe as you have ever been. I will take care of you, and I promise I would never poison your food. Look I will eat some too, just to prove it.

I stick my fingers into the stew, breathing in at the heat against my icy hands, and I bring it to my face, leaning in and guzzling it from the palm of my hand.

I shiver. It is beautiful, and to be kneeling before you, having you watch me, is perhaps even more sumptuous than a decadent meal. You are all I need. And I am all you need. We have everything we need right here, right? Even if it is just for the winter?

I lift my face from my savoury palm to look back towards you, deploring, begging, pleading, and I catch the little flicker of movement.

I freeze, my eyes running across your ice, not comprehending where it had come from. Your eyes, your mouth, your chest.

Do it again, I whisper.

Your finger twitches. Minute. A momentous effort for so little. You poor thing.

But how could I let this happen? The thermostat is cold enough. My lips are blue, and my toes are numb. How. How.

I kneel and I watch. The tiniest shake of you. A mountain of steam curling up from the bowl, wrapping around your finger like I wish I could. Sizzling.

My swears echo in the freezer.

How could I be so stupid? Distracted by my obscene thoughts. I bat the bowl of stew from before my knees and it smashes against the cold metal of the floor, brown slop splattering across the freezer, steaming and sizzling and melding. After it, I follow, flinging myself to the ground, the pain shooting dully through my cold knees, and desperately I scrape chunks of ice into my arms and drop them before you like an offering.

They fall to the floor, and I wail, scrambling back to my knees before you and balancing scoops of crushed coldness onto your stomach and chest, packing them around your finger until it takes.

I am sorry. I do not want you to see me like this. I am just a little flustered, what with the footprints and the stew and the melting and the twitching. What? The footprints? No, we don't have to worry about them, it's fine. I'm all yours, I promise. There we go, just keep that there and you'll be all better by morning.

As best I can I clean up the frozen stew, blushing under your unfaltering stare, and then I lock you up safe for the night, make sure the house is completely closed, go up to bed, and try not to think.

There are still footprints in the snow the next morning, although I am sure I covered them. Perhaps the wind blew the fresh piles away, although when I stand in the open there is no breeze against my cheeks. They walk to the window and back, as before, but this time they make their way to the door, too. It seems unlikely I missed seeing those yesterday, but perhaps I was too busy. I stand over them with my hands on my hips and I stare at them as if they will give me the answers.

They do not give any and the mountains are empty.

It is only me.

Tentatively, I walk around in my boots, placing them in the hollows, but it was a long shot I know. The soles of me slither around in the far too large space.

Just a lost stranger with their hulking big feet. Miles away by now. Frozen in ice.

Today I flatten them out before I cover them in snow. They will not bother us again. I will lock the doors though, just to be safe, before I take my cereal and milk down to you.

Nothing for you today, I am afraid. I am sorry to say that I am still not happy about how you reacted to the stew that I had cooked. Perhaps it was a little my fault for pushing the steaming bowl so close to you, but mostly it was all yours. Cereal and milk will not harm you, but I do not think you deserve it today. I will still sit opposite you, of course, for I would never abandon you, but I will not talk.

As I eat you watch me unwaveringly and I have to hide the small smile that threatens to sneak out onto my face. I am still angry, stop it you little devil. But of course, you are still mine and I take such good care of you. Even when I don't like you, I still love you. So, when I am finished with my bowl, I check over the state of your finger. Ah!

Lovely. Completely healed over. I am happy to spend a few hours hunched over and destroying my tender shoulders for you, so that I may file away at the clump of ice, so tender and loving am I.

I even come back in the evening and pass another few hours in your company after I have eaten my salad. It is not super appealing to eat chilled food in the cold I must say, but the sacrifices I make for you, darling. Shoving down an unappetizing meal and then dedicating my time to your comfort.

We are nearly there, this session might even do it, although my eyes are growing weary and the sound of the file grinding against the ice is starting to wear on my ears.

So much so that I rather start to imagine I can hear other sounds within the din. Squeaking and squealing and grating. Is that you, my love? I pull away from the ice to run my fingers across it, making sure that the file had not dug straight through and landed on your bone, but it is still encasing you perfectly. Nevertheless, the squeaking makes another appearance, and I saw you! I saw you. I am sure of it. I back right away and I kneel before you and I look up at your face, staring hard at your eyes, but you are stubborn, you little scamp, and you do not move them again.

I blast the cold and I leave.

There are no footprints the next day, but I cannot shake a feeling of concern. I spend an hour or so checking the entire house, looking in cupboards and under loose floorboards, but there is nothing out of place, so I take us each a bowl of food into the freezer, and we sit together.

It is very cold today, the blast having done its job, and I can see from across the table that your eyes are glossed over with a layer of ice. Perfect! Even so, as I bring a fork of food up to my lips, I am sure I hear something. At first, I am filled with panic, convinced somebody had got into the house after all, and I curse myself for not checking the freezer for intruders, but then it comes again.

I lower the fork, and I wait.

It is you, my love? You are grunting at me? Like a pig?

I push our plates aside and once more I am on my knees before you, shushing you and soothing you. I know the food looks good, darling, and I know you must be hungry, but I cannot feed you, my love, as much as we both crave for it. Your systems need to stay shut for the winter, encased in the ice. You must trust me; I always know what is best for my guests. In spring I will release you to thaw under the sun and I will hope that you will still love me. Or at least come back next year. I will look for you, in the mountains, when nobody else will. Now shh, calm down, you shouldn't be awake.

I comfort you until you settle and then I turn the freezer to its coldest setting, and I leave you to rest. It would not do for me to stay, I am afraid. The ice would take hold of me too, and then we would be a right pair! Who would look after you, hey? Don't worry, I will come back later. I will just take a little walk out to fetch some wood to soothe the tickle in my throat from the cold. I have to stay in perfect health for you, my love, I will not be far away I pro-

Footprints.

I stand in my door, and I stare at them, and I stare at the empty mountains before hurtling down to the cellar to check that the freezer door is still locked. It is. You are safely away. I should have trusted you. I am sorry.

I cover the footprints and I lock all the doors and I huddle in my bed until morning.

Again. A trail of them. To the windows and the doors and around and around the house. I stand in the kitchen, and I break all my plates and I scream, and I grab the bread knife and my feet are thunder down the stairs to the cellar. When I fly into the freezer the cold air steams out of the door in clouds, but I barely even feel it. You stare at me as I enter, your face so placid and unmoved, and it makes me prickle with shame and anger. I do not even reassure you as I kneel on the floor beside you and hack the knife into the ice that you live inside. It scrapes against it harshly and then it bumps against your hard skin and then it slips through it like butter and catches on your bone and then your foot falls off in my hands.

I hold it up to my cheek for a moment, the blood instantly freezing to my skin, and I want to caress it, cradle it, smell it, taste it, eat it, but I must blink away my haze and remember my duties.

I leave your staring face behind, and I take it outside and I press it into the footprints in the snow and I knew. I knew it all along. I should have just left it and pretended it wasn't true, turned the other cheek and waited until summer. But I am nothing if not a fool and nothing if not efficient.

I hold it in my hands, and it fits perfectly within the indents, snuggling up against the walls of snow and pressing into the pattern like an old lover.

Out in the cold I kneel, and I cry, and I watch the blood on my hands seep into the white and then I wipe my eyes and I march back into the cellar, and I am furious. Furious with you, frozen one. How could you? Have your stinking foot back, you bastard.

I fling it at you, and it smashes into your chest, and I hear the cracking over the anger boiling inside of me, but I lock the door behind me, and I leave you to rot.

I am alone for days. I am not accustomed to it. I have gotten used to your company. But I must remember that I am angry. So, I eat alone, and I chunter over my hot steaming stews about how much I loved you and cared for you and sacrificed for you, and for what. You do not even love me. You should, you know. I found you. Nobody else did. You are a fool, a fool. And I am a fool for thinking you would change.

Don't think I can't hear you either.

Oh yes, I hear the faint banging on the sides of the freezer, the metal echoing and ringing throughout the entire house as if you are inside the pipes. And I hear the footsteps too, limping and dragging and ringing and ringing around the building. Knocking on the windows and rattling on the doors. I hate it I hate it I hate it.

I pull the duvet over my ears, and I scream louder than you until I fall asleep.

It is dark outside when I wake, and I sit in bed, and I listen but there are no sounds. A bad dream. That is all. I let it all get on top of me.

As I make for the bathroom, I think over what I will take you for breakfast today, but the light will not turn on. I flick the switch again and again and I run into the hall, and I flick that too, but nothing happens.

My breath steams in front of me in the cold as I groan. Power out. I wrap myself in two jumpers and my dressing gown and I am halfway down the stairs when I realise.

The freezer.

The last few steps are a blur as I stumble down them and I all but fall into the cellar. I can hear the screams from inside, and when I yank the door open a puddle of melted ice pools around my feet and you fall to your knees within it, melting and disintegrating and suffering.

Oh, you poor, poor thing, I am so sorry. I dig my hands under your armpits, and I coo and soothe as I drag you up the stairs. You are soft but hard and you try to help, I know you do, but you are still half-frozen, and your ankle is leaving a smear of blood on the steps. I am sorry, I am trying, but it is too hard, and I know you are hurting. I leave you part way up and run, panting, and sweating into the dark, ignoring the footprints and grabbing armfuls of snow to chuck over you, but it melts and dissolves into nothing before you have a chance to cool off again. There is nothing else for it. I must dig deep and get you to the top. Get you outside into the cold. I try to block out the screams and the pained moans coming from you as I pull. This is for the best. You will be grateful soon.

We fall out of the back door together, and in the grey dusk I dig into the snow with my bare hands to make you a crevice. With a heave I shove your body in, and you roll into it with a groan that makes my heart ache, and I push heaps of snow over the mound of you, but it melts in my hands and soaks into your clothes.

No. This cannot be happening. It is not spring yet. It is not time.

I have to do something.

I am sorry. I have to leave you. Just for a moment. I will pull the snow up tight to your chin, cosy and cold, and you will be okay. I will not be long.

I drag myself away from you and I stumble to the electricity box at the side of the house, blowing on my cold hands to ready them to pry away the cover, but it is already loose, swinging on its hinges, the wires hanging out of it like spilled guts.

My heart stops cold as if the ice has taken it and I look across the mountains. I do not think there are wolves here and I have not heard the helicopters.

When I turn back to the box, I try to find some semblance of a problem to fix, digging my hands into the guts, but it is no use. We will not be getting electricity for the rest of the winter. The vans cannot make it up here until spring.

I come back to you, full of pity and regret, and I fall over the snow covering you, and I cry into the ice, and you wriggle beneath me, and I need you to stop. Stop moving. Stop wriggling. Stop making noise. It is not time.

Stop!

We both fall still, surprised by my outburst, and that is when we hear it.

Instinctively I jump up, crouching over you like a wolf protecting their cub and grabbing at a handful of you, ready to drag you inside and protect you with my life as I look up, scoping the situation, expecting to see a rival predator bearing down on us, but it is not an animal I see.

It's a person.

Thirty feet away. Staring at us. At me. At you.

Blue coat, red hat. Staring.

Gently, I ease you from the snow, trying not to startle them. The ice clings to your red hat but slips easily from your blue coat, and you mumble quietly at the warm air hitting your cheeks. I lean over you, keeping one eye on the figure, and I try to sooth you, pressing my cold hands onto your skin and whispering. Shh, it's okay. I've got you. I'll take care of you. I won't let them hurt you. Won't let them take you.

Slowly, laboriously, I start to drag you towards the door, urging your eyes back onto me when they flicker to the thing. You do not need it. Not anymore. You have me. I am all you need. I will take care of you. Forget that. Forget.

Ten feet from the door. Nearly there. You are so heavy, but I would do anything to protect you. Nine. Your ankle catches on a rock or a stick protruding from the melting snow and you grunt loudly. I drop you in surprise and kiss your cheeks and they make my lips burn but the sound of the snow does not stop.

Discreetly, I raise my eyes towards the thing. It is walking towards us, slowly. Almost as if it was merely wandering. Perhaps it is. Perhaps it will not care that I am slipping my hands back under your armpits.

It cares. It cares.

I pull and you groan, and it starts to run straight at us. It is fast and desperate, and it groans alongside you, but one of its legs sinks further into the snow than the other and it slows it down. Their charge turns into a desperate stumble, the blood from their ankle leaving a stain behind them in the white, but still, they encroach on us faster than I can pull. The winter has made me weak, but my love for you makes me strong. I scream and you scream, and they scream, and I drag you inside and I slam the door shut as the shoulder of their blue coat slams into the wood.

We fall back against it, sprawled across the hallway, and they bang, and they hit, and they thump, and you are in my arms, and you are melting, wriggling, panting, screaming.

BLACKBERRY WINTER
WILLIAM JENSEN

None of us were prepared for last year's snowstorm. I don't know how many lives were ruined amid the chaos and violence, but parts of town were destroyed, and people were killed. Countless others were injured, too. When the temperature dropped and sent everyone into a panic, my only goal was to keep my wife and daughter safe. Though I remain haunted by what I witnessed, I have few regrets about what I did.

My name is Cash Michaels. I am a sportswriter. Most of my articles focus on baseball. I will never get rich in my profession, but I think of my job as getting paid to watch the world series, which isn't something to scoff at. I've been doing this for almost twenty years, and I have been smart with my money, so my family and I have managed a comfortable life. I have a wife and a daughter, and we live in Anson, Texas, a small town in the middle of the state just west of Austin and San Antonio where the soil is gray and rocky, and the roads resemble giant snakes curling around the blond hills in the distance.

It's a nice place to live. We have good schools; the downtown strip underwent a rejuvenation a few years ago and now has a small-town charm combined with good restaurants and boutiques. A lot of people are moving here to retire, too. There are plenty of opportunities for swimming at Lake Lamar, hiking along the Tonkawa Bluffs, and hunting and fishing and bicycling. Our library is also impressive, and my wife and I do a lot of volunteer work there. There are several churches for every belief, and our local Boy Scouts help keep the parks clean. I've lived all over Texas and tried to live in New York when I first started writing sports, but I honestly wouldn't want to be any other place.

But now I have to reconsider everything. My wife, Rose, wants to move. Maybe to Dallas, where she's from. Maybe to Nacogdoches, where we met in college. Everything here is tainted, and both of us want a fresh start.

No one seemed nervous when the weather reports came in. Living between two major climate zones, we often get violent changes in weather. Typically, we get what are called Blue Northers: arctic winds that blow down through the plains and make the temperature drop by twenty or thirty degrees. Others call these Blue Blizzards or Arctic Screamers. But besides these forty-eight-hour fronts, it really doesn't get cold here in Central Texas. No one owns snow tires, snow shovels, parkas, or gloves. Our houses aren't built for cold weather, and our streets are not prepared for ice. And, as it turned out, the electrical company wasn't prepared either.

On the eve of the storm, Rose and I drove to the hardware store for pipe covers. They'd sold out, so we had to settle for stretches of polyethylene to make our own. Rose snatched the last two and said we should leave. It was already cold in the store like a gas station beer cave. Men and women in hoodies shuffled down the aisles with crossed arms. Everyone grimaced. The check-out line was long but moved quickly. People bought duct tape, batteries, flashlights, and bottled water.

"Come on, man, give it to me!" someone said.

I looked around, not knowing where the voice came from. Two men, both early-middle-age, argued over a pack of insulated bag covers for outdoor faucets. They tussled about sixty feet away from us. They gripped the bag covers and pulled and side-stepped as if in a primitive waltz.

"Let go! It's mine."

"I need it more."

An employee approached them with his hands raised; he asked them to calm down, and he called both men "sir."

They didn't listen.

One of the men swung a wild, messy fist and struck the other man in the jaw. He fell and rolled. Rose gawked and grabbed my arm.

"You son of a bitch."

"You should have let go."

"Sirs, I'm going to ask you both to leave immediately."

"He started it!"

The employee, a young guy with short black hair, escorted them outside where they cursed at each other as they stomped away. Rose and I shared glances in disbelief. We moved forward toward the cash register and paid.

Driving home, the dusk was gray as smog. The radio played the news. The reporter said, the schools in the county were cancelling classes due to expected snow, a rare occasion, and warned us all to drive carefully. Rose stared straight ahead at the road.

"People are crazy," said Rose.

"Yes," I said. "They can be."

"Even a little snow could be awful here," said Rose. She reached out and turned the radio off. She rubbed her hands together, probably more out of stress than from the cold. We had the heater on, which was strong and pleasant.

"I think it will be fine," I said. "Everything will melt before you know it."

"You're probably right."

"Probably?"

"Probably,"

That evening, while Rose cooked a big pot of chili, I taped the polyethylene around the faucet in our backyard and covered it with a towel to stay safe. The sky stretched out as a dirty, smokey quilt. The air tasted different, too — thinner and lighter, almost brittle like bits of ice that snap and melt in your mouth. I looked at our neighbors' houses. Lights were on. Everything looked okay.

I imagined them eating dinner, like we were about to do, playing board games, drinking hot chocolate, sitting around the fireplace that they practically never used. And though I feel stupid saying this now, it all made me happy. Rose likely thought I was insane I smiled so much when I came inside. But there is a joy to being cold—there is a joy to growing warm after being cold. And that night I knew our entire little town was getting to do just that, it was like a strange holiday gifted to us and we all received an impromptu adventure to another place. For the next twelve hours we'd be New Hampshire poets, Vermont apple pickers, or Montana hunters resting hearty after a long day. It was something different. And for me that was more than enough.

Our daughter, Shirley, seemed to have a similar mindset. She laughed as we ate our chili and said she wanted to wake up extra early in the morning so she could see whatever snow we had before it melted. She is sixteen and has long chestnut brown hair like her mother. She's a smart child who wavers between being a kid and a tiny adult depending on her mood.

"I want to make a dozen snow angels," she said. "Maybe I can build a snowman—"

"How about a snowwoman?" said Rose.

"—do you think there will be enough snow?"

"No promises. Finish your chili."

❄

After dinner, we played Monopoly, and Rose and I drank a couple of glasses of bourbon to settle in. Shirley almost won the game, but Rose rallied and built hotels in all the right places and conquered. We listened to the wind wail outside and occasionally peeked through the windows to see if there was any snow yet. We saw nothing but the night sky.

Shirley went to bed first. Thirty minutes later, Rose and I crawled under our covers to stay warm. The bourbon from earlier coursed through me, zinging my stomach and lungs and heart. Rose shuddered. I put my arms around her and pulled her close to me. She wore sweatpants and an old Stephen F. Austin State University long sleeve shirt, worn and baggy and shapeless. She rested her head on my chest.

"Do you think our pipes will hold? We should turn the faucets on, just a little bit, so there's a drip," said Rose.

"We can do that if you want."

"Should we check the weather again?"

"No. There's no point. Everything will be okay," I said.

"Yes. You're right. I know you're right. I'm just scared."

I kissed the top of her head. I rubbed her shoulder and kept holding her. I wanted her to feel as safe as possible. The heater hummed, like a giant cat purring, and I felt confident and secure. I was just ignorant.

Rose fell asleep. She breathed heavy against me, and I felt the air fill and leave her lungs. I gazed out the window. In the faint glow of the streetlamp at the corner, I saw the first flurry begin to fall.

In the morning, everything was covered with snow. I woke at dawn and stumbled out of bed toward the window and peered through the blinds. I gawked with dizziness. A thick, seamless white carpet covered the front yard, the cars, and the street. Snow weighed down the branches of the live oak by the mailbox. Snow smeared the neighbors' roofs. The sky was cloudless, and the rising sun created a pink haze in the east.

I told Rose to come look. We stood in awe for a second before we rushed to wake Shirley. This probably sounds pathetic to anyone who lives up north, but for us in Texas, snow is almost mythical. We've heard of it, but few of us have seen it.

We bundled ourselves as best we could, using socks for mittens, and rushed outside with giggles and hollers. Our jeans, flannels, and sneakers immediately became heavy and wet. But we didn't care.

Shirley made her snow angel. I threw a snowball at Rose's butt. She half-screamed, half-laughed. She scooped up snow and ice and threw it at me in retaliation; she encouraged Shirley to help her. The three of us fought bravely in our snowball battle, and by the end we were exhausted and red-faced, and our cheeks ached from smiling and laughing.

Our street was a frozen river. You couldn't even see the blacktop. Just white with slick patches of blue. Rose and I weren't going to even try driving. I figured the afternoon sun would thaw things out.

We were all on our front porch about to head inside when we heard the strange yet distinctive sound of tires spinning, skidding, and sliding.

An engine gasped and screeched.

I knew what it was before I saw it.

The three of us turned just in time to witness a black truck sputter and weave. It looked like it was floating. The back wheels fishtailed. Rose, in a motherly instinct, grabbed Shirley and pulled her close.

Then, as if in slow motion, the truck crashed over the curb and the sidewalk into a car parked in the driveway of the house northeast of ours on the other side of the road.

Metal crunched into metal. Glass shattered and spilled and chimed. A loud pop went off, and steam erupted from under the truck's hood. A horn wailed. Birds fluttered out from the trees like a scattering of buckshot.

"Shirley, go inside, Shirley" said Rose. "Go right now."

"Mom—"

"I said go."

Shirley grunted and marched inside, shaking out water and ice with each step. I think Rose and I both knew this was the start of something and whatever it was couldn't be good. Carefully, we approached the end of our driveway; partially because we wanted to make sure the driver was okay, but also out of a morbid curiosity of what awaited.

The driver's door swung open and a big, burly man stumbled out. He slid on the ice and struggled to stand, as if drunk. He held his door to keep from falling. I recognized him from the area, but I'd never spoken with him and didn't know his name. He had a beard, dark with random gray hairs poking through. He wore a trucker hat and a Wrangler work vest over a red and black lumberjack shirt. The man was breathing heavy and rapidly but managed to hiss profanities between breaths.

I was about to call out and ask if he was okay, but I knew he was. Perhaps he was rattled from the accident, but he clearly wasn't injured. Before I could speak, the front door of the house opened, and our neighbor waddled out in his bathrobe and sweatpants and no shirt. His name is Joe, and he's not super friendly. He lives alone. He's on the short side and is fat without being obese. He's bald and has a pencil-thin moustache, so Rose jokes that he's either a plumber or a used car salesman, but we found out a few months ago that he's actually a computer programmer and an air force veteran. He keeps to himself, but he's also the one house on the block who keeps his lights off and doesn't answer the door for trick-or-treaters on Halloween even though he's obviously home. On different occasions, Rose and I have heard him curse an unlucky salesman who knocked on his door.

"You dumb baboon!"

"I'm sorry, mister—"

"How many wine coolers did you have with breakfast?"

"Sir, it was an accident. I haven't been drinking, I swear. It's just the ice and—"

"I know it's the ice. Why are you driving like you're in NASCAR?"

"Sir, I am so sorry."

"Oh, you're sorry? Okay, I didn't realize you were *sorry*! Please, how about you come inside so you can have some cookies and demolish more of my property. I've got a shotgun I'd like you to meet!"

Joe's voice reverberated through the frozen air. Rose held my arm, not letting me move. She didn't want me to get involved, and I wasn't sure if I wanted to.

"Hey, buddy—that's uncalled for. It was an accident. I'm fully insured. We can call the cops and a tow truck and figure this—"

"Look around, Einstein. The roads are fucked. Everything is shut down. And in case you haven't noticed, the power is out. And the cell towers must have gotten taken out, too. Nobody is coming."

Rose and I looked at each other. We'd been outside playing and hadn't checked our phones or tried turning on anything that morning. The men kept arguing, yelling. The power going out wouldn't be too big of a surprise, but there was something about Joe's tone that made it feel like an emergency. Rose and I went back inside.

Our house was dark.

And it was cool.

"Mom," said Shirley from upstairs, "the TV won't turn on."

I went to the kitchen and flipped on the light switch, but the room stayed dim. Rose stood at the base of the stairs. She looked at me. I shook my head.

"The power is off for now, hon" she said. "It will come back on eventually."

"What am I supposed to do? That means no internet either right?"

"No lights, no TV, no computer."

"What about phones?"

Rose found her phone in the kitchen. She didn't have service.

Neither did I. We found out later that the towers had gone out before the power, but none of us realized it.

"This sucks. I'm bored."

"I know," said Rose. "Your life is terrible."

Rose crossed her arms and shuffled toward me. She stuck her neck out with her wide brown eyes. She wasn't mad or panicked, but she was concerned. She started to speak, but I interrupted her.

"It's fine" I said. "At least it's daytime. Everything will be back on in about an hour."

"It's cold, Cash. We need heat."

"Yes."

"And the roads? What about the roads? You saw them. How can we get out of here? What if there's an emergency? How could an ambulance or a fire truck get in?"

"Everything will be melted before lunch—"

"That road is frozen solid. It's more an ice rink than a street."

"Emergency vehicles can handle it."

Rose squinted. I wasn't sure if she wanted to call me stupid or cry. Maybe both. Rose is a strong woman, and she always speaks her mind, never holds back. And if she is upset with me, she lets me know. She and I communicate well, which has kept our marriage smooth, but it is never easy criticizing your partner. Rose was thinking. She wanted to articulate something to me, but I wasn't sure what.

"Cash" she said, "I want you to think. Okay, honey? Think real hard. The roads are frozen. The power is down. Do we have supplies?"

"It will be fine—"

"Stop saying that" she said. "I don't want you to reassure me, I want us to have a plan. Not just wait and see what happens. I want you to be active and know what to do if things don't just magically slap back into normal. Let's try this again. What are we going to do?"

Rose was correct. We needed to be prepared. I strolled past her to our front door, opened it, and stepped outside, into the cold, still air.

Joe was still bickering with the man with the black truck. It didn't look like it was going well. I peered to the left and the right. All I saw was snow and ice. No people, no drivers. Our town was soundless and frozen.

"Hold on a second" I said to Rose and trekked through the snow and carefully across the road, trying not to slip on the slick pavement beneath it all.

I waved my arms at Joe and the other man. They saw me but didn't say anything.

"Joe," I said, "you okay?"

"Me? I'm fine when assholes aren't speeding around the one day of the year we all need chains on our tires—"

"I said I was sorry, mister. I've got good insurance—"

"Gentlemen," I said, "no one is hurt, and anything that is damaged can either be fixed or replaced. Let's remember that."

Both men shrugged and nodded sheepishly. Joe pulled his robe tighter to shield his belly from the cold. I introduced myself to the man who crashed his truck into Joe's car. He said his name was Nolan, and we shook hands. He had a strong grip and made eye contact when he spoke.

"Both of you lose power, too?"

Joe nodded.

"Yeah," said Nolan, "we got a generator, so we're okay for now. But I'm trying not to use it too much since I don't know how long this will last. I've got one can of gas, but that's it."

"What about water?" asked Joe.

I stared blankly at Joe.

"You know," said Joe, "H20? It comes out of faucets."

"What about it?" I said.

"Do you still have water?"

"I don't know" I said.

"We still had some at our place," said Nolan, "but the pour was getting thin. We filled up the bathtub and a bunch of bottles while we could. I recommend you all do the same. You're definitely going to want water for your toilet tanks."

I stood there calmly nodding.

My insides tightened and stretched. I felt dizzy. Winter had closed the world. The roads were undriveable, we were without electricity, and we were apparently about to lose water, too. My brain bisected; one half of my mind screamed while the other stayed logical, reasonable, and calm.

Eventually, I told myself, the power would be restored. We'd have electricity and heat again. The sun would come out and melt the ice on the roads so we could drive again. It was going to be a few hours, that was all. But the other half of my head said something different: *You're all in trouble. You're not prepared.*

I knew I couldn't let that voice take control, but I needed to listen to its warnings. Now wasn't the time to panic, but it wasn't the time to act arrogant or apathetic either. I said my goodbyes to Joe and Nolan and went home.

Rose had changed into dry jeans and her one wool sweater she typically wore on Christmas Eve. She was sitting at the base of the stairs and tying the laces of her boots when I came through the door. Her brown curls curtained her face, and she seemed stressed but in control. Her nostrils moved as she breathed. She didn't blink.

I told her about what Nolan had said, and we tested our faucets. We still had water, but the flow was weak. Rose and I gathered bottles and jugs and old canteens and filled them at the kitchen sink. We told Shirley to run the baths. She squawked at first but did as she was told. All of us worked steadily. We moved without words. Afterwards we gathered downstairs in the kitchen and searched the cupboards.

Three cans of tuna.

Half a loaf of bread.

Two boxes of macaroni and cheese.

One bag of whole wheat spaghetti.

A can of black olives.

Four cans of refried beans.

Half a box of Raisin Bran. A full box of Cheerios.

Oatmeal.

Flour. Sugar. Baking soda. Hot cocoa mix. Half a box of stale cookies leftover from Thanksgiving.

The refrigerator was better stocked: breakfast sausage, eggs, oatmilk, butter, orange juice, lemons, and cheese. Our freezer had two small cartons of ice cream, waffles, broccoli, and ice. Of course, all of this would spoil soon.

"We still have gas," said Rose. "We can cook some stuff."

"What stuff?" said Shirley.

"We can make do" I said.

We huddled in the living room and played Uno and Monopoly and ate sandwiches, cheese omelets, and bowls of cereal. We draped ourselves in blankets so we resembled strange monks. The afternoon slipped away. We read books and slept; Rose and Shirley labored over a giant puzzle. But the power didn't come on.

At the end of the second day, Rose whispered to me she was worried. I couldn't blame her. We still had water in the tubs, and we still had some bread, but supplies were low. We'd gone for forty-eight hours on what we had, but neither one of us knew how much longer we could hold out on what we had. None of the snow had melted, in fact there had even been more snow in the night, which had turned to slush and froze over everything. It would still be dangerous to drive.

"We don't have enough" said Rose.

"We can live off peanut putter for another day."

"No" she said. "Enough is enough. We can't wait any longer."

"We're not starving" I said.

Rose and I lay in bed under two comforters. It wasn't that late, but we found it difficult staying awake when the house slipped into darkness. I turned on my side to look at her. She sat upright with her head hung low.

"We need some essentials. Bread. Maybe some eggs. Potatoes, if you can find any. Shirley is hungry. I'm hungry, too. Are you listening?"

"Yes."

"Tomorrow, when the sun is out, try to drive to the Dollar General. It's close. They'll have the basics."

"I doubt they'll be open—"

"If you don't go, I will."

I stared at my wife's outline. My muscles knotted up hard as stone. She sighed and fell backwards, letting her head crash on her pillow. I told her I'd go in the morning. She rubbed her eyes silently.

I left early in the afternoon. The roads sprawled outward as milky blurs before dissolving into a hard blue sky. The land was rugged and cold. Snow weighed everything down. The truck's heater blasted at the highest level, but I still heard the snow crunching beneath my wheels. I drove slowly.

Getting out of the neighborhood was easier than I expected.

After I kicked the snow away from my back tires and shoved the heavy blankets off my truck's windshield and roof, backing out was almost normal besides having to go over a bump at the curb. My street lay as a soiled bedsheet, something once white and clean and pure but now dirty and wrinkled. I turned right and came to Memorial Drive, the long stretch of blacktop that cuts from downtown Anson deeper into the Hill Country. I looked left and right but didn't see any traffic. Several sedans sat abandoned by the side, trapped in patches of icy mud, unable to pull out. I looked for pedestrians, perhaps the drivers trying to walk home, in case someone needed a ride.

I gently applied the brake pedal as I approached and turned into the parking lot of the Dollar General by the Texaco station. The store's windows were broken. Shark teeth shards protruding from the jambs were the only thing left. Beads of glass dotted the pavement. Inside, it looked as if Goths had ravaged and pillaged every aisle. Glass and debris smeared the floor. There was so much trash, random and scattered, I couldn't identify most of what I saw. Cereal and work gloves and bits of paper and cheap plastic toys. A display of DVDs had been toppled, and burst cans of beer piled beside the ransacked coolers. You couldn't walk normally down the paths. I had to choose my footsteps carefully and awkwardly, trying to maintain my footing around the clutter.

No one worked the cash registers. Two men emerged from behind a row of greeting cards and office supplies. Both wore flannel shirts and baseball hats, and their faces were pale and unshaved. Each of them carried two jugs of water.

"It's pretty picked over" said one of them. "Get what you can and hurry home. Things are getting crazy."

"What do you mean?"

"People are starting to freak out. I caught some jerk last night trying to break in. I don't know what he was hoping to find."

"Some yahoos are starting fires" said the other man. "Not sure if they're trying to stay warm or just wanting to create havoc."

"That the last of the water?"

"Afraid so, and I'm not selling it."

"I understand."

The man and his friend nodded at me and left without saying another word.

I couldn't find much. Some cheap frosted donuts, tortilla chips, a crushed loaf of Wonderbread, a few energy drinks, and canned raviolis. I carried what I could to my truck and went back for a second round. When I returned with candy bars and popcorn, an old man in a thin overcoat stood beside my truck. He stood crooked and gaunt. His only other clothes consisted of slippers and pajama bottoms. He stared at me.

"Hi" I said. "You surviving okay, sir?"

He didn't speak.

I sensed something was wrong. He didn't appear injured. I

couldn't see any wounds. I wondered if he had dementia, maybe he was somebody's poor grandfather who'd wandered off after no one visited to feed or care for him. I stepped forward, hoping to help, when he started laughing.

As cold as it was, my temperature dropped an extra five degrees. His laughter wasn't joyous. It was the sound of madness. A dissonant series of screeching strings. Blood poured out of his mouth. He didn't have any teeth.

"It's the end of times," he said. "First God destroyed the world with a flood, a glorious flood. Now he destroys us with snow. Look around. Humanity is doomed. I pulled out my teeth so the devils can't find me."

He held out a hand toward me, his fingers stretched wide and stiff. He beckoned for me. He slowly shuffled forward, laughing and drooling blood all the while. All I could do was stand there and shake my head.

"You," he said, "you can join me."

He dug his free hand into his overcoat's pocket. He motioned for me to come closer, but I backed away. He pulled out a pair of pliers.

"Let me take out of your teeth and you can be saved, too."

In a blur, I dropped the candy bars and bolted toward my truck. The old man stood and blocked me, so I shoved him, knocking him hard to the ground. I fumbled with my keys and started the engine before I even closed my door.

I was shifting into reverse when the old man got to his feet. He looked at me and grinned. He still held the pliers in his hand. He tried to run but merely hobbled. He yelled, "I'll save you" as he hurled himself at my door, but I peeled backward out of the parking lot and onto the empty, icy road. The old man collapsed with a thud.

I almost spun into a ditch on the other side of the road. I changed gears and jolted forward, my truck fishtailing as I sped north and away. I wasn't careful, and I'm shocked I didn't crash or slide off the road like so many other cars clearly had.

Then I noticed the smoke. There were fires somewhere, some

place out of sight. The clouds were large and dark. I wasn't sure what was burning, but it had to be a building. Maybe the old man wasn't crazy, I thought. Maybe humanity was doomed. I didn't hear any sirens. I didn't hear any familiar sounds of emergencies. I heard only the thump—thump—thump of my heart.

Our little Texas town finally had a winter wonderland, but it wasn't like a Hallmark holiday film or a joyful occasion. We were all desperate and cold. I didn't understand what was happening. By the time I reached my house, my teeth chattered like a madman's typewriter. I fumbled opening the door. The house wasn't much warmer inside. With the electricity not working, the place sat silent and dim. No television or music. No dishwasher rumbling. I called out but didn't hear a response. I called again and waited. After a few seconds, my wife replied from upstairs, her voice distant and muffled.

"Cash?" she said. "Is that you?"

"Yeah" I said, slightly confused on who else she might think it was.

Rose rushed out of our bedroom toward the top of the stairs. Shirley stayed close behind her. Rose's eyes were wide and blood-shot. Shirley appeared small and meek, hiding behind her mother.

"People were trying to break in" said Rose.

"They were yelling and fighting and trying to get inside," said Shirley. She was crying and holding onto her mother's arm.

"Who was trying to get inside?"

"Everyone has gone crazy. Did you see what happened across the street?"

I opened my front door and stepped onto the porch. Somehow, I hadn't seen the rest of my street. Windows of cars and other houses were broken. The black truck that had crashed into my neighbor Joe's car was still there, his windshield smashed and looking like a glass cobweb. But there were other cars, too. These weren't just abandoned. These were clearly rummaged and vandalized. A red Honda Civic parked halfway onto the sidewalk, all four doors wide open. A white SUV had rolled onto its side farther down the road.

I backtracked inside and shut the door. I locked the dead bolt, and my breathing quickened. I felt as if I were falling, that the world was dissolving and swirling together. I wanted it to stop, to be normal again.

Dusk came like a halved plum. The horizon looked bruised. Rose gathered flashlights and lanterns. I'd told Rose what I'd experienced with the old man. I told her about my conversation with the other men. She held a hand to her mouth. I told her we needed to stay inside, and she agreed.

We didn't want to frighten Shirley, so we tried to act casual. I suggested I'd read to them. I took down my copy of *Life on the Mississippi* and joined my wife and daughter in the living room. Rose had started a fire in the fireplace. The flames cast wild and flickering shadows. We huddled near the hearth, and I read to my family by the hot, orange light.

"The Mississippi is well worth reading about. It is not a commonplace river, but on the contrary is in all ways remarkable. Considering the Missouri its main branch, it is the longest river in—"

Outside, someone screamed.

It almost didn't sound human at all. The voice came as an electric scratch. Perhaps a shout of pain. Maybe it was a yell of excitement. We stared toward the front door, the windows. No other shouts followed. I worried there were more like the old man at the Dollar General, folks who believed it was the end of times, people who yanked out their own teeth.

"It's okay, Cash," said Rose, "keep reading."

"Please, Daddy."

"It is the longest river in the world—four thousand three hundred miles. It seems safe to say that is also the crookedest river in the world, since in one part of its journey it used up one thousand three hundred miles to cover the same ground that the crow would fly over in six hundred and seventy-five. It discharges three times as much water as the St. Lawrence, twenty-five times as much as the Rhine, and three hundred—"

Another scream streaked across the sky. This was different than the last. While one had been a loud, high pitched yip of noise, this was a bold war-cry. It was madness with joy in the madness.

"Daddy, I'm scared."

"It's okay, honeybun."

"Go on with the book, Cash."

"And three hundred and thirty-eight times as much as the Thames. No other river has so vast a drainage-basin; it draws its water-supply from twenty-eight states and territories; from Delaware on the Atlantic seaboard, and from all the country between that and Idaho on the Pacific slope—a spread of forty-five degrees of longitude. The Mississippi receives and carries to the Gulf water—"

A cacophony of shouts and grunts and laughter rumbled just outside our front door. Men's voices followed, low and rolling. My family and I stayed as still and silent as gargoyles. Shirley cried, but she didn't make a sound. Her tears resembled bits of glass.

"They're probably just drunk," I said.

"Can't you tell them to go away?"

I could see a confrontation going poorly. We didn't know how many there were or what they were up to. I just hoped they would move on and go somewhere else. So far they hadn't done anything other than make some noise. I'd already encountered one madman, and I wasn't prepared to meet anymore.

I looked at my wife. She shook her head slowly at me in disgust.

Shirley marched to the front door, swung it opened, and yelled into the cold: "Shut up! Everyone is stressed. Go home!"

She slammed the door and came back to her mother and me. Rose and I gawked. I wasn't sure if I was impressed or devastated.

"See," she said, "you just need to stand up to them and they'll—"

One of our front windows burst into a million shards. A brick, thrown by one of the men, skidded across the hardwood floors and the debris of broken glass. We all shrieked and dove for cover even though we sat in a different room.

"Hey, man!" said somebody "You got any beer?"

Laughter followed. Not just from the speaker, but from a small gathering. A troupe of vandals parading the neighborhood.

"Come on, bub—we're thirsty!" said another man. "If we're all going to die, I don't want to go sober!"

Someone tried crawling through the broken window. A leg, clad in denim, carefully stuck through the opening, trying not to get cut or gashed on the remaining glass.

"Cash, they're coming inside," said Rose. Her voice came clipped and shrill.

I rushed toward the remains of the window. Moonlight, pale and blue, reflected over the beads of glass on the floor. The rest of the house stayed dark as a catacomb. The man had gotten halfway inside. I slammed into his knees and hips. He pawed and pulled at my shoulders. He yanked at my collar.

All I could think of was the old man, his mouth filled with blood, muttering about humanity being doomed. The end of days. I was panicky but fast moving.

I kept shoving. One of the man's wrists scraped against a remaining shard in the pane, and he screeched as the glass sliced into him, spurting blood over the cuff of his jacket as I pushed him back through the window. He collapsed onto snow and rocks with a thump. The man scampered away on all fours. I couldn't see his friends, but I heard them breathing and chuckling.

"Daddy?"

Shirley stood ten feet behind me; her voice startled me so badly I thought I jumped an equal ten feet. She had her arms crossed, and she stuck her head forward with hunched shoulders. She shivered.

"Go back, honey," I said, "go stay with Mama."

"What are they doing? What do they want?"

I was about to go to her, embrace her, comfort her, when the men outside started making noise again.

"We want to play with you, bub!"

"I think I like this house the most."

I glared through the broken window. Figures moved. I couldn't see any faces. I wasn't sure how many there were. At least four voices called out, but there may have been more.

Shirley dashed back to her mother and the warmth of the fireplace.

I stepped closer to the window, careful with my steps on the broken glass. Icy wind blew over my face and freezing my eyes and cheeks. I clenched my jaw to keep my teeth from chattering.

"How about you all get the fuck away from here," I said.

The men laughed.

"Step outside and ask us politely," said one of them. "Come out here and we'll all be friends."

More laughter.

I heard a small click and saw a flame as one of them lit a cigarette. I focused on the cherry of the cigarette and was able to see five men. They stood in a cluster off to the side where the driveway met the front yard.

"You're all drunk," I said. "Go back home and sleep it off."

"Night's early, boss," said one of them.

"And I ain't tired," said another one.

"Hey," I said, keeping my voice loud and deep, "you don't want to fuck around with me. Now get your ass out of here."

One of them mocked my threat by repeating it verbatim in a high-pitched whine. The others giggled. One laughed so hard he started gagging.

"Okay," said the first man, "we'll go. You have a good night's sleep, sir."

I waited. The men kept smoking and drinking and whispering.

Then one of them said, "Is he gone?"

"Yeah," said another, "I think he's gone."

"Okay, so divide and conquer, right?"

The huddle broke. Two men dashed to the left while the others scattered to my right.

I flew back to the fireplace. Rose held Shirley to her chest. Shirley looked as if she were trying to dig into her mother's breast. Rose glared at me.

"Take Shirley and go upstairs. Lock the door. Don't let anyone in."

"Cash, you're scaring me."

"Good. You should be scared."

Rose stood, practically pulling Shirley up with her. They shuffled away with the blankets still draped over their shoulders.

I knew I'd have to act quick. I had to be aggressive. I would have to go against everything in my nature. But I was ready. I hurried to the garage. I wasn't sure what I was looking for but when I put my hands on the hammer, I knew I had what I needed. My brain switched to a primal muscle. I didn't even have any feelings. There was nothing left but instinct and reaction.

Inside the house everything was quiet. I didn't hear Rose or Shirley. I didn't hear the men mumbling or clomping through the bushes. I went to the back and peeped out the window. The snow in the backyard shined like fresh linen.

Two men crawled over the fence. They came heavily and clumsily. Each tumbled to the ground, landing on his stomach. They almost fell on top of each other. I watched them struggle to stand. Neither seemed to get a decent footing. They trekked across the yard, dragging their feet through the snow.

The other men used the gate door on the opposite side of the fence. They walked in a straight line and reconvened with their friends in the middle of the yard. They started scouring the far edges along the fence.

They were gathering stones.

"Hey, buddy—" said one of them, the same one who'd appeared to be their captain, "We're going to have some party tonight!"

The first volley came pathetically. Stones bounced off the walls and the windows. The men chuckled. The second attempt came faster and stronger. They threw with anger. The window above our kitchen-sink broke. The thuds against the house were loud and hard. Upstairs, Shirley let out a shriek.

I kept my grip on the hammer tight. It didn't feel as heavy as before.

"Some people like to rock, some people like to roll, but moving and a grooving is gonna satisfy my soul," sang one of the men. Everybody laughed before throwing more rocks.

Another window, the one just to my right, shattered and showered me with grains of glass. I dove to the floor.

"Let's have a party! Ooh! Let's have party. Send him to the store, let's buy some more, and let's have a party tonight!"

Once I managed to pull myself away from the glass, I got back to my knees and looked out again. Air, cold as the waves off Maine, blew inside as a constant stream. The men marched forward.

I jumped up and went to our couch and dragged it across the room.

"I've never kissed a bear, I've never kissed a goon, but I can shake a chicken in the middle of the room," sang the one man.

I shoved the couch against the backdoor as a crude barricade. My spit turned thick and coppery, like sucking on a dozen pennies.

"Let's have a party," they sang as a dissonant chorus. One of them tried the door, bumped it into the couch and couldn't budge it. Then they began crawling in through the broken window.

A leg, almost dainty, glided inside and stepped onto the glass covered floor.

I dove and smashed the hammer onto the man's knee. The bone

shattered upon impact. The leg went limp and docile as the man blared an ear-piercing screech that was more mechanical than human. He kept screaming. His friends pulled him back out and tried to calm him. He kept howling, panicked with torment. Then he started to gag and vomit and cry.

"Stay the fuck away from my house," I said.

"He broke Scout's leg, man. The guy took out Scout's whole fucking leg,"

The man, apparently named Scout, whimpered and gasped. One of his friends rushed to the window headfirst and grabbed the windowsill to help pull himself in. I brought the hammer down on his knuckles twice before he could do anything. His hand exploded in two bursts of blood and cartilage and bone. He howled and grabbed his wrist and gawked at his fingers that were now splitting away from the rest of the hand.

"My hand, look what he did to my hand,"

The man screamed.

I swung the hammer into his face. His teeth and his nose disappeared into a red pulp. He collapsed with a gurgling sound and spat and drooled red over the snow as he choked on his blood. The other men stood and gawked.

I sprinted away.

"We got to get him now," said their leader, "We can't let them identify us."

I ducked into the shadows and hid in a corner near the front of the house by our staircase. I stood still and held my breath. The men outside mumbled and cursed before coming inside to find me. I heard their boots on the broken glass. The wind moaned and rattled the blinds. The house had been cold all day, but now the wind was turning the place into an igloo.

The men searched for me without speaking. But they didn't move discreetly. They huffed and puffed and pawed at the counter tops and pushed over lamps and chairs. I heard one of them open the refrigerator, grab a soda, pop it open, and slurp. Another one lit a cigarette. The tobacco scent flooded the house.

I knew I couldn't take all of them. But I had to do something. The important thing was to keep them away from Rose and Shirley.

I had to lead them away.

I sank to the floor and kept my knees to my chest. I stayed small, compact, invisible. Footsteps tapped nearby. They came closer. Closer still. Even closer.

Musk, like woods and ash and sweat, filled my nostrils.

I waited until I saw the boots. He left muddy footprints wherever he went; his gait was neither fast nor slow, trying to be quiet but failing.

In a seamless and graceful motion, I kicked my leg out in front of him, tripping him, as I held out the hammer, claw-side up. It was almost like ballet.

The man, husky with meat and flab, dropped hard and sudden.

His face connected with the hammer's claw with a wet crack. The metal jammed into his eye and cheekbone, and even when he thrashed and squealed, the hammer stayed stuck to his head.

"Take it out, take it out, oh shit," he said.

I heard the others charging through the house. I bolted to the front window they'd broken earlier and jumped through, nicking my cheeks and neck in the process. I didn't feel the impact when I hit the ground. Rocks and ice and the hard earth.

"Get him, look what he did to Rammy, oh fuck,"

"My eye, oh God—not my eye,"

I didn't glance back. I ran. Cold air spread into my lungs and coursed through my blood. The chill didn't bother me. I couldn't feel it. The men chased me, barking profanities and threats.

"Motherfucker!"

"Dead-ass fuck-face!"

"Tiny little bitch!"

I kept running. I screamed for help as I cut across someone's front lawn, trudging through snow. My legs became sluggish as if filled with sand. A wooden fence waited about fifty feet away, and I was going to have to scramble over it to get away from the two remaining men. I wasn't sure if I could do it. They were gaining speed and closing in. I tried to push myself, run faster and harder.

I trampled over dead rose bushes and threw my body as high and far as I could, but I managed only to get my arms and part of my chest over the top. I tried to pull myself, drag myself over to the other side, some other stranger's backyard to get away, to get far away. The wood dug into my sternum, scratched at the flesh in my armpit, the bottom of my biceps. I'd been running in just jeans and a t-shirt, so my skin was blue and covered with goosebumps.

Pull, I thought. You need to pull yourself over. Wherever you have any strength left, you need to use it and use it right now.

And then they were upon me.

I let out one last cry, a shameful plea for help. They pulled me down and threw me into the snow. I started crawling, kicking. I felt hands grabbing at my shoulders. The other one kicked me in the ribs and hips. Each blow came dull and without pain, just sudden pressure and release. The snow, so cold, burned my lips and cheeks. Some got in my mouth and melted and tasted good, almost refreshing.

They turned me over, and one of them punched me across the jaw. I wheezed and he hit me again, this time directly in my left eye.

"You're a real Rambo, ain't ya?" said the man who'd punched me. I recognize his voice as the de-facto leader. "We're just trying to have some fun."

"Fucking jerk."

"So now we need to double our fun," said the leader. "First we're going to cut some things off."

The other one laughed like a donkey. I couldn't see either one well. They wore beanies and had puffy cheeks. The leader had a bushy mustache, wild and unkempt. He seemed fairly muscular under his coat, but the other one was a butterball but taller than his friend.

"Take his nose, Drev. Cut it off and make him eat it."

"Don't use my name, asshat."

"Sorry, I just—"

"It's fine," said Drev, "I like that idea. You hungry, asshole?"

The butterball laughed again.

"Baby's gonna eat his nose, baby's gonna eat his nose."

"Shut up," said Drev. "We're going to make this slow. We're going to make this last. I'm going to take your nose, and then I'm going to take your ears."

Drev and the butterball giggled. They shared a glance, like a married couple when they're thinking the same thing.

"And then," said Drev, "I'm going to—"

Drev never finished his sentence. He never finished anything ever again. His head snapped away in a loud puff of red rain and gore. There was only the top of his neck and throat and a bit of his jaw left. Blood gushed. I couldn't hear anything other than a high-pitched whistling. Blood covered my chest. Drev's body collapsed to the side. His left arm draped over my hip.

The butterball stuttered. He stared at Drev's body. I swatted the dead man's arm off me. The ringing in my ears faded.

"Oh shit, oh shit, oh shit," said the butterball, his voice barely more than a whisper. I turned my head to look up and see Joe standing in his bathrobe and slippers with a giant shotgun in his hands. Smoke curled from the barrel that had just unloaded a shell of buckshot into Drev, removing his skull in the process. Joe was panting and sweating, and he kept his jaw clenched. He looked at me and aimed the shotgun at the butterball.

"Please, mister. I'm a good guy, I swear."

Joe looked at me.

I nodded and gave a two-finger wave.

Joe pulled the trigger and blew away the butterball's guts and spine.

❄

Joe and I walked back together.

We didn't talk much. He called me a "real asshole" a few times, which I couldn't disagree with. Our neighborhood looked different. Not just dark and cold but wrecked and ashamed.

Stranded and abandoned cars aligned the roads. I noticed a lot of the houses had broken windows, some boarded and some not. I smelled smoke but couldn't see any. Joe muttered about riots, but I honestly didn't care enough to ask.

As we neared our homes, I told him we'd have to get our stories straight for when the power came back on and the police showed up.

"What is there to get straight?" he said. "The power went out; the assholes ran amok. A couple of them threatened your life and my life and I defended myself."

"The other one didn't have a weapon," I said. "Can't they prove that?"

"The cops are going to be busy with paperwork until their grand-children graduate law school," said Joe. "Look, a few bad guys got what was coming to them. No one is going to look too deep into that."

"There were a few others that tried to break into my house. They may still be there," I said.

"Want me to come with you?"

"No," I said. "I'm sure they're gone. I got to them with a hammer."

"A hammer? You're a goddamn barbarian, Cash. You're a fucking animal."

The power came on the next day.

The Red Cross set up a relief center at the high school a few miles down the road. Rose and Shirley and I listened to the emergency broadcast on repeat and decided to try to make our way out. As we slowly rolled north, I picked up pedestrians trudging through the snow. Everyone was cold and quiet. Their faces exhausted, stunned, and pale.

Some of the snow had melted into slush. The roads were slightly better, good enough that I saw other trucks carefully roll by, loaded with passengers. Ice lay in patches along the blacktop. Smoke billowed from various spots across town. Helicopters flew above us, and sirens blared in the distance. Other pedestrians, dressed in robes and blankets, trampled through the snow and the brush. Everybody was trying to get somewhere.

A MOTHER'S REMORSE

JAY T. DANE

The car ride up to the cabin was uncomfortably silent through the deserted backroads. Kathrine's worry had only grown during the long drive. Her daughter, now sat in the passenger seat staring out the window, hadn't said a word to her since she'd announced that they would be going up north for the holidays this year.

She tried to be patient, but it was no easy task explaining to a sixteen-year-old that she would have to do without her friends over the winter break. It wasn't to punish her. Kathrine wished she could see that. She had made this decision because she needed to get away from the city. She needed room to think and to breathe without feeling like everyone around her was breathing down her neck at every moment.

A trip out north to a more rural setting would surely help her get her head straight.

The snow began to pick up as she signaled to turn onto a gravel side road. They were almost there now, and they'd be settled in for their vacation shortly. Everything would be okay.

Despite the unsettling mood in the vehicle, the scenery rounding the bend toward the cabins was beautiful. A wonderland come to life through the ice and the branches surrounding them. The isolation would take a few days to adjust to, but to Kathrine, the idea seemed peaceful.

The cabins were in view now; they were cozy wooden buildings fit to belong in paintings frozen in time. The office to check in was just up the road, and it was just as cozy looking as the cabins.

She parked, keeping the car running. She looked over to her daughter. "I'll be right back, Mia. You okay?"

Mia didn't move her eyes from the window. "I'm fine, mom."

Kathrine sighed and got out of the car.

Inside the check-in office, the woman behind the counter looked up and smiled at her as she opened the door. She stood up from her chair. "You must be Mrs. Benton, it's so nice to meet you. I'm Amanda Cresner."

Kathrine smiled and shook Amanda's hand. "Yes, it's nice to meet you, too, Amanda. Please, call me Kathrine." She shifted her eyes around the office. "It's very beautiful up here, I'm surprised there aren't more visitors around this time of year."

Amanda waved her hand. "Oh, it's mostly the weather that keeps folks away around this time. The snow can get pretty heavy and it's quite a ways back into town to get anything." She handed Kathrine a key. "But don't worry, I've got your cabin all stocked up with supplies and there's some food for you in the storage freezer in the cellar, so you'll be all set for your stay. If you need anything else at all, don't hesitate to call me and I'll get whatever you need for you."

Kathrine smiled. "Oh, well thank you so much, that's very generous. It's just me and my daughter for the week so we should be alright, but I'll keep that in mind."

Amanda smiled again and sat back down in the chair behind her. "It's no problem at all. I've got the two of you checked in and you're all set with your key there for cabin number three. I hope you both enjoy it here."

"We're looking forward to it. Thank you again, Amanda." She started for the door.

"Of course, Kathrine, I'll see you both around."

Kathrine gave her a wave as she left the office.

Key in hand, Kathrine already felt better about things. She was certain the time they had up here would fix everything and that Mia would eventually agree with the decision.

She got back in the car and looked at her daughter, who hadn't moved, "Are you going to be okay?"

"That depends," Mia huffed, "are we going home?"

Kathrine sighed and drove them to cabin number three.

The cabin was just as nice on the inside as it was on the outside, with rustic decor and cozy looking furniture. The only problem was the cold silence that radiated through their temporary home. This wasn't what Kathrine had had in mind, not at all.

This trip was supposed to help them, but Mia, her sixteen-year-old daughter, still wouldn't speak to her, not even after she'd tried to make her favourite dinner. Both the gesture and the food had gone untouched.

It had gotten dark outside, and in the warmth of the dim light in the kitchen, Katherine cleaned up the dishes. She wished there was something that could help, she wished she would have another dream that would tell her what to do.

Surely, if she went up and talked to Mia, they'd be able to talk things out and it wouldn't come to that.

She hung the drying towel back up on its peg and wiped her hands on her pants. This trip had been so last minute and a complete surprise to her daughter, of course she was going to act out about it. She was sixteen and it was her winter break.

A wave of chills ran through Katherine's spine as she walked down the hall to Mia's room. There was nothing to be frightened of, but there was something about this place that made her feel as if she was being watched.

It had happened before.

She stood outside her daughter's room, which Mia had retreated to immediately upon their arrival, with her heart heavy in her chest. There were no flickering lights, no cold spots or anything, just washes of orange light over the wooden walls.

She stood there in the silence of the hallway, just looking, looking, looking at the engraved trim work on the wood. She wasn't in control of her own body. Her breathing was forced, her head felt heavy, the hallway itself was suffocating her, she—

The door flew open, and she jumped.

"Mom? What are you doing?" Mia's brown eyes looked angry but softened to concern the longer Kathrine stood there.

"Mom?"

Kathrine broke out of her state. "Yes I- I'm fine I just, how did you know I was out here?"

Mia's face turned to worry. "I heard footsteps. I thought you were going to come in but then I just heard loud breathing for a few minutes and it... it kind of scared me."

Kathrine furrowed her eyebrows. "I didn't mean to scare you, honey, I'm sorry. I must have just zoned out. I was wondering if I could talk to you because... I know going on this trip is hard for you. I'd like to explain myself, and see if there's any way I could make it up to you?"

Mia looked annoyed again, but didn't say no. She walked back into the room and sat on her bed, her clothes and her things were already all over the place. At least she was making herself at home.

Kathrine took this as a sign for her to come and sit, so she walked into the room and perched herself on a rather old looking but comfortable chair by the window and folded her hands in her lap. The chair was adorned with old lace doilies, which reminded Kathrine of her own mother's house. A thought both odd and comforting.

She began picking at the delicate lace as she spoke. "I know the last little while hasn't been easy for you, and I know that a lot of that is my fault. I booked this trip for us because I thought that some time out in the fresh air and the quiet would do us both some good, but I see now that it was selfish of me. We're different people and you need different things than I do. I can't ask you to forgive me... I know that I took you away from a lot of things, over the holidays no less, but I just needed some time. I needed some time to think and get away from things."

Mia fiddled with a blue sweater that she'd thrown over her bed. "I just had so much going on, Mom. My therapy appointments, my piano lessons. I was going to go to Christmas dinner at Anna's house and I was so looking forward to that. I was getting better."

She couldn't stand how hurt her daughter looked. "I know, I know and I'm so sorry, but I called your therapist and your piano teacher, and they know you'll be coming back in a week or so. And Christmas with Anna, I know she's your best friend, but she'll understand. You can tell her it was my fault that you weren't there. I couldn't leave you on your own and I had to get away. After your dad left and the incident at work—"

"Dad left because he couldn't handle you and your psychic crap anymore." There were tears in her eyes. "Work? Mom, you got fired from work because you kept telling your coworkers that you had a vision of something bad happening to them." She waved her hands in the air at the word 'vision'. "I know you believe in all that, Mom, but it's too much for other people and you don't see that. I'm your kid and it's too much for me. The visions, the dreams, all of that, that's why your life is falling apart, Mom. You can't just tell people horrible things and expect them to be normal about it."

The sinking frozen feeling surrounded her again. "Your dad left because he's an arrogant man who won't listen to reason when it's right in front of his face. My coworker? I don't even know how you found out about that, but she had it coming. The spirit world is unforgiving to abhorrent souls, and she was one of them! This isn't '*psychic crap,*' Mia, this is a gift I've been given and everyone else around me refuses to see it."

Mia ran her hands through her dark hair in frustration. "You're the problem, Mom! I don't understand why you can't see that, but you have to stop with the visions and the paranoia. You're getting worse and you refuse to believe anyone."

Kathrine stood up, not quite feeling like herself. "There is no problem with me," her voice rose, "we're on this trip for me to figure things out and make things better. You're my daughter and you had to come with me. If you don't like it, then too bad for you. I came in here to help you and you're throwing my actions back in my face. I can't help you when you're like this!"

Mia stood up too. "I'm not, I'm telling you the truth. You make everyone around you miserable because you scare them, Mom. You scare me!" The tears were running down her face now. "I'm miserable and now I'm stuck here with you in this old, creepy cabin for over a week. There's not even enough reception for me to be able to talk to anyone from home. We're in the middle of nowhere."

Rage overtook Kathrine. "Oh, I make you miserable? You never think about how all of this makes *me* feel. I have a gift and people think I'm crazy, do you know what that's like? *That's* miserable. I'm here to fix things, and we'll leave when I say we're leaving."

"You're running away, Mom. That doesn't fix anything." Mia's voice was quieter now, "You need help." The last word was almost a whisper.

Kathrine was too stunned at her daughter to make an angry retort. Instead, she walked to the door. "I have all the help I need."

She closed the door so quietly it barely made a sound. The light in the hallway flickered.

The heavy feeling didn't leave her. The walls were thin, and she swore she could hear Mia crying occasionally. She wanted to fix things, but everything was only getting worse.

It was true that people feared her gift, but she never thought that her daughter would be bothered by it too. She shouldn't have been bothered by it. She was her daughter after all! Not her father's. Hers. Katherine's.

She got ready for bed in the silence of the dark, the only light in the cabin came from a small antique lamp on the nightstand in her room.

In the dim of the bathroom, she stared at herself in the mirror. There was something wrong here that had followed them from home, and she knew that it had something to do with her daughter. Kathrine needed a way to fix her, to get her on her side. It was the only way.

She had stared so long that it seemed her face was starting to change in her reflection. A single word came to her: *Rebirth*.

Yes...if there was a way to get Mia to understand where she was coming from, she needed her daughter to be reborn. Perhaps in doing so, it would give her the same abilities that she herself possessed.

This would fix everything.

She walked down the hallway to her room adjacent to Mia's. The fear that had gripped her earlier in the evening began to fill her again the closer she got to the end of the hallway. It grew stronger and stronger until it was almost too much for her right outside Mia's room.

The light from her room illuminated the panels on the door as she raised her hand to them. Upon touching the door, blackness tried to overtake her heart.

In that moment of frozen terror, she realized with horror that her own child was the negative presence that was following her around. It oozed through the door like a plague so thick she swore she could see it.

A creak on the other side of the door sent her spinning into her room, nearly slamming the door as she went. This would not do; she would not let her only child be possessed by some demon that caused chaos and unrest in their lives.

She would fix this.

Kathrine crawled into bed, willing wholeheartedly that the dreams would come to her and tell her how to save her daughter, her family. She needed them to come again to remind her.

The slow tick of the analog clock lulled her to sleep, and she dreamed.

It came in bursts and flashes. Mia's eyes were black, not the eyes of her daughter.

The outbursts, the exhaustion, the detachment, it all made sense now. Her daughter was possessed by evil, it was all so clear now. The girl sleeping in the room across from her own was not her child and she hadn't been for some time.

Put her to sleep, put her to sleep so she can wake up.

Save her. Save her.

Flashes of the sleeping pills she'd been prescribed. The storage freezer in the cellar. *Put her to sleep, put her to sleep to fix her.*

The cold, the cold would drive the demon out.

Black tendrils coming out of Mia's body as Kathrine laid her, unconscious, in the freezer. She needed to go to sleep so that she could be reborn.

Fix her, fix her, save her.

Kathrine woke up in the blackness of her room. Now, she knew. There was no other way to get her daughter back.

The next day went by without much incident, Mia still wasn't speaking to her, but she had to come out of her room at some point. It had been over a day since she'd eaten anything, and she was bound to be hungry by now.

Kathrine spent the day sitting and planning. The dreams had come to her with a solution, and she had to figure out a way to carry it out. It wasn't something that she wanted to do or felt comfortable with, but the dreams knew that it would save Mia from the evil that held her. She would *have* to do it.

The sleeping pills were in her room in her suitcase, untouched for the most part. They did help her sleep, but they made dreaming difficult, so it wasn't often that she used them. The bottle sat mostly full in the month that she'd had it.

Kathrine didn't know how many sleeping pills became harmful for a person to take at once. She knew she'd have to be careful; the last thing she wanted to do was *kill* Mia; just the evil inside. The regular dose she was supposed to take was two maximum per night, so maybe five? Ten might make her sick but settling on seven or eight sounded correct.

She was almost grateful that the creature inhabiting her daughter made her stay in her room, it would make preparing everything a whole lot easier. To her knowledge, the two of them were the only ones staying in the cabins, so the only thing she would have to worry about was running into Amanda when she took Mia to the cellar.

The weather seemed to be on her side for that, too. The snow had picked up to near whiteout conditions and it got dark fast around here in the winter. The cover of night, along with the blizzard, should be enough for her to execute her plan without interruption.

Kathrine got up from trying to read her book. It would be easier to crush up the pills before Mia came out of her room.

The crushing feeling of doom and claustrophobia was stronger than ever when she went through the hallway to her room, but she tried her best to stay focused. She was trying to fix this; she would fix this.

The bottle was shoved in the bottom of her toiletry bag. She quickly grabbed the bottle and nearly ran back to the kitchen before setting it on the counter and staring at it.

The prescription label stared back at her in bold letters in the dead silence of the room. Kathrine felt cold and shivery as she opened the cap. Every movement she made felt too loud and too big.

She took the pills out one by one, counting out eight with shaking hands, then putting one back.

In a mechanical state, she put the pills into a plastic storage bag and grabbed the rolling pin that sat in a holder above the stove. Slowly, she crushed the pills into a powder, taking care to not make any overly loud noises.

Kathrine felt cold all over. It felt wrong. What she was doing scared her, yet she knew that if she questioned the dreams, then she would be denying her own abilities. The visions came to help her, she had to trust them.

The pills had been ground down to a fine powder, now she just had to wait for things to fall into place.

The cozy cabin now felt heavy in her bones, the sound of the wind blowing outside made her feel frozen all over. Every creak in the wooden walls spoke of evil in her ears.

Mia appeared in the kitchen late in the afternoon, her face held the heaviness of exhaustion. The bags under her eyes were significantly worse than when they had arrived at the cabin. Her hair was messy and the blue sweater she wore seemed to swallow her.

"Hey, Mom." Her voice was quiet and raw as if she'd been crying.

Kathrine tried to ignore what was obviously a sympathy tactic from the demon. "Hi, honey, how are you feeling?"

Mia stepped further into the room and sat in one of the big leather chairs. "I'm okay, just hungry and really cold." She looked around the room. "Do we know if the heat is on or not?"

Kathrine shook her head. "It is a bit cold in here. I can check with Amanda later to see if there's a way to fix the temperature, but you're probably freezing because you haven't eaten anything. Did you want me to make you something to eat?"

Mia nodded. "You're probably right. That would be nice, thanks, Mom."

Kathrine smiled through the pit in her stomach. "I'll go check the storage freezer and see what's there. I think they've left us with some frozen meals."

Mia smiled. "Okay, thank you." She rubbed her face with her sleeve.

Kathrine got her coat and her boots on with her heart pounding, jumping when she heard Mia behind her. "I know it's kind of early, but if you get yourself something too, we could have an early dinner if you want?"

Kathrine smiled. "That's a great idea!" She sounded too excited in her own ears.

Mia touched her arm as she put her gloves on, and she nearly reeled back. The darkness seemed to crawl up her veins. "You okay, Mom? I'm sorry, I know I haven't been the easiest on you lately." She looked sad.

Kathrine smiled bigger and pulled her arm back as discreetly as she could. "I'm okay, honey, I'm just glad you're out of your room."

Before Mia could reply, she pulled open the front door and made her way to the cellar. The wind nearly toppled her over, the snow and dark made it impossible to see, but the cellar wasn't too far away.

She rounded the wooden deck, holding onto the railing. Around the back of the cabin, the cellar door loomed in front of her. It wasn't a traditional ground cellar, it was just a back door in the cabin that led to a cellar room that had been blocked off from the rest of the building, for insulation purposes she assumed.

Kathrine pulled the door open, surprised at the weight of it. The dark and quiet of the room mixed with the blustery whistling of the wind made her shiver. Could she really put her little girl here? But as soon as her eyes adjusted, she pulled the chain hanging from the ceiling to turn on the light.

The concrete room was dim in the single orange lightbulb by the entrance, the cold too much for her to bear. The freezer sat alone in the far corner of the room.

She didn't want to touch it. It felt as if at any moment, the door would close behind her and she would be locked in the room forever. It was common knowledge that evil could sense when someone was planning to evict it. It always became more powerful.

The lid of the freezer creaked as she opened it, and she gasped in fright. She shook her head, she *had* to get it together.

There were indeed a few frozen meals and other things stacked up in the freezer, but even with everything inside, she could see that her daughter would easily still fit inside if her legs were bent. The plan would work, the plan would work. It had to work.

Kathrine took a deep breath and chose two boxes at random, too caught up to pay attention.

She quickly walked out of the room, slamming the door behind her. The loud boom made her jump again.

She shifted the boxes of food to one arm and grabbed the deck railing, taking a moment to stand there and take a few breaths. The dark felt like it was closing in on her.

Standing up straighter and setting her shoulders, she walked calmly back to the front door. This would work.

She took one last breath before pushing open the door and going back inside.

"Hey, Mia, we've got," she looked down at the boxes in her hands, "lasagna or macaroni with extra cheese for our choices."

Mia looked up from her chair. "I'll take the macaroni if that's okay."

Kathrine pulled off her boots and hung her coat back up. "Yeah, of course. You sit here and I'll go heat them up for us." She grabbed the boxes and walked towards the kitchen. "It really is freezing; did you want a hot chocolate or a tea with your food? I think I saw some in the cupboard."

Mia's eyebrows raised. "I'll take a hot chocolate, thanks. Do you want some help?"

Kathrine's heart pounded. "No, no, I'm alright. You sit and try to get cozy, maybe find something on TV we could watch."

Mia sat back in the chair. "Okay."

Kathrine felt a wave of relief wash over her. She couldn't have anything go wrong.

The relief didn't last long. Her anxiety peaked as she took out the bag of crushed pills from the drawer where she had hidden them. The microwave felt like it went on and on forever as she waited with nerves piling in her stomach. This had to work.

The ding made her jump when the timer finally went off. She was on autopilot as she dumped most of the powder over her daughter's food. She was starving, but looking at those crushed pills over the food almost made her lose her appetite. Quickly, she stirred it in and shoved it to the back of the counter to cool while she made the hot chocolate. When that was done, she dumped the remaining powder in and stirred.

This had to work. This would work.

She brought it out to Mia along with the macaroni before going back to get her own lasagna. A crime show they usually watched together was playing on the TV. She wanted to faint.

It was nearing five o'clock by then, the full darkness had taken over the sky. It should have been a cozy evening shared by the two of them, but Kathrine was riddled with worry. Trying not to stare as her daughter ate the medication laced dinner filled her own body with a sense of dread that somehow the evil knew. It knew, and the plan wasn't going to work.

It had to work.

Half an hour after she'd eaten, Mia looked like she was fighting to stay awake. Her head rolled back a few times as she tried her best to stay sitting up.

She looked over at Kathrine apologetically. "I don't know why, but I feel like I can't stay awake to save my life right now. I know we were gonna stay up and watch this together, but I've got to go to sleep, Mom." She looked confused, "Maybe I just need a bit of a nap and I'll feel better later." Her eyes looked bruised now.

Kathrine's voice was too high pitched, "Aw that's okay, honey, maybe some rest is a good idea. I'll be right here if you decide to come back. I'll get your dishes for you. Head back to your room."

Mia nodded and rubbed at her face. "Okay, Mom. Thank you."

Once Mia left the room, Kathrine let out a sigh. Now all she had to do was wait.

Nobody ever talks about how heavy an unconscious body is. Even a smaller one feels like a ton of bricks when being carried. Kathrine had found this out the hard way.

She wasn't a religious woman, but she prayed to anything that would listen that Mia wouldn't wake up as she dragged her limp body through the cabin. If the plan didn't go right, then this would be the end of everything.

The wind howled outside in the darkness. It was a true blizzard now. The sheet of white out the window might hinder her instead of helping her, but there was nothing she could do about it. She carried on moving Mia through the cabin, troubled.

Not enough. I didn't give it enough pills.

Mia's body would wake up soon if Kathrine kept moving her around so much. She had to hurry. All she had to do was get her to the cellar and everything would be okay. Her baby would be okay, and this would all be over soon.

She put on her boots and her coat in a methodical fashion, not fully paying attention to what she was doing, and opened the front door. Immediately the snow began to blow inside and the wind froze her to her core, causing her to shake along with her fear.

The porch light flickered.

She lifted Mia and cradled her to her chest, "It's going to be okay, Mia," she whispered. Her words were swallowed up by the sound of the storm.

The cold hit her bones like a wall as she walked outside, not bothering to close the door behind her. The one thing she could be grateful for was that there was nobody else here. No one would see her.

She carried her daughter through the freezing cold. The cellar door felt like it was miles away. The porch lights continued to flicker.

The walk was slow, her heart pounded, but soon the door was in sight. Shifting Mia to balance her weight better, she pulled open the door.

The room seemed darker after the sun went down. She pulled the chain to turn on the light, but the room still seemed dark to her. A trick from the demon to keep ger from completing what had to be done. There was darkness seeping into everything, everywhere.

Kathrine huffed as she propped Mia up against the wall, as gently as she could manage. Her body was going to hurt tomorrow. All she knew was the cold and the tension, but it would all be over soon.

She pulled open the lid on the freezer, confident that things would be okay. The darkness couldn't scare her when she was this close to saving her daughter, now it only fuelled her.

She hefted up Mia's body in her arms again and gently placed her in the freezer with all the frozen meals. "Everything will be okay, honey. I'll see you soon."

She leaned down and kissed Mia's forehead before closing the lid and shutting her inside. An immediate wave of relief washed over her; it was done.

It's done, I've saved her from evil.

Kathrine breathed out a sigh, shut out the light, and closed the cellar door.

Everything was going to be okay now.

She woke with a start in the small hours of the morning. The howling of the blizzard had stopped outside, the only sound was that of the ticking clock on the wardrobe. She was alone, yet she knew that she wasn't the only one in the room.

Kathrine looked around with sudden dread filling her chest; she didn't have her contacts in. She couldn't see. She was too afraid to move or switch on the lamp.

Someone was standing in the corner of her room.

She felt frozen, unable to react.

The figure shifted forward in short, quick movements. Kathrine couldn't bring herself to scream, only a low squeak came from her chest. As her eyes adjusted to the light, she could see that the figure was short, with what looked like long hair and a sweater that was way too big.

She squinted. "Mia?" Her pitched voice cracked through the dark silence.

"Mooooommmm? Mooommmmm? Can't... feel... can't—"

Kathrine woke with a start, her heart pounding. It was only a dream, only a silly dream. Her dreams could be wrong sometimes. Mia was fine, she would be waking up soon now and everything would be back to normal.

She went out about her day, still wracked with the paranoia of her nightmare. She was starting to calm down when a knock on the door late in the afternoon sent her heart racing again.

She opened the door to find Amanda standing on the porch, of course it would be her. The blonde woman smiled. "Hey Kathrine! I just came to check on you and see if everything was alright, that was one heck of a storm last night, wasn't it?"

Kathrine smiled nervously. "Oh, it was. That wind was something else. Mia and I hunkered down for the night with some meals from the cellar freezer and tried to get in an early night." She remembered to ask, "We were wondering if there was a way to turn up the heat. We had blankets and everything, but it did get quite cold in here."

"I'm so sorry about that, the thermostat should have been set to twenty-one degrees Celsius when it gets this cold. It's right in the living room if you want me to check it for you?"

Kathrine stopped when she saw the porch light flickering

violently. She tightened her grip on the door. "Oh, that's alright. It's not a big deal, I can figure it out." She smiled.

Amanda smiled back but Kathrine noticed her concern. "Okay, well... if you need anything, you know where to find me. I'm glad you're both okay."

Katherine waved as Amanda made her way down the steps. "Thank you."

She stepped back inside and slammed the door shut before leaning against it. She couldn't let anyone near this place until Mia was back.

When she opened her eyes, there was a figure standing in the living room entrance. Her heart stopped as the lights blinked haphazardly. It was Mia, but there was something wrong.

Her long brown hair was messy and filled with small chunks of ice. Her eye sockets were hollow and purple, her cheeks were nearly green with swelling. The tip of her nose was black, and so were her toes and her small fingers poking out of her big blue sweater. There was a long scrape across her forehead. Her lips were blue.

Kathrine nearly screamed.

The figure reached out a hand. "*Moooooommm.*" Her voice was strained.

Kathrine squeezed her eyes shut, it wasn't real, it wasn't real. Mia was going to be okay, and everything was going to be fine. She had *saved* her. When she opened her eyes again, the figure in the form of her daughter was gone.

As the evening grew darker, so did her fear. There was something in the cabin with her that was terribly wrong. It wasn't supposed to be here, it wasn't supposed to exist. She wanted to run to the cellar and check if her daughter was okay, but she knew that she couldn't disturb the process. Whatever demon had possessed her would be gone soon and everything would be okay, the things that had happened today were only apart of the dream.

Everything would be okay; everything would be okay. The more she told herself that, the less the phrase seemed like words at all.

Kathrine had turned every light in the cabin on to keep the demon out, but the lights flickered on despite her efforts. She'd checked the thermostat; it sat at 21 degrees just as Amanda said it should be, yet the cabin continued to grow colder. She had long ago stopped trying to go on with her day, she could only sit with her back against the wall, shivering in paranoid terror.

She could hear occasional whispers seeming to mock her for her fear, they all sounded like Mia. All she wanted was her daughter back.

Kathrine sat with her knees pulled to her chest and her head in her hands. She couldn't bear to look at the room anymore. The lights and the whispers would drive her mad soon. Something was wrong.

"Mom?"

Kathrine jumped and looked up. Mia was standing before her, her face and body still deformed with severe frostbite as it had been earlier. She wasn't supposed to come back like this.

Her eyes were wide in terror as she stared up at her daughter. Mia's voice was like a whispered croak, her hair dripping melting ice onto the wood floor. "Why'd you do that to me, Mom?"

Kathrine stuttered, tried to stand, and failed. "I-I had to save you; you're being manipulated by evil. Honey, I had to save you from it." She suddenly became aware in her pleading that she could see her breath.

"I'm dead, Mom. You killed *me*." The sound of droplets filled the silence.

Kathrine shook her head. "I didn't kill you, you're confused, sweetie. You- you're gonna wake up soon, Mia, and everything is going to be okay."

A wave of cold went through the room and Kathrine was lifted to her feet. Mia blinked slowly. "Listen to me, Mom, listen. My body is in the freezer now. Before I died, I woke up in the dark... in the cold. The frozen. I felt so sick... couldn't feel anything. I couldn't move. I couldn't... *breatheee.*" Her voice rattled something terrible. She put a hand on Kathrine's face and suddenly looked very sad. "Didn't know where I was. Couldn't talk... couldn't move. I died. You *muuurdereeed* me, Mom."

Kathrine's chest pounded as she looked into the ghostly, devastated eyes of her daughter. *What had she done? What had she DONE?* No. No. Oh, no. She shook her head wildly, but the frozen hand on her didn't budge.

A sob tore through her throat. "I *saved* you. I had to get rid of the evil, I had to help you. I didn't- I didn't mean for this. I never meant for this." Her tears burned her face as they froze to her cheeks.

There was something else in Mia's eyes. "You did no saving, Mom, only... *judgiiing.* The only evil was in your mind, and you killed me for it." Another slow, rattled breath.

Kathrine put her hands in her daughter's icy hair and wailed. "I didn't want this, not this, not this! I wanted my little girl back!"

Her daughter's blackened fingers dug into the sides of her face with both hands. That strange, sad look stayed in her eyes. "All I needed was time... to *talk.* You tore it away, and now I will take everything from you, too. *Everythinggg.*"

Kathrine felt her very bones grow stiff with cold, she couldn't breathe. "Please, please, Mia, I didn't mean for this to happen. I didn't want this." Her brain felt foggy and slow.

Mia's face contorted. "You wanted to save me. Now I will *saaaveee youuu.*"

Kathrine tried to push her away. "Please, no. Mia, *please.* I'm sorry." Her last words were no more than a breath as her body went numb and everything turned black.

Albert Farley had seen a lot over the years working as the Bruce County forensic pathologist, but nothing so crazy as this. On his autopsy table was an older middle-aged woman, who had been brought in with her daughter. The daughter had been frozen and suffocated after being stuffed in a large freezer. It wasn't clear what had happened to the mother, so an autopsy had been requested.

Upon cutting open the woman's chest, Albert saw something he had never seen in his sixty-two years of life. So bewildered, he paused the autopsy and made a call to the coroner.

The coroner, Andrew Lawrence, made his way downstairs, entering the exam room where the autopsy of Kathrine Benton was in progress. "Hey, Al. What's got you so wound up?"

Albert shook his head. "Her heart. Her heart is completely frozen into ice."

CHILLDREN

G.M. GARNER

Unexpected calls never fail to stoke my anxiety these days, and tonight is no different—especially since it's half past midnight. With no small amount of dread, I set the bookmark between the pages of my novel and rise from my armchair, the house phone's obnoxious jingle dominating the air.

Could it be the doctor's office with some dire unforeseen health warning? Surely not at this hour. A friend caught up in some imaginative situation, needing me to swing by and play taxi three cities away? That could be true if I were twenty years younger and still had anything resembling a social life.

Alyssa is an option, but one that makes no sense. It's been more than three years since our divorce. She's certain by now to have removed me from any emergency contacts or next of kin records. If it were her on the other end, something inconceivably terrible must have happened. Again.

I retrieve the handset from its cradle and press the answer button. With a beep, the line opens. "Walter Morris speaking," I say.

For a moment, there's nothing save for the faint static of the line.

I pause, await a response, and then open my mouth to speak again. Before the breath leaves my throat, someone replies: "Hello?"

The word is said in such a pitiful fashion that it forms ice in my veins. It's a woman... no, a girl. Young. Her voice wavers. Crying, perhaps. A sniffle? I imagine a lone figure sitting in the middle of a dank, secluded basement, clutching an old phone to their ear and begging, *please, take me home.*

"Hello there. Who—who is this?" I stammer, clearing my throat of stuck phlegm. Again, the response takes an uncomfortably long time to arrive.

"Hello?" the girl repeats.

"Yes, hello. I'm here. Who is this? Can I help you?"

"Hello?" she says again. The same tone. The same timbre. That same distraught tremble in the voice—like a recording being played back.

"You know you shouldn't be calling people this late with nonsense," I say. "It isn't funny. Don't call here again." I hang up, place the handset back on the cradle, and return to my armchair, glimpsing at the mistletoe I've hung above it as a marker of the holidays. A somewhat ironic marker, I suppose. I don't know why I bother putting up decorations anymore; it's not like I entertain others or even have others entertain *me*. What's there to celebrate? Still, each year I continue to add seasonal touches to the house. The wreath on the door, a few stretches of garland here and there. Purple tinsel—it was always Katie's favorite color—stretches across the mantlepiece, where I keep those old family photographs turned to face the wall. They come in useful at times, when I close my eyes and can no longer picture our daughter's face—though each time I steal a glimpse, I can't help but wonder if Alyssa's gaze was always so pregnant with accusation.

And all of it, from the festive decorations to the phone and the photos, feels like an inside joke I'm coming to acknowledge holds a punchline aimed squarely at me. Alyssa always did refer to me as a walking anachronism—one foot in modernity and the other planted squarely in a past that's probably best left buried. I suppose she's right.

The phone remains silent for the rest of the night, but I find it impossible to return to my battered and time-worn copy of Moby Dick—just another of the childhood treasures I still keep around. My agitated mind wanders, echoing back to that strange, desperate voice, and I steady myself with a nightcap before drifting off into an uncomfortable sleep.

Around 8pm the next evening, the phone rings again. I decide to let the answering machine screen the call, its robotic voice offering a stock greeting: *I'm sorry, there is no one available to take your call. Please leave a message after the tone.*

The speakerphone beeps and offers the line's constant hum. When a caller doesn't want to leave a message, this would usually be followed by another swift beep as they hang up. But tonight, that trembling drone seems to flood from the cradle's tiny speaker, creeping into the room to swim around me as I stand and wait for someone to speak, slowly sinking—deeper, deeper—into the encroaching sea of static.

A chill in the air washes over me, raising goosebumps on my arms, and I can't tell if it is a legitimate winter breeze or just a psychosomatic response to my discomfort in the moment because while I can't hear a voice among that static, I *do* detect breath. Human breath.

And I become more acutely aware of my solitude than ever before.

The breath isn't heavy. It's not lewd, like you might expect from a nuisance caller, nor even pregnant with the anticipation of someone who doesn't realize they've gone to voicemail. It's just... there.

Or maybe it isn't.

The call cuts off at the same moment three loud knocks sound from my front door, the answering machine's disconnecting beep emphasizing the first of the impacts.

My cellphone vibrates in my pocket. I check the notification and see it's coming from the smart doorbell mounted at the front of the house. I wait a moment, anticipating another knock. When it doesn't arrive, I press the notification and launch the doorbell's video feed.

My driveway. Nothing else. My car remains parked in its usual spot on the left, the center of the image filled with nothing but the path to my front gate, rendered visible by the camera's night vision and the single streetlight next to the road. The silhouette of the tree line surrounding the fields beyond looks disturbingly flat in the darkness, like a cheap cardboard cutout in the background of an underproduced stage play. From the doorbell's audio feed, there's only the faint sound of a dog barking somewhere in the distance and—

"Hello?"

The girl bellows from the cell's speaker so loudly that I fumble in surprise, dropping the phone to the carpet below. She sounds exactly as she did before. That same uncertain shake. The same pitch. The snippet of sound is even the same *length*, distorted and infinitely more disturbing filtered through the phone's tinny speakers.

My scalp tingles and the rest of me quickly follows suit, skin tightening all over as if contracting in preparation for a screaming leap from my body. Though the phone is on the floor, I can still see the video feed as I grind my teeth and try to will my hammering heart back to a steady rhythm. There's no one there. Only the glowing eyes of what I guess to be a cat, slinking around the edge of the gate and disappearing into the dark with one quick, darting look at the camera.

Whoever this is, they've opted to escalate their harassment—moving from mere phone calls to actually showing up at my home. The cat was probably startled by the human presence, opting to move away from whatever giggling teenager was now scrambling off my property on hands and knees—thrilled, for some godforsaken reason, that they've scared the living shit out of some washed-up miser they don't even know.

The fear drains from me, replaced with rage as I stomp my way to the front door. I pull back the curtain and stare, head pulsing with blood, through the side window as I flick the porch light on... but there's nothing. They've already escaped.

My breath condenses on the glass, informing me that yes, the house is indeed well on its way to freezing. I head to the basement and check the furnace, but all appears to be operating as normal. A broken thermostat, perhaps? I take a quick tour of the rooms upstairs to check for open windows and get a feel for whether hot air is circulating anywhere.

Through the window of the spare bedroom, I spy a large rectangle of light hanging in the darkness below. Inside of that rectangle, my closest neighbor, Alan, sits in his lounge, a broadsheet newspaper opened wide.

Just a few minutes later, I'm trudging my way toward Alan's house. It's a stone's throw, but the homes out here are spread out enough to guarantee a measure of privacy. Long driveways, high fences, big gardens. The streetlights overhead offer little respite from the dark, managing only to punch a few feet into the woods that line the side of the road opposite me. Beyond the woods, the scenery opens up to wide fields and the expanse of Broker's Pond.

On a night like this, you can almost see the shimmer of the water as it floats above the trees, carried into the air by moonlight. This was why we moved here—plenty of open space for Katie to play and explore. She could get dirty, climb trees, boat on the pond with her brother if we actually got around to having another child. But that wasn't to be, and all I'm left with is my private space among a Great British countryside that feels anything but great.

Soon enough, I'm standing on Alan's front porch, puffing miniature clouds into the frigid air and rubbing my hands together, wishing I'd chosen to wear gloves as well as my coat.

"Hi, Alan," I say, raising my hand in greeting as he opens the door, "sorry to bother you this late, but I saw you were up and... well, do you have a few minutes?"

"Walter!" A friendly smile spreads across his face as he steadies himself on his cane. "What can I do for you?" He pauses there, smile rigid, before my discomfort in the cold outside becomes obvious. "Oh," he gasps, "forgive me, you must be freezing. Come inside and have a drink."

"Thanks, Alan," I say as he steps aside and welcomes me in. It's been at least six months since we last talked—properly *talked*—but the gentleness of Alan's nature makes it feel like we could have sat together only yesterday. Pushing his mid-eighties, Alan is creeping up on twice my age, but the generational difference has never posed a barrier to the ease with which we get along. Our shared love of Blues music certainly helps.

"Oh, you know you can call me Al, Walter," he says. "And while I have you here, I just wanted to say how awful it was to hear the news. Terrible business, just terrible. I—"

"Well, it... it was a long time ago now, Al," I say, not wishing to take this particular line of conversation any further. Not here. Not now. Not again. "Let's not get into it. Please."

He pauses, head cocked to the side. His eyes flit back and forth, like they're searching some invisible file cabinet, and with a sharp inhale, he opens his mouth again. "Oh, of course, yes, yes it..." He dips his head, taking on a more sheepish posture before looking up at me again. "I'm sorry, Walt. Don't mean to rub salt in old wounds. Come in, come in. Take a seat."

Al's home is well cared for, but clearly the empty nest of a single elderly man. An old mahogany bookcase lines the far wall of the living room, a gallery of creased spines and yellowing paper. Small stacks of broadsheets clutter the space next to a retro record player, freestanding speakers tall and proud despite the dust that chokes their acoustic cloth, muting the soothing vibe of Otis Rush as he croons about a love he just can't quit.

Al motions to the couch opposite his armchair and moves to the liquor cabinet, resting his cane against the side as the clinking of glasses begins.

Before sitting down, I glance between the open curtains behind the couch, spying my own house looming above the line of hedges at the rear of Al's garden. The faint light of the upstairs landing escapes from the window of the spare bedroom, and already I feel it beckon me back to my seclusion.

"Just a quick visit, Al," I say. "Listen, have you had any trouble lately? Anyone giving you a hassle? Teenagers, maybe? Knocks on the door, things like that?"

He hands me a tumbler containing a good three fingers of bourbon, then shuffles his way to his armchair. "Hmm... no," he says, shaking his head as he sits down. "You know me. Just ticking on day by day over here."

"Hmm." I nod, cradling the glass in my hands. Something in me feels strangely disappointed that my elderly neighbor isn't suffering the same treatment I am. It would be company, at least.

"I remember we used to do that when I was young." A low chuckle. "Knock on doors and run. Sometimes we'd even hide right under the steps. *Right there.* Hold our breath and try not to laugh. It meant you could knock again almost straight away. Send 'em crazy. All fun and games until an angry neighbor shows up at the door and dad gives you what for. *Show some bloody respect, boy!*" He shakes his fist in the air, comically, then stares at his bourbon, swilling it in the glass as though searching for divinations in tea leaves. "Not like we learned, though. We'd be right back out the next night, on our way to another belting."

He looks up at me. "Thing is, Walt, we did respect our elders. We just weren't thinking about anything more than having a bit of fun. What youngster *really* thinks about the other side of the equation, eh? It's just... fun." Al seems to get lost again for a moment, before snapping back to lucidity. "Anyway, no, it's just the usual here. I read my papers. I listen to records. Enjoy some of the ol' nectar." A sly wink as he lifts his glass in my direction. "Sometimes a friend comes to visit."

I raise my glass in solidarity and offer him a smile in return.

"My boy called to say hello, but that's..." His brow furrows as he disappears into thought again, eyes quickly glazing over, and I can only imagine what kind of mental knots he must be trying to untangle. But as quickly as he left, he's back, opening his arms wide, a motion intended to encompass the entire room. "Good reason men like us live in places like this, Walt. Sometimes it's better to be out of the way."

"Couldn't put it better myself," I respond with a sigh, then down the rest of my bourbon in one swig. The warmth of it as it spreads through my core feels blissful, and it tunes me in to the chilly temperature of the room. "Bit cold in here, isn't it, Al? Everything okay with the heating? Are you covering the bills and all that? I don't want to be rude or anything, just—"

"Yeah, it's been chilly lately," he says. "Just figured it was these old bones getting ready, you know? *Acclimatizing*, you might say."

"Oh, nonsense. You might be an old fart, but you've clearly got a good bit more in the tank." I divert from the casual grimness of Al's insinuation, but I'm not certain I believe my own.

"Well, it was good to chat, Al. Thanks for the drink—and look, if you ever need anything, I'm just across the way, okay? You get that boy of yours to sort the heating out, all right?" He assures me he will, and before I walk out the door, I turn to find him glassy eyed in recollection once again. "Oh, and Merry Christmas to you and the family."

As I trudge back to the light of my house, I think to myself that I ought to get more of a handle on my self-imposed isolation. Even before I became this reclusive, it seems I've never been great at getting to know people; I've lived next to Alan for more than a decade and didn't even know he had a son.

❄

I don't sleep much these days. Maybe four or five hours a night. But after returning from Al's, the continuing chill in my home, coupled with the early onset of the winter dark, makes me long for the warmth of the bedcovers and I'm drifting off by ten thirty.

Yet as I straddle the boundary between waking and dream, the sound of a short, wheezing intake of breath snaps me back to consciousness.

The blackness of the room seems to fizzle and throb as I stare into it, clutching the quilt with knuckles I assume would be white could I see them. I strain to listen, wondering if the breath may have been my own—an agonal outburst from a body out of rhythm. That must have been it, and I curse myself for allowing nonsensical spectral notions to set me off.

I reach for the bedside lamp and flick the switch. Nothing; just a click.

I try again, rocking the switch and jiggling on the cable, but the light is dead. It's then I realize what was so uncanny about the depth of darkness in the room: on a normal night, it would be diluted by the glow of the street light outside snaking its way around the extremities of the curtains. Tonight, the dark is absolute.

My cellphone, perched in its usual position on the table at the right side of the bed, begins to vibrate. An incoming call from an unknown number. I reach for it and unplug the cable, feeling the shift of weight across the mattress as I roll back into position. Before I can answer, the phone stops vibrating and then—

In my left ear—*right next* to my left ear—

"Hello?"

They're in the room. I unleash a flurry of obscenities, yelling with fright as I spring from the bed and make a mad dash for the door. The light from my phone's screen is dim, but it gives enough illumination for me to find my way and, panting and whimpering, I crash into the hallway.

Staggering forward with drooping, uncoordinated paces, I unlock the phone and switch on its torch, allowing me to descend the stairs as something thumps and slides across the floor above. I thump hard into the front door, no further plan in mind than to run screaming into the night, and scrabble with the keys that hang from the lock. Something slams into the sidelight window and my tongue rattles inside my mouth.

Instinctively, I back away. A small hand, like a series of sticks stuffed inside a sagging green bag, squishes, palm first, against the frosted glass and slides down, the squeak setting my teeth on edge and I scream—dear Lord I can't help but scream—as I follow that hand down to the abominable, rotten face that glares up at me from the cold stone floor of the porch.

I turn to run toward the kitchen, only for the movement of a tiny figure in the doorway—the hint of a tattered purple dress draped over angular limbs, skin mottled, loose, *wet*—to send me scrambling back up the stairs. My ankle twists on an upper step, sending a stinging burst of pain through my leg as I stumble through the nearest doorway and into the spare bedroom. I slam the door behind me and, in the gloom, slide a nearby chair beneath the handle. It should hold. It's got to hold. Then I limp to the window.

An encroaching frost spreads from the bottom of the glass, and beyond I can see the bright, floating loge of Alan's living room.

He's standing at the window and with frantic movements I wave, shouting, "Alan! Alan for God's sake look!" He doesn't move, doesn't signal that he sees me, and so I toggle my cellphone's torch on and off, on and off, as I move it in a circular motion with my arms.

Something about Alan's stillness alerts an impetuous dread and I stop gesturing. Instead, I lean closer, until my nose touches the freezing cold of the window and my hitching breath spreads its own moist distress signal against the glass.

A look of terror sits frozen upon Alan's face, his hands fastened to the handles of his living room window. Literally *fastened*. Icy tears streak glittering trails from eyes as lifeless as his dull blue skin, crawling down to frame a mouth locked in an eternal silent scream.

And then I see the figure in the room with him. Tiny. No more than eight years old, at a glance. Pajamas old and faded, long out of style. A puffy, slackened face, discolored and slightly too big, as if someone mistook the season and slipped a grotesque adult mask onto a child. Yet the thing's bulbous eyes and the thick, swollen tongue that slides in and out between its crooked lips declare the visage is no mere costume.

Worse is that despite the disfigurement, the likeness between Alan and the child is strikingly obvious—and sorrow seizes my heart as I come to understand why I didn't know Alan had a son.

Good reason men like us live in places like this, Walt.

The child-thing stands there, stock still, gaze fixed on Alan's rigid corpse.

Then, in an instant, fixed on *me*.

My stomach lurches and I yell in surprise, pulling the curtains closed to cut myself off from that damnable sight and it, too, from me.

I slide to the floor, resting my back against the wall. My head feels light, swimming, and the urge to cry overtakes me as soon as I hear a timid knock upon the bedroom door.

Scratching.

"Hello?" she says from beyond. Exactly the same as every time before. An impossible repetition.

It takes a moment before I realize the other sound, the keening mewl I can hear ringing in my ears, is coming from my own throat. My legs rub feebly against the carpet as my body wills itself to crawl —an activity of which I'm only vaguely aware on a conscious level. Yet to be made completely mad with fear, mercifully detached from this living nightmare, is a luxury I'm denied.

Something clicks there, in the dark, and the door creaks open as the chair pressed against it slides to the floor. I grip tight on the phone as slowly, slowly, a pillar of the utmost blackness widens, opening a passage into some infinite, inexplicable void. From that void creeps a chill that slithers across the carpet and bites through my toes—penetrates my clothing and skin and sets my teeth chattering, my breath condensing in the room's thinning air.

And as I bring the phone's torchlight down to the lower portion of the doorway, my hands trembling, it reflects a glow from the luminous skin of the broken, grinning thing that slides from the murk and into the room, arms outstretched.

It can't be. "Please, God, no!" I shriek with sheer, unbridled terror, the hands and head of the thing rounding the foot of the bed to reveal, swinging below lank hair and milky eyes, a necklace that now exists—*should only exist*—in grief-stricken photographs, shattered memories and the depths of the earth.

Without ceremony, the light dies, plunging the world into abyssal darkness and leaving me only with the glowing afterimage of her monstrous, emaciated form as Katie reaches out for me, slick and dripping as the day we lost her. The day I failed her.

And as the fetid stench of stagnant water and decaying moss floods my nose, the breathy scrape of a dead voice crawls into my ear:

"Daddy... I'm so cold."

FIND A BOY

DAVID RIDER

The boy ran.

His shoes kicked up powder from the unplowed road. The icy wind bit his face when he cleared the vehicle and scrambled into the shallow ditch. The snow there was deeper than it looked. The ground beneath was rutted. He stumbled. Were he twenty years older, his ankle might have given; but at ten-years-old his bones were a youthful rubber, and his leg only wobbled. He came out of the ditch and into the open field.

That morning, his mother had said something about it being in the "single digits," but spouting numbers in relation to weather meant nothing to him. He was that age; an invincible age before cold temperature meant anything. His father understood that mentality, and warned, "You *wanna* freeze your balls off, huh, dummy?" He'd shrugged on his winter coat, the dark blue one from Sears with the orange lining and fur-rimmed hood every kid wore then, but no gloves. He refused them. And didn't feel like waiting for his mom to search the closet for last year's knit mittens clipped to the string that she would feed through the sleeves. To risk sending her to the closet also meant risking an order for him to put on galoshes. He was in the fifth grade. All of that was baby stuff. So he left the house into the single digits, dressed like it was late spring with a little winter coat.

A bitter headwind drove particles into his eyes and face, feeling more like dry sand than wet snowflakes. His bare hands were already numb, and his feet, protected only by threadbare tube socks and the flimsy fabric of his Adidas, were on their way to freezing. He was barely a hundred feet from the road.

A man emerged from his vehicle to go after the running boy.

"Are you okay?"

Dan blinked, snapping from his trance.

Kris turned down a CD player blaring Van Halen's *Balance*. "Where did you go?"

"Nothing. Nowhere." He swung his gaze from the view out the Mazda's passenger window. He tried on a grin for her benefit but it didn't take.

"For fuck's sake, don't smile like that in front of my family. It'll make you look creepy and weird. Not exactly the best first impression."

God, you're fucking mean sometimes, he thought. Instead, he said, "You can be mean sometimes, you know that?"

This made her smile. It lit up her face more than the time when, during a recent pillow talk session, he'd whispered how her eyes were the prettiest he'd ever seen. Her toothy, beaming expression loudly declared that pushing his buttons was something she took great pride in.

"It's why you love me, right?"

He looked away, back to the flat, snow-covered Illinois country-side. Away from the casually mean, and toward the hypnotic and frightening. Seeing endless rows of plowed fields whizzing past his window on family vacations—always perpendicular to the highway, stretching into infinity—had mesmerized him for as long as he could remember. His brain became entranced with the geometric, visual effect of each straight crop row melding into the next.

As for *frightening*...

"Did I ever tell you about the time I was abducted as a kid?"

Hearing the man give chase made the boy scream.

The sound was snatched from his lips, as if an invisible, icy fist smothered it out of existence. The next frantic intake of freezing air through gritted teeth seared his throat and lungs. Screaming again wasn't going to happen. Until that moment he hadn't known teeth could feel cold air. What if sucking oxygen through them on a day like this caused them to become brittle? Could they shatter like icicles? He closed his mouth and breathed through his nose. His nostril hairs and snot stiffened into crystalline burrs.

Their chase fouled the white, virgin field, describing a straight line leading away from the county road, just as the car's progress had left a fresh, two-grooved path in the snow before stopping. From a bird's-eye view, it told a story in a ninety-degree angle: a pair of parallel lines in a white landscape headed west, stopping at a sedan, then formed a new line created by two dots heading due south into endless white.

The details of the chase would remain untold for nineteen years.

"Bullshit."

"Have I ever lied to you? I was abducted by a guy when I was ten and a half."

Her eyes went from the road to study his face. She appraised him anew before her gaze flitted back to the traffic around them creeping along on I-80. Any trace of her previous smile vanished like a warm breath against cold glass.

The album's third instrumental track faded, and the interior of her MX-3 was silent before Sammy Hagar's vocals returned.

"I...haven't thought about it in years." His hand went to the oh-shit handle on the door, knuckles whitening with his grip. "It's funny what triggers it. Probably this weather. Or this snowy farmland hellscape."

"Hey, I grew up on a fucking farm, asshole." Her pretty eyes narrowed.

"Sorry."

"Don't pull any of that city shit around my family. They won't have it and neither will I."

"*Sorry.*"

She didn't stop. "You know what my father would say when we left Chicago after seeing a Cubs game, or visiting the Museum of Science and Industry? 'Good to be back in Illinois.' Every. Single. Time. That's what you're about to walk into and shake hands with."

That's asinine, he wanted to say. What he went with was, "I said I was sorry."

"Just tell your little kidnapping story."

The boy was a fast runner. Whether it was gym class or beating feet away from bullies after school, he prided himself on his impressive speed. His favorite *Looney Tunes* character was Speedy Gonzales. If one of the fleet-footed mouse's cartoons came on on a Saturday morning, it always made the rest of his day better.

But little Speedy never had to sprint through snow.

The drifts in this field looked higher than what covered the road. They were so high it didn't feel like he was running at all. His speed had been more than halved. He was moving no faster than Speedy's cousin, Slowpoke Rodriguez.

A desperate glance at the expanse ahead threatened to sink his racing heart. He was heading toward *nothing*. The cloud cover and falling flakes turned the sky greyish-white to the horizon. The hazy fog from earlier this morning hadn't burned off way out here. It blurred and blended sky and earth. Without buildings or trees to denote distance, he had only the vague visual of the plowed field's straight row directing him into the void—and even that was being erased.

He hadn't tied his shoes tight. His movements worked snow into the sides and under the tongue. Too frigid to melt, it settled in and under the arches of his feet. The socks weren't going to help.

He lost feeling in his toes first.

"I was walking to my friend's house."

She went back to needling him. "You had friends?"

"A best friend. I told you about him."

She frowned.

"Carl? My buddy growing up?"

"I guess."

"I've mentioned him a few times."

"Okay."

He sighed. "Anyway, he invited me over to screw around. So I headed out into a blizzard. Like this one, but worse. *Way* colder."

"When was this?"

"Couple months before I turned eleven. February." He didn't bother with the year. They were the same age and had at least that much in common. "So, I was literally half a block from home when this guy pulled over and offered me a ride. He was in a dark green sedan. A goddamned *boat*. Like all the four-doors back then."

"And you actually got in his car?"

"I..."

"Like a fucking moron. How dumb were you?"

"Look, he knew what he was doing. He didn't ask a yes or no question. It was, 'Come on, it's cold. Lemme give you a lift.' And I said, 'That's okay. My friend's house is only three blocks away.' And he said, 'Come on, in this weather three blocks are three miles. Hop in.'"

"And you actually did. Nice."

"You know how it was back then. Kids hitchhiked all the time."

"Not kids *our* age! We were supposed to be smarter than that! The Boomers who hitchhiked grew up licking lead paint, then their brains rotted while waiting around for Rush fucking Limbaugh to rally them to the Dark Side!" She steered her car into an exit lane and took the curving ramp off the highway faster than she should have. The MX-3 fishtailed, just for a second, before its treads caught the salted road.

His grip tightened on the door handle. "Jesus, slow down! I—"

"What?" she said, grinning. Then saw his face. "What?"

"What did that sign say?"

"The Minooka Exit. Why?"

"...Nothing."

"Whatever. You got into a friendly stranger's black sedan. Like you wanted to live the Ides of March song. And...?"

"It was green, I said. And at first it seemed like he was taking me to Carl's. He drove in the direction I told him. But when I said to turn right, he didn't. He went left, and headed to the boulevard. And I go, 'Hey, wait,' and he said, 'Do you like WLS?' and turned on the radio."

"God. Damn. *Everyone* listened to that station, didn't they? Kids and perverts alike."

He nodded. "And I'll never forget what was playing: 'Convoy.'"

"Oh, *God.*"

"The song ended when he turned onto the highway and I knew I was in big trouble. And that was when popular tunes would play again and again every hour or so. We were driving so long 'Convoy' had actually started again. That's when I bailed out of his car—"

"Wait, back up!"

"What?"

"I have questions," She scoffed. "Jesus! Don't blow your wad early. Like always. I wanna know about the *guy*. You're glossing over—"

"Because I don't remember much about him!"

"You spent an *hour* in a car together! How do you not—"

"I was too afraid to look at him, alright?! I don't know, I guess he looked how every white guy in his twenties did back then. Long hair hanging over his eyes. Mustache. You know how he looked? He looked like those guys who spent their Saturday afternoons under the open hood of their muscle car working a wrench and drinking Schlitz. *Those* guys."

"But what did he say?"

"What did he *say*?"

"Yeah. Didn't you talk?"

"*I* said I wanted to go to Carl's house. When that didn't work I said I wanted to go home. I said Mom was serving bologna sandwiches and Fritos for lunch."

"Jesus."

"I know."

"What'd *he* say?"

"He..."

She waited.

"...He spoke in a different voice than when he offered the ride."

His words sank in and silence filled the car. The last song on the CD had ended and the player wasn't set on replay. The sound of the radials sluicing through icy slush came from below. The Mazda slowed at an intersection. When it turned west onto a county road, the sound returned with its acceleration.

"What do you mean 'different voice'?"

"The guy sounded *different* after I got in his car. Like he used one voice to pull me in. One he rehearsed. To sound normal. He never used *that* voice again."

She shuddered. Her eyes stayed fixed ahead, targeting the safe passage-promise offered by the twin grooves of past traffic.

"His *real* voice—that's how I thought of it at the time—came as a deep mumble from his throat. Like he didn't want to use his tongue or lips to form words. And he kept calling me a...."

"A what...?"

"Boy!"

The man's voice carried in the chill air; against the wind, somehow, crossing the distance between them and beyond. It came from his throat, originating there as if a belch rather than spoken word.

"Boy! Stop!" Two belches. Guttural sounds. Disturbing in their clipped non-enunciation.

The sounds made him push through the snow with renewed energy. The cold may have canceled the feeling in his toes but that, in its way, helped his progress. His feet chuffed forward, shoveling through ivory drifts; the three-striped Adidas sneakers becoming determined blue plows.

His heart responded somewhat differently to the man's voice.

In his experience, those giving chase stayed silent. From the age of six until now, walking his half mile home from school, he knew bullies to speak in threats and warn against running. They beat your ass and bloodied your nose, and if you took your lumps and stayed down they went away cackling. But as the older antagonists aged out of elementary school to be replaced by those in his own grade, he discovered two crucial things: first, he had developed surprising speed, and second, chunky, lumbering punks can't run far.

He would walk across the school grounds and cross the street into their dark territory where they circled in wait. He would come within twenty feet, acting resigned to his fate in the moments before they spat their threats. He wore the frightened face they expected. The one that calmed them. And when they started to say, "I'm gonna kick—" he broke into a sprint and juked past them before the last two words were uttered. They always gave chase. Even the ones his age, the wiry ones built for speed like himself, couldn't keep up.

Many a Friday afternoon included a run home (for some reason, they always seemed to want to get their licks in before the weekend).

But the running was always a silent affair; an exercise in concentration where all will was devoted to escape or pursuit; the pounding of sneakers on concrete the only sound. To speak and to threaten while in chase mode was a waste of energy understood by both predator and prey.

This man didn't understand those rules.

He bellowed and ordered.

This was both encouraging and terrifying. Mixed with the uncertainty of just how long he could keep up his pace, his emotional state spiked ever closer to panic.

The man and the boy had stayed evenly matched across a football field's length of frozen tundra. The thick haze ahead only allowed them to see the next hundred yards. Nothing beyond.

"Boy!" the man shouted again.

"He said it a lot during the car ride, but he said it to himself."

"I don't understand." Her eyebrows met in confusion.

"He repeated it over and over. Like a mantra."

"He said 'boy' over and over?" She slowed for another stop sign.

"Not exactly. At first, I couldn't tell *what* he was saying. The music from the radio wasn't very loud, but neither were his whispers. I only heard them between songs."

She rolled into the intersection without using brakes, and steered left, not bothering with the turn signal. The Mazda's rear end swung wide and skidded. Before tires touched road again she said, "Wheeeeee!" more to herself than him.

He tightened his jaw and ground his teeth. His leg muscles rigid as both shoes stomped a brake pedal that wasn't there. For a third time, his right hand threatened to wrench the handle from its door mount. He growled, "Jesus *fuck*."

The red car swayed and straightened onto a thin strip of pure white. No grey road showed, although the indication of it could be seen in exactly one previous pair of tire tracks that had traveled in the westbound direction they were headed. The grooves of this path were being filled in by the falling snow. They might not exist in the next thirty minutes, but for now they were deep enough to prove there *was* a road.

She cackled like a witch—or perhaps, he thought, more like a punk from his dim past who'd left him crumpled on the sidewalk after an epic beatdown. Until this second, he hadn't equated her mental bullying to the physical harassment that had instilled anxiety in him during childhood.

"You were saying?"

It took him a moment to remember where the conversation left off. Once he did, he considered what would've been his next words, then dismissed them. He shook his head. "Nothing. He was muttering shit and when the car slowed enough, I jumped out."

"Wait wait wait!" She taunted him with one of her grins. "You were going somewhere with that. You don't get to just clam up now."

"And *you* don't need to get all *Road Warrior* in the damn snow! If we skid off the road, where the hell would we be then? At least I keep a goddamn bag phone in my car in case of emergencies!"

"Well, *you* didn't want to drive, remember? And news flash: they're portable. You could've brought it with and plugged it into my lighter."

"I said I didn't want to drive *today*. Period. It's stupid to go out in weather like this. And I don't like being in the middle of nowh—"

"Oh, so I'm stupid now?!"

"I didn't say that."

"You said my driving is stupid. And you called my family stupid for living in the middle of nowhere."

"*I didn't*—"

"Yeah, you did. You called my family a tribe of no-tooth, no-chin, moonshine-swillin' hill folk! You picture them as extras from *The*

Hills Have Eyes, don't you? You think they're named after planets? I'll bet you hate farmers in general. Is that it, Dan? Shit, I think it is. You hate the people responsible for putting food on your fucking table! Admit it!"

He stared at her.

She stared back, wide-eyed, nostrils flaring.

After a few seconds, he whispered, "Fuck you."

Her lips curled back and she brayed like a mule, teeth bared, painting the car's interior with her laughter. She slapped a hand down on his leg, midway between knee and thigh, then seized it in a surprisingly painful grip.

He winced.

When she relaxed her fingers, she slid them further up to his inner thigh. Her pinky finger grazed his package before she pulled her hand away, offering a tease, nothing more. "Go on. Tell me. What was the pervert mumbling?"

Dan exhaled and answered her.

She hadn't heard him. "What?"

He said it again, in the way his abductor had spoken—pushing three syllables from his throat, past his tongue, not bothering with pronunciation. His lips almost didn't move at all, as if using them caused discomfort.

"I'm still not hearing you."

Dan spoke the words the same way, louder this time but also articulating his lips to be understood so he wouldn't have to repeat them. "Find...a...boy."

She went fully silent.

Though he hadn't wanted to repeat it, he took her silence as having not heard him yet again. "*Find a boy*. He said it probably hundreds of times during the car ride. *Find a boy*. Like a mantra."

He saw the shudder in her arms and hands, positioned at nine and three on the wheel. The way they trembled in unison from shoulders to wrists. Heard the hiss of her breath and the way she held it.

She locked her dead-eyed gaze ahead, not speaking.

"He said it like he had followed orders. A soldier on a mission, repeating the words of his superior officer. *Find a boy.* But I'm sitting there freaking out because I didn't know what was next. He had already *found* a boy. He was taking me somewhere. But to where and to who, I didn't know. Because what was *next*? So I start to cry. I mean, we all went to the school assemblies. We all learned about Stranger Danger. A guy we didn't know stood at half-court in the gym and said, 'They'll offer candy to lure you in.' And he warned us about not getting in their car. But that guy in the gym never told us what would happen if we *did* get in the car. The *not* knowing a possible outcome didn't terrify me until I *was* in a car. By then you're thinking back and realizing no adults *ever* told us what would happen. That made it worse. That made it something so frightening that grown-ass adults didn't talk about it. And my guy, my abductor, he didn't offer candy. Not at first. And not until he realized I was blubbering. That's when he looked at the glove compartment and mumbled, '*Open the box.*'"

She listened without facing him.

"And when I opened it, I found a gun. A huge revolver. And an open package of candy. And he said, '*Butterscotch helps,*' in that creepy voice of his. He said, '*Butterscotch* always *helps.*' And him stressing that word...it...it broke me. Because now I knew other boys or girls had taken this trip with him. And I pictured them going to their own assemblies at their own schools and finding themselves in this exact same seat. And they'd also burst into tears. And they'd also seen the gun and been offered his shitty butterscotch candy. And I wondered if their parents knew what had happened to them. Or if mine would ever know what happened to *me*. And more importantly, would *any* adult actually talk about what happened to *any of us*?"

She hadn't moved again. Not since her body and arms had shuddered at his words. She'd shown no reaction to the rest of his story since.

"After I saw the gun, I knew it was time to go. He'd locked the doors when I got in, but I'd noticed the button on the passenger door behind him hadn't gone down like the others. I scrambled over the seat and yanked the door handle and tumbled out of his moving car. Then I ran."

Her gaze stayed trained ahead. The car cruised at an even forty. Too fast for these conditions, but steady on the straight, unseen road.

"So, yeah. *Find a boy*." He glanced at her blank face. "You asked."

"The thing is, Dan," she said, her voice as toneless as her expression, "that's really not the end of the story..."

He'd kept his fists clenched as he ran and couldn't feel his fingers. They'd become crimson phantom appendages with deadened nerves lashed by the razor wind. His legs ached with the continuous effort, yearning for level ground without shin-high drifts so he could put actual distance between him and his pursuer. For all he knew, his feet were gone. All sensation ended at the ankle bones. He whimpered and, for the first time, stumbled.

Sheer momentum kept him going.

Now the man closed the distance. While his long stride was an even match with his prey's speed, his edge ultimately proved to be the protection he wore against the weather. The skin around his eyes, behind the balaclava, was his sole exposure to the cruel elements. If the blizzard got worse and the current wind speed doubled to sixty miles an hour, he might have a problem. But his outerwear was sufficient to this task. He closed the gap by degrees.

Something melted out of the thinning haze.

A distant line. Dark grey shapes, at first. Ruler-straight across the horizon. Consisting of irregular, varying heights.

"*Boy*," the man mumbled, closer than ever.

Trees...a line of trees. The field's plowed acres *did* have an end.

"*Stop.*"

The boy whimpered again. Rather than feeling elation, the trees signaled an end. They provoked dread. His pursuer would catch him there. They might as well be a brick wall. A finishing line where he would be finished.

But no one catches Speedy Gonzales.

"*Boy.*" The man sounded ten feet away.

The tree-line grew larger. With details to focus on, he now realized how graceless his movements had become. How the trees, how the horizon, jumped and quaked. How he wasn't running smooth like Speedy.

Because Speedy never got tired.

"*Boy!*" Even closer. And...angrier.

Tree tops filled the upper half of his vision. The dead foliage their branches had shed in the fall were replaced by new leaves resembling vertical inch-high piles of whiteness. Crowned with snow, lined with it and defined by it, they appeared beautifully alien. These were ice plants that grew on an ice planet. Against the light-grey background of the landscape beyond, they were a miraculous wonder. And there, in the field past the ice trees...another miracle...

...A house.

"*BOY!*"

He hadn't noticed the barbed wire fence until he was on top of it.

"...And I think *you* know it's not the end of the story."

He blinked at her tone. "What are you—"

"Don't act like you don't suspect, Dan."

She eased off the accelerator, letting the hatchback slow a few hundred feet from an intersection. A major road, plowed and salted, bisected the smaller one on which they traveled. Their stop sign came up fast.

She had no intention of stopping. Even if she wanted to, she couldn't have in these conditions. She'd only allowed the car to decelerate enough to gauge the approach of any traffic crossing their path. An eighteen-wheeler rumbled past, heading south, doing fifty-five. It churned up a mist of salty spray in its wake. Seeing no other vehicles in either direction, she gunned the engine. The front tires spun, grinding snow, seeking purchase. Then they found the bare road and shot across. The truck's trailing mist hit the car.

Dan couldn't see through the glass to the road ahead. His teeth ground together and his body stiffened. Once again, he seized the door handle in a death grip. He caught a sign through his side window identifying the north-south highway they'd crossed as Route 47. The sight of it triggered another inexplicable, autonomic response in his chest.

She hit the wipers. They cleared the windshield in two swipes.

No tire marks ahead.

Logic suggested the car was still on a road. The snow blanketing everything, everywhere, offered a contradictory suggestion. This was a paradox; a drive-thru thought experiment about quantum mechanics. Schrödinger's Road. It may or may not exist. There were no houses, therefore no mailboxes on either side to gauge a possible paved corridor. Utility poles to the left were the only guide as to where safe travel might be found.

It was his turn to shudder.

She glanced away from the illusory roadway. "I've been watching you. And you've known since Minooka. Or, at least...you suspected."

His throat was dry. "What are you talking about?"

"And back aways, again, when we passed all those willow trees. You recognized them."

Had he? He'd been telling his story, gazing out the passenger window while looking for comforting patterns in the fields like the day he'd been taken. Yes, a building and parking lot had registered in his peripheral vision to the left, but what his eyes landed on through her side of the windshield was a grove of weeping willow trees. They were so unlike the elms the car had passed since leaving the inter-state that he took note of them. But was it more than that?

"And these, up here," she continued, tilting her head back to point with her chin. "What do you see?"

He looked ahead to a cluster of immense, silver cylinders near a weathered barn coming up on the right. "Silos?"

"Grain bins, but nice try." Her voice got lower. "Look familiar?"

His heart thumped.

"Why don't you finish your story, Dan." It wasn't a request.

He didn't answer.

"You said you jumped out of the car. And ran. Across farmland, right? And the man chased you?"

He didn't nod.

"Across the fields. Through the snow. Until...?"

He swallowed.

"Until *what*, Dan?"

"Un-Until I ran into..."

"Ran into what?"

"Barbed—"

"Barbed wire," she blurted.

His blood chilled.

The boy spotted the wire stretching before him too late, almost invisible against the backdrop of trees. Steel posts ran the length of the tree-line, sunk within a deadfall thicket of frozen leaves and limbs. The grey wires strung through them, paired with the strip of forest beyond, served as clear indicators of property lines.

Instinct took over, triggering the honed reflexes of a boy accustomed to speed and evasion. He ducked and launched himself between the upper and middle strands of wire. His head and shoulders shot through unscathed, but the metal barbs caught his arms as he torpedoed through in corkscrew fashion. The fabric of his coat ripped. The skin on both hands were scraped deep; jagged white lines etched into red flesh too frozen to pass blood. Then his jeans were snagged at the cuff, his forward momentum halted, causing a sudden descent to the ground. He thought his skin was already too numbed by the polar air to feel anything more, but his face-plant into the deep frost presented a new fact: there's always another level to the cold. When he lifted his face from the chilled drift and turned on his side, he saw he hung suspended by one leg. The denim of his jeans was twisted and held fast by a sharp barb in the middle strand.

He could see the pursuing man wore a heavy, quilt-lined coat over his flannel shirt. He had on thick gloves and a black balaclava, his breath puffing from the knitted mask. He wore work boots suited to the cold and ice, and his legs were insulated in padded, snow bib overalls. Moving steadily in the boy's wake, he took careful, measured strides up their chosen row. He stepped where the boy had, each of his footfalls covering twice as much ground.

Now, mere steps away, the man reached for the boy's leg.

He wheezed out a hoarse cry, expelling air from raw lungs. He was panicking; his long, cold run, the resulting fatigue caused by it, and the sudden stop, brought him close to hyperventilation. His hands scrabbled and flailed in the sharp, stinging coldness. He twisted wildly. He maneuvered his free leg, pushing against the lower strand with the sole of his shoe for leverage. When his wet heel slipped, it gave like an elastic band. The taut wire snapped back and thwacked the boy. A barb at its apex stung his ass cheek like a thick needle.

And there he was.

Trapped.

He had a choice—and he *recognized* the choice. Identified it. The one that looked most likely was also the most unimaginable. This was a dichotomy for a simple reason: he had seen this scenario on TV countless times. So how *could* it be unimaginable?

He and his father were faithful viewers of *Wild Kingdom*. "*Mutual of Omaha's Wild Kingdom*," the show's zoologist host Marlin Perkins always said, working in a contractual plug for the show's insurance company sponsor. How many times, over the years, had they watched the mild-mannered Perkins narrate an animal's violent death? One week, the nature show might feature footage of a lioness chasing a gazelle across the savanna. The next, it was a pack of hyenas cutting a young wildebeest from its herd. Each time a nimble animal escaped slavering death growling at their backside, the boy would cheer, "Yay!" But when an animal was brought down on their living room TV in full color, his father exclaimed, "Got 'em!" What was truly inconceivable to the boy were the moments when one beast caught another and they laid together on the plain, heaving and exhausted. As the frequent target of neighborhood toughs, he couldn't understand a prey's utter surrender in those moments. Was that really all they had to give? A hundred-yard sprint, a tumble in the dust, only to accept fangs over their throat?

The man grabbed the boy's ankle...

Got 'em!

...above where his pant cuff was snagged.

His adrenalin surged, infused with more terror at the strength of the grip on him.

If Speedy were on Wild Kingdom *and Sylvester caught him, he wouldn't just lay there. He'd fight back.*

So as the man bent to inspect the snag, the boy aimed a kick upwards. The masked head jerked this way and that to avoid the ensuing strikes. When the heel of his Adidas landed a glancing blow to the man's forearm, he grunted, *"Boy!"* in frustration. He tried again for the man's face, but the kick went too high. The top of his shoe scraped along the upper strand. The man dodged, even as he freed the boy's other leg. As he withdrew his foot, a shoelace looped around a barb and held.

The wire pulled back with his leg. The man didn't notice. He straightened, lifting his captive like a prize trout pulled from a river. The boy tugged his knee closer. The barbed strand tightened like a metal slingshot band. The boy lunged and seized the lace and yanked the knot loose.

THWACK.

The wire swatted the man across the strip of exposed skin under his mask. A barb sank into an eye and plucked meat from it as the strand twanged back. He screamed and threw his hands to his face.

Now set free, the boy scrambled to his feet in a flurry of motion.

"Boy!" the man groaned once more, clutching the leaking ruins of his eye.

Ándale, he thought, running through the trees to safety.

"...The people in the farmhouse called the county cops." Dan's tone was robotic. "But by the time they came, the man was gone. His car was, too. I heard one of them say over the radio it looked like the tire tracks just ended, but it was hard to tell with the blowing and drifting." He exhaled through his nose, his lips a grim line.

His story was over.

She reacted with a sneer; a profane curl of her upper lip. "The tire tracks didn't just *end*. You know cars have a reverse gear, right?" Her words were laced with acid. He opened his mouth to object, but she cut him off and continued. "Everything you're seeing here," she took a hand from the wheel and ticked an index finger back and forth like a metronome's pendulum, "is my family's land. They've worked it since the 1800s. I never told you that, but it's true. And this house, here, on the right, is where my Aunt Sigrid lived."

The car sped past an ancient house with two wagon wheels half-sunk into the ground on either side of a driveway. A garage with a bowed roof, defeated by time and elements, was next to the house.

"That's where she kept her car. It actually belonged to my uncle who didn't come back from Vietnam. But she never drove it. Never learned how. Too big, she said. A huge boat of a vehicle. But once my cousins and I got our licenses, we took it all the time. Sometimes to the DQ in Morris. Sometimes to Joliet to shoot pool. And some-times...farther."

Dan shifted in his seat.

"We stayed away from my oldest cousin. He wasn't right in the head. Especially after what happened to his folks. After their house burned down with them inside, he lived in the barn. We never went into that barn. We knew better. We'd heard the sounds. It started with animals. But when I was around ten, the noises that carried across the fields at midnight...didn't sound much like animals anymore."

"Bullshit, you're such a—"

"But family is family." Her glare stabbed through him. "And out here we take care of our own. When one of my cousins got a part-time clerk job with the Grundy police, she found an old case file. She also found something the local papers hadn't reported: the name of a kidnapped minor who'd been recovered in '76."

"You're so full of—"

"That was the year my oldest cousin lost an eye. He wouldn't tell the rest of us how. But he did tell my father. You see, my father had promised to take care him after his folks died, despite his *nature*. And taking care of him included preventing anyone from ever coming after him and tarnishing the family's history."

"Kris—"

"So about seven months ago, my father came to me with a name. And he had a very specific request. Well, not a request... an order."

His throat went tight.

"*Find the boy.*"

The words hung there. For them to echo was impossible, but they didn't fade because his mind replayed them a second time, and a third. Then she said them again, this time without moving her lips, coaxing them from her throat in a soft growl. She did this with widened, intense eyes. Eyes unlike the ones he once thought were the prettiest he'd seen.

"You... You need to quit fucking with me."

"I knew you wouldn't believe me, Dan, you sack of shit."

He kept his gaze locked on hers.

She didn't glance away.

The car continued forward through the snow, now accelerating faster than forty.

He twitched his eyes away, willing her to do the same—to look toward the road—but saw she wasn't going to do it.

"You need proof, don't you?"

Forty-five now.

He swallowed hard. Even without a winter storm, these weren't safe driving conditions.

She drew her eyes away, finally, focusing on the road almost as if an afterthought.

Fifty.

"Open the box, Dan."

He didn't, couldn't, move.

"You'll find two things inside. Care to guess? Hurry up, we're almost there."

"Stop it. I'm serious. You're not funny."

"A gun," she whispered, matching his volume. "And butterscotch candies."

"Fucking stop, goddamnit."

She gave him a demented grin, pulling her head back so her chin became part of her neck.

For the first time he didn't think he knew her at all. She'd never taken a joke so far. And yet, still, he tried to get her to break, tried to smile.

Instead she shouted, "*Open the box!*"

He did.

He kept one hand on the door handle and snapped open the compartment latch with his other.

He saw a gun.

His heartbeat spiked.

The car shot past a concrete silo on the left, revealing a sprawling ranch house and a windmill and a horseshoe driveway lined with vehicles.

But rather than downshift to slow the Mazda, she tapped the

brakes. The car began to slide. Her obscene grimace melted away, along with the not-quite formed, maniacal, throaty laughter. Instead, the flailing of her arms and the slapping of her hands on the wheel filled the skidding vehicle.

Dan threw himself from the car as it left the road.

His head struck the metal pole of a mailbox as he tumbled.

The MX-3 bounced into and out of the snowy ditch. It roared toward a nearby maple tree. The front hood buckled between eye blinks as it crashed into the wide trunk, coming to an abrupt, startling stop. A shower of snow shivered from the branches above, shook loose like salt from a shaker. Steam jetted from the crushed radiator.

Silence.

Then a scream from inside the house.

Dan sat up in the ditch, dazed, taking stock. His head hurt. His heart thundered. His right hand came out of the snow when he lifted it, but it dangled limply by the wrist, broken and floppy. Something was in his other hand, hidden in the drift.

He tried to stand, found he could, but his eyes refused to focus. The world blurred and doubled. The falling flakes, thick like styrofoam packing peanuts, didn't make it easier to see. He couldn't maintain his balance. Legs unsteady, his shoes shuffled forward, displacing the snow. He arrived at the open passenger door from which he'd bailed, bent on its hinges, and his concussed brain couldn't reconcile what he saw.

Kris's lower face had been skewered and removed by a tree limb coming through the windshield. It had punched through her and the driver's seat. The airbag inflated below it, having not deployed until the front end hit the tree. Blood gurgled up from her open throat, turning the airbag red. She blinked at him. Her eyes were wide and aware but didn't comprehend what had happened.

His spinning mind tried and failed to perceive her emotional state. Hard to do with only half a face.

Then, hearing shouts and calls from the house, she glanced to her left.

The family was emerging from the front door, into the snow.

Her gaze shifted back to him.

His mind filled in the thought.

Found the boy.

She died.

His left hand jerked up from his side.

He fired the revolver before conscious thought told him he'd even grabbed it before jumping from the car. He fired it again and again, toward the figures running toward him. A large shape collapsed. A smaller one dropped next to it. The others scattered as if to surround him. To outflank him. And so, he turned to run around the side of the house, firing twice more.

The backyard was half an acre of white limbo and little else, leading to the whiteness of more acreage and straight rows stretching into the blizzard. The wind flayed his bare face and ears. It rippled through clothes unsuited to frigid temperatures. The chilled powder worked its way into his shoes.

His thoughts were equally cold, despite the burning turmoil in his head. Imagination and logic collided, unbalanced and seesawing, neither gaining the upper hand. He did what felt best. That which came naturally. He ran.

His imagination said, *Away from the danger.*

His logic added, *And if there's nowhere safe, you have one bullet left.*

He ran into the snow and was ten-years-old again.

COLD CASE

NEIL WILLIAMSON

Michael Phayre knows he should've checked the contents of the manky file box, but he didn't. Not when he collected it from old Porteous's ratty room-and-kitchen up in Springburn. Not on the shoogling trolleybus down the Keppochhill Road in the freezing Glasgow rain, either. Even when he'd humphed it all the way up to the fourth floor of the George Square office building and was standing there staring at Porteous Junior's neatly gilded name as he waited for the door to be answered, it wouldn't have been too late.

Had he stopped and thought for a just wee moment, he might have saved young Andy and his wife the agonies to come. But he didn't stop. He didn't think. It didn't occur to him that the *sundry extant case files* itemised by the solicitor might include the old man's notes regarding the Jeannie Colquhoun case.

And really, it should have.

Robert Porteous had been a meticulous and righteously committed policeman. Once. Before his sense of duty over Jeannie had curdled into obsession. Who'd've guessed it had still festered in him after all these years? Not Michael but...aye, he should've.

It had been a bad, bad business at that. The worst. None of them who'd been there had got away unmarked by it.

Probably he ought to feel responsible, but what good would an apology be to Andy and May? It happened and that's all there is to it. Life's cold like that.

Andy Porteous was in high spirits that morning. That was Andy anyway. Affable, good natured. Quick with a joke, but never snide with it. *No a bad yin, fur a Hun*, as Michael's old Da would've said.

As it happened, the Glasgow Rangers had been on a wee run of form, but that wasn't the reason. Andy was simply a blithe boy by nature, and you can get a long way in life just by being pleasant company.

That's the thing about happiness, though. It may feel like a lovely bubble filled with sunshine and rainbows when you're in the midst of it, but all that colour and brightness tends to blind you to what things are like for everyone else.

"Come!" Two voices shouted in unison from behind the frosted glass.

Fixing a smile, Michael did as he was told.

Andy's rooms weren't large—just the reception and the young fella's inner sanctum separated by a panelled partition—but they were a million miles away from the sorry circumstances his father had ended up in. Having just come direct from the one to the other, Michael could make that comparison with certainty. Andy'd done well for himself since the estrangement, and nobody on Earth could begrudge him.

Entering, Michael found Andy perched on the corner of the reception desk and May settling onto the chair behind it. A shared spark of laughter lingered in their eyes. Michael didn't speculate. Their being newlyweds was the reason he'd knocked after all.

"Michael!" Andy said. "Come in, come in."

"Get you a wee coffee, Michael?" May was beaming. Michael knew that lovely smile was just for show, but he allowed himself to bask in it for a second anyway. Then he told himself to get real. Lassies didn't smile like that for dour old duffers like him.

"No, I'm aw right, thanks," he demurred, hefting the cardboard box onto the warmly gleaming desk. The lid of it was dust furred, the handwritten label washed out to an indigo-brown stain, and the box slumped to the side where the corner had been nibbled away by miscreants unknown.

May pulled a face.

Sure enough, it was a nasty business to dump in the middle of all their shine and polish. Though, Michael reflected, it was far from the worst of what had been found up in the former Detective Inspector's filthy hovel.

"Here they are then," he said, keen to get on. "His *cauld* cases. You absolutely sure you want them, pal? Yer faither had no paying clients at the end. If you ask me, this dross should go straight on the midden."

Andy's smile twitched. You'd hardly notice unless you knew him. A glimpse of the stubborn steel that, whether he'd admit it or not, was the spit of his old man's.

"You're maybe right, Michael," Andy said breezily, "but my dad let people down. If there's anything I can do to tie up some of his loose ends and finally bring peace of mind to some of his old clients, then I consider it my duty."

Michael saw May's gentle touch on Andy's sleeve. What Andy really meant was there was no way he'd pass up an opportunity to prove he was better than the old man had been. It was a fire that raged in him and would never go out. What better way to demonstrate that for a professional investigator than neatly wrapping up the old man's unsolved cases?

Michael shrugged, more than content to leave Andy to it if that was how the lad's mind was set. He had a court summons to serve in Knightswood anyway.

If he'd known what the contents of that box were, though, *even then* things could have been different.

As it was, he said: "The midden, mind." Then he buttoned his Crombie coat and tipped his bunnet at May, and left their bright bubble in favour of the dreich Glasgow weather.

People had all sorts of stupid notions about what it took to be a Sheriff officer. Delivering writs and summonses. Recovering debts or, if they couldn't be recouped, enforcing repossessions or evictions as dictated by the grand old Scottish legal system. You'd have to be a hard man, considering the kind of bastards you'd be delivering that justice to, right?

Most folks, taking one look at Michael's bulky frame and his pummelled dough features or hearing his gravelly voice, assumed exactly that. True, he could handle himself if it came to it, but that wasn't what made him good at his job. Ninety percent of the time, an ounce of something that sounded like empathy got the job done surer than the cosh in your pocket. Anybody could pretend to be the hard man. It wasn't nearly so easy to fake compassion. It was a skill that Michael reckoned he'd just about perfected.

The house he visited in Knightswood was one of those nice wee four-in-a-block maisonettes and its owner, Mrs. Burns, was a nice wee lady. She and her husband had bought the house as newlyweds after the first war, never guessing there was even greater strife waiting just over the horizon. Old Jimmy Burns had worked as an actuary before enlisting in 1940 and had always been the one to take care of their money. But the Jimmy who'd come home in '45 had been a different man, she said, secretive and sullen, and he'd frittered away their savings over the subsequent decade and a half.

In Michael's experience, men could very easily be both loving and secretive at the same time. It hadn't been a changed man who'd returned, just what little was left of the original one. But he held his peace and let her continue.

Nellie'd only found out about it all on Jimmy's passing earlier that year. The amount she owed would've made a banker blush. She only had her sewing money? What was she to do?

Michael cradled a willow pattern cup with a digestive biscuit balanced on the saucer as the lamentable tale unfolded. The house around him was spick and span. Not a blemish on the Axminster. Not a smudge on the Edinburgh crystal sherry glasses. Even the wally dugs on the mantle gleamed. She was a proud woman, Mrs. Burns, but she was long past her wits' end with the hand she had been dealt. And it hadn't helped that she'd stuck her head in the sand until the law had come knocking.

Michael sipped his tea and nibbled his biscuit, careful to catch the crumbs in his palm. Then, when Nellie was wrung out from the telling, he offered sympathy and reassurance that the courts *might* be disposed to some measure of leniency since the initial fault anyway was not of her own making. But she had to be sure and turn up on the appointed day and time. He laboured that point, made her repeat the date and place back to him. Promise that she'd be there. Because that, after all, was the entire purpose of his visit.

Mrs. Burns cried then, tears of relief dabbed brusquely away. She managed a tight little smile to show that she at least felt less isolated in her misery now. Then she said something unexpected.

"You've a reassuring manner with women, Mr. Phayre. Your wife is gey fortunate."

Michael merely nodded and took his leave. If he'd done a decent deed, he felt no particular pride in it. The job was done. On to the next one.

Since the trolleybus routes largely followed Glasgow's arterial roads, getting from Knightswood up to Maryhill promised a tedious ride back into the heart of the city centre followed by an equally long one out again. On the other hand, Michael had a good pair of shoes and wasn't yet of an age to be averse to a bit of exercise. He'd been a constable after all, in his youth.

But it was for exactly that reason that he hesitated over setting out to walk. Because the quickest route would follow the course of the Forth & Clyde canal where it skirted Dawsholm Park. And the canal wasn't a place he ever liked to revisit if he could help it. Especially not in winter. The rain had temporarily turned into ash grey sleet, but it was easing off now, and if he managed to get this last job done quickly enough, he'd have time for a pie and a pint at the Horseshoe before getting back to the Sheriff Court in the afternoon. As long as he didn't go as far as the locks, it'd be okay.

He managed in the end to devise a route up to the witness's address on Cranbrook Drive that meant he barely glimpsed those slack waters, but his thoughts were stained like spilt petrol for the rest of the day.

Which was why Jeannie Colquhoun was on his mind when Andy Porteous telephoned him at home later that evening.

"I know you were there." Andy was uncharacteristically breathless with agitation. As would anybody, Michael reasoned once he understood, who'd just read the details of that rank rotten affair for the first time. "Tell me everything you know. Leave nothing out."

Michael worked out what must have happened—it could only have been that damned box—and that it was already too late to pretend ignorance. Andy was a terrier with a case. There'd be no peace.

So, he told him everything, and left nothing out.

Jeannie Colquhoun had been a draper's assistant in the town of Bonnybridge, near Falkirk. It was an unremarkable wee place and she'd been a forgettable wee lassie. A good worker, friendly and conscientious, according to her employer. A plain girl, according to her pals, but a faithful friend. She'd liked to put on a bit of lippie and have a dance at the weekends, but she'd never been going to steal anybody's husband.

A good girl, a wee treasure, an angel, according to her devastated parents when Michael and a WPC named Paula Provan had accompanied Inspector Porteous to interview them in their home on that bleak morning in 1946.

How had Jeannie ended up twenty miles to the south-west in Glasgow? That was the first big question. The canal that skirted Bonnybridge on its way to link the rivers Forth and Clyde had once been an important shipping connection between the east and west sides of the country but, long since superseded by the railway, it had fallen into disuse and disrepair. And, since her body had been found frozen to the ice of that same waterway, it had naturally been the focus of the police's investigations. There had to be a connection on or by or under those miles of murky ice, or among the few boatmen and lock-keepers that still frequented those silent banks.

If there was, none was ever found.

Who had she met when she'd slipped out during her lunchbreak that January afternoon? Nobody'd ever come forward. There'd been no official boyfriend and, if she'd been keeping a lad quiet, she'd kept that secret absolutely. She'd simply nipped out on the Wednesday and there'd been no trace until the discovery of the body was reported early on Sunday morning.

She didn't even take her coat. Those were the words of the draper, Brownlee, that later became inextricable in Michael's mind with standing in the foggy pre-dawn on the canal's edge at Maryhill Locks. At that point in time, Jeannie had only just been reported missing. Even so, those words—spoken in a police interview a week later—were the ones that came back to him whenever he recalled staring down at that dirty thick ice.

She didn't even take her coat.

It had been hanging on the hook in the shop's back room at the end of the day, her purse and house keys in the pockets. So she'd only been wearing her shop dress, plain brown shoes and American tan tights when she went out. And a yellow hair slide with a daisy on it.

Jeannie was found naked under a square of carpet underlay. It was tucked around her like a tatty, grey bedsheet. They had to use brazier coals to thaw the awful thing off her. Her clothes were never found.

There had been swans in the frozen darkness. Restless, keeping their distance, but watching. Like ghosts.

Nobody'd knew what to make of the state of the poor lass. Michael, at the ripe old age of twenty-three, had already seen his fair share of everything from domestic violence to gangland razorings, but nothing came close to what he witnessed that morning. The way her face had been obliterated by repeated impact with a never-identified heavy object. Her fine brown hair ripped out by the roots. The way her fingers had been gratuitously broken. The arms and legs, yes, there could have been a reasoning there. The clavicles, even the pelvis. All of the larger bones snapped and displaced so that she could be arranged so inexplicably in that almost perfect swastika shape, if that could be called a reason. But her white fingers? There'd been no sense in that at all beyond pure sadism.

What manner of mind would be capable of it? Nobody there could answer that. What manner of mind would despise a young woman so completely as to tie her up tight enough to leave rope abrasions around her ankles and wrists and neck, and long enough for the bruises rained down on the soft parts of her body to purple and yellow, yet to leave her private areas alone? What kind of mind would inscribe enigmatic quotations all over her body in Signal Red coloured gloss paint?

Sun arise on painted wings. What could that mean?

Nobody could even begin to fathom it. Not then, and not since as Jeannie's case gradually got buried under the snowstorm of violent crimes against women that proliferated in the city in the decades that followed.

Andy Porteous went quiet on the other end of the line, but Michael could hear him breathing. Forced, shuddering. Angry. Michael had been that angry too, once. They all had been. And the anger had grown as the days and weeks stretched into months, into years, and no culprit was brought to justice. If the crime itself was an outrage, the failure of the police to bring justice for it was surely every bit its equal.

They'd kept the mismatched, lurid details out of the newspapers since only the killer could have known them. The injuries, the Nazi iconography, the slogans or whatever they were. The hair slide finally turning up miles away in Sighthill Cemetery. There were so many oddities about the death, in fact, that it had felt like only a matter of time before someone would let something slip and they'd have him on the scaffold. But men had come and gone through that interview room. Bad men, decent men, frightened, bewildered. And none of them ever had.

Those details, though, had tainted all of them that had stood there in the frigid fog that morning. Sunk in through the skin, right into the marrow of their bones so that they all felt like they'd never be warm again.

In due course, some of the officers had tried to move on, getting themselves assigned to different cases, seeking transfers to other divisions, but the damage was already done. The cracks began to show. Signs of some taking to the bottle, rumours of marital strife. The fiscal depute—who'd only ever seen the photographs—was sectioned after jumping into the Clyde from the Jamaica Street Bridge.

Those few rendered unable to turn away by their sense of duty had continued to wrestle with the puzzle of Jeannie Colquhoun, and every one of them—decent, bad, frightened, or bewildered—had ended up defeated.

Old Inspector Porteous worst of all.

Michael went his own road, growing a crust that was cold, abrasive, and impossible to penetrate. A different sort of bubble, he supposes, thinking about it now. The heat death of his soul.

He still dreams of swans though. Their gimlet eyes watching from the gloaming. The looming outlines of their outstretched wings like cemetery angels.

"There must have been more discussion about the crossword clues," Andy said once Michael was done with the telling. He had that same way of skipping past the tragedy to focus on the puzzle as his father'd had.

That was when Michael knew for sure that the lad was destined for the same fate as his old man.

"Andy, son," It was already too late, but the words had to be said. "Drop this one. It's too long in past. Leave it there, eh?"

"How the hell couldn't you solve this?" Andy repeated several times before hanging up the phone, his anger at such an affront going unpunished blazing down the line. "How could you fail her?"

Afterwards, Michael poured himself a hefty dram of Johnnie Walker and sat with the wireless on. A melodrama, something about family secrets. It was just babble but it was better than the cold, crackling silence.

The next morning, Michael considered paying another visit to Andy's offices but, in the end, he didn't. He wasn't the boy's father, thank Christ. It wasn't his responsibility. He'd tried.

What else, he thinks now, could he have done that would have made any difference at all?

A month later, May came to find him.

Michael was in what was becoming his usual corner seat at Baldi's, working his way through a plate of rigatoni and a half bottle of Valpolicella. Italian food had been a fairly recent discovery for him. He wasn't sure what had attracted him through the doors of the little *ristorante* that had recently opened in his neighbourhood.

Maybe it was just that it was new. That the city was changing. After a lifetime of stodgy meat and potatoes, he found that he liked the fulsome flavours. It was colourful food, like the checked paper table-cloths and the vase of crysanths and the yellow lanterns that hung outside the entrance. Like the youthful waitress whose red lips always seemed to be humming a pop song as she flitted between the busy tables, switching effortlessly to boisterous Italian to answer the owner's querulous commands. It was a place vibrant with colour and life.

Michael chose the corner table because he could watch it all in the diffused reflection of the fogged-up window. At a distance.

"Michael?" May wore a powder blue wool coat which she clasped at the neck with an ungloved hand. Her face was pale except for the pink scalds of her cheeks. There was no smile for him today. "Can I talk to you please?"

"Of course." What else was he going to say? He gestured to the empty chair.

"Not here." She winced. "I need to talk to you in private. Please."

Michael would rather not have taken May back to the flat, or anywhere where it was just the two of them together, an ugly man, a frightened woman, but she was insistent. At least, he thought as he ushered her into his darkened hallway, he kept the place tidy enough.

When they entered the living room, those sharp blue eyes of hers took in the armchair, the side table, the whisky glass and summed him up in a blink, but she made no comment, just went to the other chair and perched on its edge. She waited, stiff and brittle, while he fussed around switching the lamps on and lighting the gas fire.

"Get you a coffee, May?" he said. "Something to warm you up?"

"I'll take a whisky," she said.

He found a clean glass, cracked the seal of a new bottle and poured her a generous dram. One for him too.

"This is about Andy, then?"

May took time over her first sip. There was an unfamiliar hardness to her features. In all their acquaintance she'd been Andy's pretty girlfriend and his regular comedy foil. Here, she's something else entirely.

"Tell me," May cradled her tumbler like it would warm her hands, "about Paula Provan."

Michael examined the liquid in his own glass, the orange-blue shiver leant to it by the unsteady fire. Then he said, "You didn't get Paula's name from those old case notes."

"No," May said. "In fact, it was conspicuously absent. She's mentioned at the very beginning, and then just like that she vanishes from the story."

"Paula left the force," he said. "I don't know what happened to her after that." It was a poor lie. He'd known, he'd just never done anything about it. Tracked her down, taken care of her. He could have done that for the last lassie to have smiled at him like she meant it, but he hadn't.

May leant forward. "I do, I interviewed her."

"Right," he said, relieved they wouldn't have to dance around it. "So, you know what Porteous did?"

"I know what he did," she repeated. "But what I really want to know is why."

Michael recognised the tension in her, the need to *fix it*. She wasn't even thinking of herself. Not yet. This was about doing right by Paula, and maybe about saving Andy.

He wanted to ask her: *has he hurt you, hen? Or even just been getting, you know, irrational? Angry?* But instead he gave her the answer she was asking for.

The Inspector's desperation to understand the inexplicable thing that had happened to Jeannie Colquhoun had driven him to explore some wild theories. Everything from cod psychology to secret German cabals to black magic. At one point, he'd employed the crossword compiler from the Glasgow Herald to make sense of the cryptic riddles that had been slathered across the lassie's skin. A desperate gamble and, when that bewildered fella had inevitably failed to come up with a solution, Porteous had arrested him instead.

That was when it came out that Porteous had, in secret, been staging re-enactments. Simple ones at first, but as the questions of how and why *a man could do these things* had continued to elude him, it turned out that he had been edging closer and closer to a complete simulation of the crime.

Michael never heard what had been offered to Paula Provan to aid the Inspector with his clandestine investigations. All he knew was hypothermia had set in by the time they found her, and he never saw her smile again.

The old boys club that formed the upper echelons of the Police service had paid her off for her part in the misadventure. They'd pensioned Porteous off, too. And, considering his twenty-seven years of otherwise sterling service, the Inspector's madness was expunged from the records. Not only for his sake, but for the sake of the force and the men that served in it.

They decreed that no-one needed to know about the things he'd kept in the bottom drawer of a locked filing cabinet. The clothes resembling what Jeannie had been wearing on the day of her disappearance. The curling black and white photographs. Of Paula wearing those clothes, or some of them, or none, displaying the writing scrawled all over her body. Of Jeannie, one in a garden, smiling shyly, and dozens at the scene, in unflinching detail. That pulped white face against the grey ice, wearing a frozen crown of black blood. Clipped to them, a yellow hairslide sporting a daisy.

"It was how things were done," he told May. "How they've always been done when men see the violence other men do and pretend not to understand it." He gulped his whisky down, relished its all-too-brief heat. "But it's really not that hard to understand, is it? There's no mystery to the *how* and the *why*, they just dinnae like the fucking answer."

May was hunched around her glass now.

"Men like Robert Porteous," Michael could see that she understood that by this he also meant his son, "will drive themselves mad looking for any other answer rather than accept the obvious one. But the obvious one is all there is. Men. We're all capable, we're all culpable. We're all beasts at heart." The words tumbled heavily from him like chunks of ice he'd been carrying around inside himself for forever, but there was no relief in getting them out. He was still as cold as ever.

"I think you'd better go now, eh hen?"

Without another word, May placed her glass on the floor, got up and left, failing utterly to disguise her hurry. Michael heard to door snick open and slam shut.

He was alone again.

Sitting here now, he wonders whether May still believes she can save her Andy. Or if, maybe, she's running instead. She isn't naïve enough to believe there's still a bright bubble to hide in anymore.

And he's sorry for that. Sorry that it's come to this. If he'd known what was in those files that first day, they wouldn't be here. But he didn't. And here they are.

If the world's a cold place, he might just be the coldest thing in it. But what can he do about that?

Nothing.

He gets up and turns the fire off, the lights too. Then he pours himself another dram and settles back in his chair. In the dark, in the cold, his skin tightens. He begins to shiver. The shivers quickly become convulsive, whole-body shakes. In the silence, he hears a crackling, like thick canal ice giving way to reveal the gelid, slow-moving murk underneath.

In the corners of his vision, he can make out pale shapes. Watchful ghosts. Spreading their wings wide like shrouds. They whisper and hoot softly and shuffle closer. Their condemnations hanging frigid and everlasting in the cold air.

WAIT UNTIL NEXT WINTER
MARCEL FELDMAR

S hane stood at the edge of the clearing, looking up at the clouds, heavy with snow. Thankfully nothing was coming down yet. They'd spotted the lake just after sunrise, even though the approaching storm was obscuring most of the light. Lauren stood next to Jodi, who leant weakly against a tree, while Shane moved cautiously on to the frozen surface, testing the solidity. Dex stood at the edge rubbing his gloved hands together.

"Damn it's cold," He mumbled.

"Thanks for the update," Lauren snapped.

They'd planned to do an easy two-day hike, knowing with the weather and the fact they were doing it off season it might take longer. Starting near Twin Falls they made it to Laughing Falls easily. From there, the goal was to head straight down to Red Chairs and from there down to Kicking Horse, near the Trans-Canada. But then the first storm hit, throwing everything off course.

On the evening of the second day, they were starting to feel a little anxious. Dark, heavy clouds were rolling in. Dex tried to reassure them, but Jodi wasn't hearing it.

"There's someone following us." She'd whispered as they moved down the mountainside, sliding up closer to Dex.

He laughed a little. "'Someone' ... as if there's anyone else stupid enough to be out here."

"Okay ... some*thing*. Whatever it is, it's not good."

"There's nothing. Let's keep moving towards the water." Dex said.

"Dex..." Jodi started, but then her voice trailed off. Dex was already walking away, and he wouldn't have listened to her anyway.

She took a deep breath, looked nervously behind her, and then started to follow the others hoping this wouldn't become an *"I told you so"* moment.

The winds shifted a few hours later, bringing a soft mist of icy rain. They were starting to realize the lake was farther than expected.

"We need to set up camp. Find shelter by the trees." Lauren said. "Stay warm, get a little rest, and as soon as it gets light, we continue."

They set up a tent, and moved together, trying to find comfort between the four sleeping bags. Shane rummaged through backpack and pulled out a heavy black flashlight, shining it in a slow arc across the tree line. The white beam reflected off the fluttering shadows of the snow that had just started falling.

There was nothing out there. No animals, no people, no city. Just endless snow. As it got darker and colder, Shane started letting his mind wander. What if there was nothing else? What if they had already frozen to death and this was limbo?

"Shane?"

He turned to face Lauren. "We shouldn't be here."

"What do you mean?"

"I don't know," worried Shane. "I feel like this place wasn't meant for us."

"We'll be okay," Lauren whispered, and slowly the wind became a lullaby.

They drifted off for a couple of hours, only to be ripped from almost dreams by a shrill pained cry.

"Jodi!" Dex shouted, jumping out of the tent and standing in knee-deep snow within seconds.

Lauren and Shane scrambled from their tent to find Dex frantic.

"Jodi's *gone*. I heard her screaming..."

"Footprints." Lauren interrupted, pointing towards a trail in the snow.

They ran, Dex in the lead, into a mess of branches heavy with snow. Clouds were moving fast over the mountain and the temperature was falling. It wasn't going to rain; it was going to snow. Hard.

Lauren spotted her first, on her side, half buried in a mound of snow and pushed against the trunk of a fir tree. Her jacket was torn, clawed apart, and there were scratches on her arms and blood on the side of her face.

Then Dex dove towards her and pulled her towards his chest. "Jodi..."

Her eyes fluttered open, she gazed up at him blankly, then they closed again.

"Is she alive?" Lauren asked.

"I think so. It looks like a bite mark, above her ear," he said, observing the row of strange puncture marks surrounded by blood already congealed.

"Jodi, you need to get up." Dex whispered with a little shake.

They managed to get her standing, and slowly made their way back to the tent.

"We can't stay here; the storm is going to hit. We need better shelter, or a way off the mountain." Lauren stated.

Jodi steadied herself against a tree, gathering strength.

"What happened?" Shane asked.

Her hand moved up to the wound on her head. "No idea."

She was shaking, but they knew it wasn't from the cold.

"I had to go to the bathroom, went behind a tree. Then there was a noise... like something heavy falling behind me." Jodi continued.

"Did you see it?" Dex asked.

"No, just shifting shadows. Dirty fur. Like a bear or a wolf, but it wasn't either. It was so fast ... and its teeth..." Jodi stopped, shakes became shudders, and she doubled over, sobbing.

Lauren sat with Jodi as Dex and Shane packed up.

Jodi stopped a couple of times, and Lauren carried on helping her off to the side, waiting as nothing came out but dry heaves.

"I'm dying," she muttered as Lauren helped her up.

"You'll be okay." Lauren couldn't tell if she was being encouraging or hiding her own worries.

Jodi's skin was pale, and her lips were losing color, her forehead burning up. The infection, or whatever it was, was coming on faster than it should, Lauren thought. It had only been a couple of hours since the incident.

Then Jodi started getting worse. Dizzy spells and stomach pains making it even more difficult for her to keep up.

"Everything hurts," she said, sitting down on a snowed over tree stump. "I'm not going to make it, babe."

"You're just delirious... you'll be okay," Dex replied.

"I don't know," Lauren fretted. "She's burning up. We need to get her help."

They stopped, and Shane knelt and started to rummage through his backpack. He pulled a map out, handing it over it his shoulder to Dex. "Can you figure out where we are and where we need to go?"

Dex fumbled through the pages in the dog-eared guide, while Shane stood, fiddling with the buttons on the phone. He shook his head, looked up towards the sky, then back at the phone. "No good."

"What?" Lauren breathed.

"No service..." Shane pointed up. "Maybe we should try to move above the tree line? Dex, how far is Twin Falls?"

Dex snorted. "Too far. We should keep going towards Red Chairs."

"Are you sure? I think we passed that. Maybe we should head south? That should lead us to the highway," Shane argued.

Jodi gave him a weak smile, and Lauren nodded in agreement, giving Shane's arm a squeeze of solidarity. They'd been involved for almost two years and had barely spent any time apart. They'd been traveling and hiking all across North America, discovering their love of the wilderness while strengthening their feelings for each other. Shane's attention to detail combined with Lauren's willingness to take risks created a solid team.

"We got this." Lauren whispered.

Shane nodded. After last summer's rafting adventure down the Colorado River, managing to get lost, and then found again, he was pretty sure they could get through anything. He looked over at Jodi and Dex. Not the river rafting types. He wondered why they were even on this hike. If they hadn't met at the start of the trail, they would have never met. And if the girls hadn't hit it off immediately, they probably wouldn't have decided to take the hike together.

"Look, we need to move." Shane stood, facing Dex.

"Who made you team leader?" Dex asked, lobbing a hastily made snowball at Shane.

Shane sighed, "If you have a better idea, I'm all ears. I'm pretty sure if we don't hit the highway, we should at least come across a campground on the way. We probably won't find any campers, but there might be shelter."

Dex gave a noncommittal shrug and stared back at the way they'd come. "Whatever. Maybe we should split up."

"Seriously?" Shane said.

"Look, If you and Lauren want to keep going towards the highway, I think I can make it back to Laughing Falls with Jodi. At least we know there's shelter, and probably a satellite phone or something set up in the cabin, right?"

Shane stared, astounded. "You think separating the group is the best idea?"

Dex looked over at Jodi, who had managed to stand, and then

back at Shane. "Why not? You and Lauren can keep going towards hopefully the highway. And it'll be easier to follow the path we already took, so we go back. Whoever gets help first sends it towards the others."

"That's not a good idea, man." Shane shook his head. "No way we split up. Not in this weather."

"But if we all go, we could all get lost. If we split up, there's a chance someone will make it." Dex insisted.

"No," Lauren said sternly. "We're in this together and we get out of this together."

"It's obvious who's side you're on," Dex muttered.

"It's not about sides." Shane growled, "It's about what's right."

Slowly, with Dex helping Jodi, the four moved down the snow-covered trail towards a thick line of trees and towards what they hoped would be the highway.

After the first line of trees was cleared, they walked into a wide clearing. Their pace was picking up.

"Damn it." Shane stared down at the phone. "Nothing. I think the storm might be messing with the signal."

Squinting through the cold glare, Lauren gave an excited whoop.

"The lake! We're almost there."

"So cold," Jodi whispered as they walked. "So hungry."

The sight of the lake gave them a burst of adrenaline. They'd been prepared for bad when the trip began, but they hadn't expected the worst.

Dex had made sure they were armed, although he was mad that Jodi had gone into the woods without taking his rifle, and even more furious he hadn't been able to kill whatever creature had attacked her.

They were closer to civilization than it seemed, but many of the roads in the area had been closed and there was no cell reception at all. As far as they were concerned, they were in the middle of nowhere, which was getting colder and darker by the minute.

As they neared the lake, Shane saw a thick plume of smoke rising over the trees in the distance. Not a forest fire, but smoke from a chimney.

They all felt a slight wash of relief as the first drops of rain started to fall.

"It's at the other side of the lake." Dex said. There was a moment of silence.

"That's too far. For her," Lauren said, giving Jodi a worried look.

"We could go across," Dex proclaimed, stepping on the ice.

"Are you crazy?" Lauren blurted. "Not a chance! We'll head around the edge. Help me with her."

They slowly worked their way around the frozen edges moving towards the rising smoke. As they trudged along, stopping often to help Jodi while ignoring Dex's complaints, Shane noticed that the smoke didn't seem to be any closer.

A voice shouted. "This way! Over here!"

The rain was coming down harder, and Shane knew it could get worse any second. He squinted through the falling drops. It was a man in a uniform, arms waving above his head.

"It's a ranger!" Lauren exclaimed. The distinguishing red jacket cut through the weather.

They made their way over, following the ranger. He made a beeline for the thicker trees standing off the path as the group followed. It was a little rough– legs catching on hidden branches, feet slipping on stones under the snow– but the man knew where he was going. He led them to an outcropping of rocks where he pushed a few smaller trees to the side, revealing a cave-like crevasse.

It was small but there was enough room for them to stand together, sheltered by stone.

"Good thing I found you when I did," the ranger said, pulling back his hood. He gave his four rescues a disapproving shake of the head. "You were heading in the wrong direction. Would've ended up in treacherous forest before you'd make it to my cabin. The smoke can be a little misleading, the way the wind pushes it around the trees.."

"What are you?" slurred Jodi, swaying slightly.

"Your friend's not well," The ranger said.

"No... but... why are you here?" Lauren stammered, only now taking in the stature and voice of the man before them.

"Adrian. Adrian O'Conner. Canadian Ranger. I'm stationed at the cabin you were attempting to get to. And you are?"

"Lauren. This is Shane and Dex..." She introduced as they awkwardly waved. "And Jodi here was attacked. Bit by something last night. She needs medical attention as soon as possible."

"We can head to my cabin, weather the storm. I don't have much food, but I've got some. And a decent first aid kit."

"Do you have a phone?" Lauren asked.

He sighed. "I do, but it's been acting up. Between this location and the weather, it's been really hard to get a signal out. I might be able to get the two-way radio working, but I'm not sure if anyone is in range."

"And that's how horror movies start," Dex muttered under his breath.

Adrian looked off in the distance. "The cabin will be good until the storm blows over, then we can get help."

Jodi slumped against Dex, who almost fell over from the sudden shift in weight.

"I don't think we have a choice at this point," Dex grunted.

The four followed Adrian through the trees towards the lake, then down towards the cabin.

"How long have you been out here?" Lauren asked Adrian as they walked.

"This time, about a month."

"This time?"

"I'm up here every winter. And every winter I find people like you."

"People like us?" Lauren echoed.

He gave her a sideways glance. "Unprepared for the weather."

"Don't go out too far, Dex." Shane shouted behind them.

Lauren turned and saw Dex walking out on to the frozen lake. "Dex!"

Dex glared but walked back. "What?"

"People have fallen through that ice, and some of them have never been found." Adrian warned. "There are bodies all over this mountain."

"And I'm sure you know where," Dex spat.

Adrian walked straight up to Dex and pointed a finger that almost touched his chest.

"Listen," he said so quietly the other three couldn't hear. "You may die up here, but I'm not the thing that's going to kill you."

Then he turned and continued walking, finishing his thought so everyone could hear. "Listen to me and you might survive."

They walked in silence for a few minutes, when Lauren sidled up to Adrian.

"Do you know what attacked Jodi?" She prodded.

"Yes," he said. "We need to keep moving."

The possibility of them making it back to the cabin without any further mishaps vanished as the rain switched to snow.

"Should we take cover?" Lauren asked, worried about Jodi.

"No. Not a good idea," Adrian ordered. "Keep your eyes on the trees. I've got yellow blazes marking the way."

It wasn't too bad at first. The flakes were large and flat, drifting listlessly to the ground. The outstretched fingers of fir and pine above them helped keep their trail clear. But then the wind started pushing against them as they moved down past the trees into clear field. That meant there was no protection, and nowhere to hold the markings they had been following. Any semblance of a trail had been covered by snow and the edge of the lake was no longer distinguish-able from the land. They trudged through, heads down, eyes focused on the ground right in front of them as the rest of the world was obscured by the swirling and unexpected white.

Without warning Jodi stopped, and pulled on Dex's arm, making him yell in surprise.

Jodi's eyes were wide, and she stared at Dex, words not quite making it out of her mouth.

"Guys!" Dex shouted.

Adrian had been leading the way, but abruptly stopped and started back. "What is it?"

"I saw something," he said. "Off to the side, in the forest. Like a shadow, a big one, moving through the trees."

Shane and Lauren, huddled together, looking back towards the snow covered pines.

"It's just your mind playing tricks on you," Adrian said quickly. "Probably snow falling to the ground, or wind. Auditory illusions, nothing more."

Jodi looked at him, not quite trusting his response. "I don't know..."

"I heard something, too. And it's not the first time. It could be what attacked Jodi," Shane said, catching up.

"C'mon. We're almost there," Adrian pushed forwards. The others lined up behind him, using his body for a shield. Wool scarves wrapped around their faces, hoods pulled down low.

Dex yelled into the air, frustrated. "We should have stayed in that cave."

"If we'd stayed, we'd be stuck up there!" Adrian shouted back over the wind. "It's right around the next bend. The lake ends, then there's just a stand of trees between us and the cabin," he explained. "One last push."

And they pushed, moving through a life sized snow globe. It seemed the entire mountainside had turned against them.

"All this shifting of snow and rain has created layers of hidden ice. That's going to make it tricky to get back into town even if you do make it to the highway. At least for a couple of days," Adrian shouted through the maelstrom.

Jodi was also shouting, her fever breaking slightly, the ice and cold hitting her with a sudden clarity. "Dexter." She reached out and grabbed his arm.

"What?" He answered, surprised.

"Don't leave me."

"I'm not leaving," Dex said. He grabbed her arm and pulled her next to him. He didn't want to be lying.

Then the cabin appeared out of the storm like a winter mirage. The windows glowed orange, and the chimney breathed a thin plume of cedar smelling smoke.

Jodi felt a swell of elation, but it was suddenly diminished by an overwhelming feeling.

I'm not going to make it.

She shook her head, took a deep breath. She wouldn't believe it. She didn't want to.

"Come inside, quick." Adrian interrupted her thoughts. He opened the door, and the wind and snow pushed them in.

"Don't leave me, " Jodi whispered against the back of Dex's neck, falling against him.

"Nobody's leaving."

They entered the best warmth they'd ever felt; Lauren and Shane first, and then Dex and Jodi, carried over the threshold. A honeymoon of pain. She wasn't crying anymore, but she wasn't conscious, either. Adrian came in last and locked the door with a series of bolts.

"We'll gather in the living room by the fire." Adrian said. "I'll check the phone and radio while I heat up some soup and get the coffee brewing. You should get into warm clothes fast. We've lost most of the day, and we need to be set up before night. It's going to be a long one."

Shane and Lauren moved next to the fire while Dex fell on to a couch; Jodi was placed on another. He pulled a rough wool blanket over his head and tried to find a silent space in his mind. Nothing but stillness and quiet.

Something had attacked Jodi. Something had been following them.

It was going to be a long night, Adrian had said.

Dex pulled off the blanket, frustrated. "Is the coffee done?"

"Almost," Adrian answered. "Shane, could you try to build the fire up?"

Shane nodded as Adrian knelt by Jodi, wiping the wound on her head while handing her a couple of pills and a glass of water. "It's some amoxicillin and a couple of 222's which should take the edge off."

"The phone?" Jodi mumbled, as Adrian got up and moved back towards the kitchen.

"Still no good. I've got the two-way on, but it doesn't seem like anyone's in range."

Jodi closed her eyes and lay back into the couch. The light of flickering flames and the aroma of coffee filled the cabin making it almost cozy.

"Thank you," she whispered, with a tiny smile. And then: "I'm hungry."

Adrian finally came back with the coffee, and Lauren turned her back to the fire. She gazed out into the darkness through the living room window, holding the steaming mug next to her face like a safety blanket.

"Do you think whatever it was will freeze out there?" Lauren asked, turning to look directly at Adrian.

Adrian leaned back in his chair and gave Lauren a sad look. "I doubt it. I'm pretty sure that thing has been out there for a long time." Adrian paused, looked towards the front door before continuing, "Longer than this cabin has been here."

Lauren narrowed her eyes, "What are you not telling us?"

Adrian stood and moved to the fireplace, standing between Lauren and Shane. He grabbed one of the long iron pokers and shoved it into the soft glow of embers. There was a crack of wood and a hiss as water shifted to steam, like a threat and a whisper.

"We are in the wilderness, and that comes with challenges. But we should be okay. No need to worry about what's out there," He said, staring into the softly smoking fireplace. "But I think we do need to worry about keeping this fire going. We're going to need some more wood."

"I know you saved us, and I'm thankful," Shane looked around, "We're all thankful. But I think you know what's out there. And I think we do need to worry. Jodi could be dying, and you might be the only person who can help her."

"Okay." Adrian moved back to the chair and sat, leaning forwards. "There is something out there. It's been out there for a long time. I've never gotten a good look at it, but I've seen what it can do."

"Are you talking like bigfoot? Some kind of mountain monster?" Dex asked.

By the fireplace, Shane slowly lowered his head into his hands, elbows on his knees. He was feeling a little faint, a little like something in his reality was shifting and he was slipping into some surreal nightmare version.

"Not bigfoot..." Adrian started.

"Wendigo." Dex finished.

Adrian gave Dex a wry smile. "Also no. Older than that, I think. Or perhaps from somewhere else. Wendigo comes from cannibalism. This thing feeds on something else, and when it attacks, it doesn't eat... it destroys."

"And you haven't called in your ranger friends to help hunt it down?" Lauren questioned.

"I have, and nothing has come of that. There's no sign of it when springtime comes around, and when bodies are found, there's no evidence it was anything other than a wolf or a bear. Your friend is one of the only people I've seen survive an attack,"

Adrian paused for a second. "And I don't know if she'll survive for much longer."

"What do we do?" Lauren asked.

"We make it through the night and try to get into town tomorrow morning. First light."

Lauren moved to the window to peer outside. The shadows from the forest seemed to wave towards her, mixing with the light from the cabin, creating a mottled bruising on the layers of snow stretched between them and safety.

"And I used to think the snow was so pure." She sighed.

"It is." Adrian said as he shifted his cup of coffee back and forth between his hands. "It's what's in it that's evil."

They moved to the fire for more warmth and sat semi-circle around Adrian. He stared at the flames, and it seemed as if they were whispering words he wanted to say. Lauren felt like they were kids camping in the night and telling ghost stories, and for the first time the fear was replaced by a twinge of excitement.

"That thing appears every winter, but for some reason as the winters are getting warmer, it seems to be getting stronger, and more aggressive." Adrian stopped to poke at the burning wood, sending a tiny whirl of sparks up the chimney. "As if it's angry and taking it out on us. Five years ago, it attacked my wife. Near where you were, at the top of the lake. Winter storm, we were caught off guard. It came at her while I was setting up a tent. I've been tracking it, hunting it, ever since. This is the closest I've come."

The three stared at him in shocked silence.

"And your wife?" Lauren asked, voice quavering.

Adrian looked up at her, "Tamara. She got bit. Infected. Like your friend, only much worse. She didn't make it."

Adrian stopped as something hit the window. He jumped up, pulled the curtains aside, but there was nothing there. "Branch, probably. Wind blows the loose ones down."

He left for the kitchen, and began rummaging around in a cupboard. The others just watched him quietly.

"Do you believe him?" Lauren whispered.

"I don't know," Shane replied. "I mean, I believe something's out there. And something may have attacked his wife, but..."

"Okay," Adrian announced, holding up a key. "You all know how to shoot a gun?"

Dex nodded, but Lauren and Shane looked at each other, slightly worried.

"I used to shoot, a long time ago," Lauren said. "But I don't think Shane's ever held a gun."

"Well, not a real one," Shane mumbled sheepishly.

"Doesn't matter. Now's not the time to have misgivings." Adrian moved to a cabinet by the front door, unlocked it to reveal a rack of rifles, and a couple of handguns as Dex whistled in appreciation. "Now it's time to survive."

Adrian took one of the rifles and stepped back, "Choose your weapon, but keep the safety on. Hopefully none of you will need to use these." Adrian made a gesture towards the cabinet and the other three moved closer.

Dex grabbed a pistol.

"Be prepared," he muttered, sticking it in his waistband.

Lauren grabbed another rifle while Shane reached for a handgun. "Just point and shoot, right?"

"Pretty much. You'll be okay," Lauren said. "We'll be okay."

As if to punctuate her comment, the lights flickered briefly, and the wind outside picked up, sending debris across the roof.

What if this was how it all ended? Just a slow cold descent into oblivion?

Dex went to check on Jodi, who was lying still on the couch, buried under a blanket. Her forehead was hot, but not as hot as it had been.

She shivered under his touch, and he sat next to her, gently stroking her hair. "How are you doing?"

She reached up silently, grabbed his wrist. Her hands felt colder than winter. "We're all going to die."

Dex felt the chill from her fingers seep inside and wrap around his heart.

"No. We've got this."

He took a couple of the pills from the bottle beside the couch and helped Jodi wash them down with some water. "We've got this," he repeated. Quietly, he stood to join the others in the kitchen.

"How is she?" Lauren asked

"I think she'll be okay."

None of them believed him.

They moved around the cabin, securing the windows, making sure both doors were locked and bolted. It was a decent sized cabin. Solid. Secure. But there was still a feeling of uncertainty drifting through the rooms. Uncertain of what was out there, uncertain of what the night would bring. The only thing they were certain of was that sleep was not an option.

"Maybe this will help?" Adrian offered, holding up a bottle of whiskey. "Just a sip, right?"

Dex took the bottle happily. "Maybe a couple of sips."

Shane and Lauren sat on opposite sides of the kitchen table, guns within reach. Adrian moved the chair into the center of the living room, positioned between the window and the front door. Dex put his gun down on the coffee table and sat on the couch with the whiskey.

A burst of wind hit the side of the cabin, pushing the wooden chairs on the porch back against the wall with a faint rolling knock and thud. There was nothing to see other than the constant shift of shadow and white.

"More coffee?" Lauren asked as she stood.

"Wait." Dex stopped her, hand raised in warning.

"What?"

"There's something... did you hear it?" Dex asked. "Out there, in the snow."

"Just the wind." Adrian reassured.

"But it wasn't. It was more rhythmic. Something moving, alive. Like heavy footsteps, not random," Dex insisted.

Shane moved to the window and breathed a foggy circle onto the cold glass, then made a frowny face with his fingertip. "How do you know?"

"What?" asked Adrian.

"I mean, you told us there's something out there, right? And now there's nothing out there. Which one is it?" Shane demanded, facing Adrian.

"There's something out there, but it's not close enough to worry about, yet. I have traps and tripwires set. We can relax, as long as one of us stays alert."

"That's fine," Lauren said. "As long as we skip the monsters. I've made it through worse weather."

Lauren watched as Dex and Shane exchange a glance.

"C'mon," she sighed. "Either we trust Adrian and his ability to survive up here for the last five winters, or we don't. I need to sleep."

Before anyone could respond there was a sound from outside. A low, soft moan slid in through the crack under the door.

"What was that?" Lauren whispered.

"Your monsters," Dex whispered back.

"Dammit, I swear I saw something move." Lauren said slowly, backing away from the window.

Dex pulled the curtain back, peered into the swirling darkness. "It's the storm. Blowing through the trees. Just branches creaking."

He didn't want to turn to face the others, worried they might be able to tell he was lying. Worried they might be able to see the fear in his eye.

Another moan, but this time it increased in volume, becoming a sharp cry. It sounded farther away, but the tone carried an unmistakable anguish.

"It's a person," Lauren said. "We need to help them."

"How do you know it's a person?" Dex asked.

"Listen," Lauren held up a finger, tilted her head slightly.

"What kind of person would be out there?"

"The kind who needs help, Dex." She glared.

Dex quickly defended. "Or the kind who wants to *kill* us."

"Please?" Lauren pleaded.

"Fine." Dex growled as he grabbed his gun and angrily zipped up his parka. "Shane?"

"I'll come with. Shane should stay with Lauren," Adrian said, and grabbed his jacket.

Lauren watched them head towards the door. A wave of fear washed over her.

Adrian paused for a second, looked back at her. "We'll be quick."

They left without another word. Shane locked the door behind them.

"We need to help," Lauren said.

"You're not going out there," Shane said quietly, moving next to her. "You heard what Adrian said, It's just the wind. Sounds playing tricks. What did he call them?"

"Auditory illusions."

"Yeah. Those."

Then, as if angered by their disbelief, a scream of inhuman sharpness cut through the storm. Lauren threw her hands to her ears as Shane winced in sonic pain.

It echoed through the snow, bounced off the trees and hit the cabin intensified and reverberating, then stopped as suddenly as it started. Shane and Lauren slid to the ground, backs against the wall, heads just below the window. They could feel the cold seeping in and silently moved closer together, searching for whatever warmth they could hold between them.

Outside, Dex and Adrian heard the same horrific screech and crouched down under the cover of darkness and snow.

"What the hell was that?" Dex asked.

"Something we don't want to mess with right now," Adrian spat, through gritted teeth.

"Is it coming closer?"

"No. We're okay," Adrian muttered.

I hate you for taking her, he thought to himself. *I hate myself for letting you go.*

He stood up straight, and reached out and grabbed Dex by the shoulder, "Look, this isn't your fight. You've got a wounded friend, and you need to take care of your own. You need to get back inside."

Dex just looked at him.

Adrian took a deep breath and exhaled slowly. "Okay. Let's walk around the cabin. Carefully."

The snow kept coming, and Adrian knew something else was coming, too.

This time, he hoped, *I'll be ready.*

Dex nodded, and the two of them continued walking around the cabin, sticking to the tree line. The muffled sounds of heavy things falling in the thick drifts kept a staggered time just out of sight, peripheral shadows blurred by the snow melting on their faces.

"What's out there?" Lauren asked, standing next to Shane while they tried to see through the impenetrable wall of whirling, endless snow.

"I don't know." Shane turned to look at her. "But it's not good."

"Quiet...did you hear that?" Lauren whispered.

"No..." Shane answered. "Should we go back out there?"

His voice wavered slightly, worrying Lauren. Before she could answer, there were three sharp raps at the door.

She ran to open it, letting in Dex and Adrian shaking off snow.

Dex was visibly shaken. It was obvious the stories from earlier and the endlessness of the snow was getting to him. Adrian stood next to him, "Nothing in the traps. Everything seems secure, but this storm is going to make things difficult for us."

"I think maybe we all need another shot." Lauren said, moving to grab the bottle from the table.

Shane closed the door behind them quietly and watched Lauren. As she turned, she paused and gave him a look of understanding.

"I'm not getting drunk; I just need to dull this edge," she promised.

"We should take it easy," Dex said quietly, surprising everyone. "We might need to stay sober for this one."

Without waiting for a response, he walked back to the couch and sat next to Jodi. Her breathing had mellowed but she was still shivering, skin still cold to touch. She shifted a little as he sat, but her eyes remained closed. She moved again, mumbled something about bears, and then rolled over, her back to Dex. He leant over and pulled the blanket up to cover her more.

"We need to make this fire bigger," he said as the others joined him in the living room.

"I think I really need to try to get some sleep." Lauren said.

Adrian nodded. "It's a good plan. We take turns keeping the fire going and keeping watch."

They drew straws. Dex was up first.

As the others tried to make themselves comfortable, Dex added a knife from the kitchen to his arsenal. "Just in case," he told Adrian.

Adrian just nodded, and then turned to face the wall.

The room filed with a silence broken by the crackle of fire and a constant howl of the wind outside.

A howl that was so much more comforting and hypnotic than the shrieks from before.

Shane stared at the flames, while the other three lay quietly, waiting for anything resembling sleep to find them and maybe take them away.

Slowly, they all drifted, under slow flames and the hushed whispers of windswept pines. Perhaps it wasn't sleep, but it was close.

❄

The wind shifted, and Adrian's eyes opened. It was three in the morning, according to his watch. He knew what was coming, but he also knew it didn't matter. There was no warning to give, no preparation to take. The wind always came first, pushing through the small cracks in the wood, the space under the door. Down the chimney and over the glowing embers on the grate.

Then the scratching. It could've been some nocturnal creatures moving over the rooftop, jumping from tree to cabin to tree, but Adrian knew it wasn't. There was nothing to do but let it pass and hope it didn't get worse.

This night it did.

Adrian stood, everyone else remained asleep.

He grabbed his rifle, zipped up his jacket, and quietly let himself out into the freezing tempest.

As soon as the door closed, Shane's eyes shot open. He'd heard something, and he wasn't sure what. He stared at the wall feeling a sudden fear, an unwillingness to turn around. As if there was something there he shouldn't see. Was it someone at the door?

"No. Imagination," he told himself. "It's the storm."

It wasn't the storm.

There was something on the roof.

Shane sat up, looked around. The fire was going, but Dex was sitting in a chair, turned to face the front door. He had fallen asleep. Shane rolled his eyes.

So much for first watch.

Lauren was on one couch, Jodi on the other. Adrian was... gone.

Shane slowly stood up, tiptoed towards the bedroom, opened the door a crack. No Adrian.

He moved to the window, peered outside, and then he saw it.

A shadow, thin and fast, swinging down from above the window, across the porch, and up again.

Like a tail.

Something hit the door.

Shane stumbled backwards, tripping over his feet, and fell on his ass, visions of a hundred horror films flooding his mind.

Do not invite anything inside.

Lauren woke when Shane fell next to her, jumping to her feet. Dex, oblivious, muttered something and shifted in the chair.

"What happened?" she asked, helping Shane to his feet.

"Nothing. Freaking myself out," he said, as he moved back to the window and pulled the curtains aside.

He peered out, then dropped the curtain and moved back to the couch.

"Shane?"

"Just shadows and snow," he said.

Nothing was said for a few minutes. Lauren went to the window to see for herself. It was all darkness, except when the falling snow reflected the light shining out.

"What's out there?" She whispered.

On the couch, Jodi coughed. It didn't sound as if she was getting better.

"Adrian?" Lauren turned, calling out quietly.

"He's not here."

"Did he leave us?" Lauren worried. "The guns? Supplies?"

Shane checked the rack before moving into the kitchen. "Food and water are still here, but he took a rifle."

"Where did he go?" Lauren asked.

"I don't know. Maybe to kill us," Shane said.

"Shane, nom" Lauren countered.

Shane gave a non-committal shrug, smiled, and let out a slow breath before he started to brew a pot of coffee. "Probably not, but it's best to be ready for anything."

"It's not funny," Lauren growled. "Make it extra strong."

Dex soon woke up, not knowing if he'd been asleep for one hour or five. He came to feeling something was wrong. He couldn't tell if it was real or remnants from a barely remembered nightmare. He leaned forwards, his hand reaching for the knife he'd stashed underneath the cushion.

A strange light washed in through the windows. Grey daylight. It cast a surreal glow over the interior of the cabin.

He hadn't meant to fall asleep. Feeling slightly embarrassed he looked around quickly to see if anyone else had noticed. If they had, it didn't matter. There was something else going on.

Shane and Lauren were on either side of the window in the front room. Lauren held a shotgun, up and across her chest. Shane peered through a crack between curtain and wall, a rifle at his side.

"Adrian?"

"He's outside again." Shane said turning around. "Somewhere."

It's happening, Dex thought, jumping up and grabbing the shotgun from the floor. But really, he had no idea what was happening.

Something outside. A bear. Monsters. Death…

"Shane?" he whispered, only to be shushed by Lauren. She motioned for him to go check on Jodi.

Before he could move, it hit. Like a small earthquake.

Something had struck the back of the cabin with a heavy dull thud, muffled like a snow-covered battering ram, shaking the walls. glasses rattled, and then silenced.

"What the…!" Dex exclaimed.

"Check on Jodi," Lauren interrupted. "Now!"

Dex quickly headed to the couch, where Jodi lay curled up on top of the blanket. Her eyes fluttered periodically.

"Dex?" she mumbled.

"I'm here."

"I'm hungry."

Dex sat next to her on the couch, and then it hit again. Harder.

The sound was still thick and dull outside, pushing through layers of snow, but inside pictures clattered against the wall and something fell and smashed on the kitchen floor.

Jodi's eyes opened wide, and she sat up on her knees. "It's here."

"What's here?" Dex asked, feeling a sliver of terror creep in with the cold.

"He's come for me," Jodi said, and then she slumped back down on to the couch. Her breathing short and fast.

Dex stood and shouted towards the others. "Shane! What was that?"

"Just the storm, branches falling. It's intense out there."

"That can't be it. Jodi's freaking out! There's something out there, she said it's *coming* for her..."

"What's coming for her?" Asked Lauren, moving to the couch.

"I have no idea, whatever's out there." Dex said.

There was another crash, and the front door slammed open bathing Adrian in a swirl of snow and darkness.

Before anyone could react, he took three steps towards the center of the room with a shotgun in his hand. He barked a sharp order directing Dex to get Jodi into the kitchen with Lauren and Shane, then moved behind the couch to push it towards the front door.

The living room window quivered, then glass shattered. Shards falling into the living room and into the night. The cold air rushed in, filling the room with a blast of frozen terror.

The silence held everyone in a static stillness for an endless minute, until there was a cough from Jodi. She stood there, swaying next to Dex. Her skin a deathly shade of green. A slight trickle of blood dripping down the side of her face from the wound in her head.

"I don't feel so good." Jodi's voice broke the silence, and she started to fall.

Dex grabbed her, and slowly lowered her to the floor. He knelt beside her. "Jodi?"

"Look," Adrian said. "I've got an old Chevy at the bottom of this first hill. About a thirty-minute walk in good weather. I'm pretty sure there's enough gas to get you in to town, but you should go now."

"*Now* you tell us?" Shane blurted.

"The storm wouldn't have let you get close before, but now it's probably the best option," Adrian explained. "If you stay, it's going to be really bad."

"Why did you come back?" Dex asked suspiciously.

"I need to kill it." Adrian said and tossed a set of keys under-handed towards Dex. He sat down in the old leather chair without offering anything more, pushing it into the corner with the heels of his hiking boots. He held his shotgun across his chest, determined. The silence came back. Heavier, and thick with uncertainty and fear.

The winds outside picked up and inside the electricity suddenly struggled, faltered, fought, and then came back strong. The shadows cast by lightbulb and fire vanished into a second of emptiness, and then flared back into soft blurred shades of comfort and grey.

And in the silence Jodi whispered words that made everyone feel cold again. "It's not going to let us go."

Then an even colder sound slipped across the open room. A sound causing ice and shivers. Something was at the back door. Trying to get in ... a scratch, a staggered battering on the wall, and it stopped. A tense electricity filled the room.

Dex stood and moved towards the front door; Adrian's keys held tight in his hand.

"What are you doing?" Shane demanded.

Dex stopped in the doorway. He closed his eyes. "Barricade the door behind me."

"Dex?" It was Jodi. "Don't leave."

Dex stood with his back to everyone. He had the keys to the truck in one hand, a gun tucked in his belt. He lowered his head and felt a shudder in his chest. An unfamiliar sensation. He remembered lying next to Jodi at the motel in Banff before the trip. And before that, when they first met. Hawaii at the waterfalls, watching the sun rise. He remembered her whispering how she felt about him. He clenched his empty hand into a fist, felt a tear threaten to fall.

He moved slowly out on to the porch. His breath cut a thin line of vapor into the outside.

"Everyone leaves."

Behind him he could hear Adrian cock his shotgun and Lauren doing the same. He glanced back, Shane had his sights set on whatever the door would open to.

"Yeah," Shane muttered. "But we're leaving together."

Dex took a step back, letting the broken door swing open wider. A draft of snow swirled in, leaving soft spots of water as it melted on the cabin floor.

"Can we make it down to the truck?" Lauren asked quietly.

"With Jodi?" Dex said. "I doubt it."

Behind them claws scraped against the kitchen window. A pause, and then something hit it hard. A slight crack appeared on the edge of the glass.

"Dex..." Lauren warned.

"Fine," Dex growled. "We're in this together. But if I die, I'm never going to forgive you."

"I can live with that," Lauren said tartly.

Dex turned and moved towards the kitchen as Adrian stepped in to take his place at the door. Gun raised; eyes focused on the path leading towards the porch.

"Anything comes in this window," Dex snarled, picking up a hefty utility knife, "gets stabbed in the throat."

Jodi slowly walked towards Dex, slightly stumbling. Lauren moved up to grab her as Dex shook his head, motioned for them to both go back into the living room. "I've got this."

Jodi swayed a little, then leaned against Lauren before she staggered back to the couch. She sat abruptly, pouting and whining.

"Jodi?" Lauren asked. "What's going on?"

She stared up at her, the pout turning into a scowl as she rubbed her belly. Shane watched; the words she had said earlier came back to him ... *I'm hungry* ...

"What's wrong with her?" he hissed.

Jodi started to stand, unsteadily, and lean in towards him but stopped as a heavy thud reverberated from outside the front door. In the kitchen Dex spun on his heel; outside it was all black and specks of white.

Adrian stepped into the doorway, facing the darkness. His legs spread slightly, shotgun at the ready. There was a time when he thought he might be able to live a normal life. Have a family. At least, have a wife. It's not like he hadn't tried. But between death and divorce there hadn't been much left for him. He'd given up on that. But he wasn't ready to give up on this.

"I'm not going to let you take her." Adrian whispered into the empty air, towards the darkness of the forest. The edge of the frozen lake just beyond. "Not again."

"What do you mean?" Lauren asked, moving behind Adrian, her gun at the ready. He didn't respond so she turned towards Shane.

Shane started a shrug but was interrupted by a sharp crack, almost like a gunshot, from the back door.

They all turned, the door was still shut, but now it split down the middle, shards of wood angling out uncomfortably. Then something hit it from the other side, and it split in half. What came through then was a mess of fur, teeth, and darkness. It bounded, screaming, towards them. Snow swirling around an elongated body and wild saliva splattering the floorboards as claws dug into wood.

Three guns burst into deafening life, hoping for death. Two shotguns and a rifle. They weren't sure how many bullets were spent and how many hit, but the thing reared backwards slipping on its own now blood slicked and matted fur. It twisted, knocking over the shelves in the hallway and suddenly changed course. Adrian had turned, moving towards it, pumping the shotgun, but it was faster than imagined and had slipped around the corner into the kitchen.

Dex screamed, and fell against the table, hitting his head, and slumped down to the floor. Lauren stepped around behind him and unflinching, raised her weapon and fired a shell directly at the thing's head. It fell backwards, blood spurting up, a viscus brownish green syrup and splattering down over Dex's prone body.

It shuddered on the ground and lay still for a second.

Shane took a step towards the kitchen, rifle aimed at the crea-ture's head. "Is it–"

Before he could finish his sentence, the thing let out a shrill scream, and turned slithering and skittering back towards the gaping hole it had come in through.

"Don't let it get away!" Adrian shouted, running after it through the back door and up the hill into the trees. Shooting as he ran, he vanished into the flurries and wind.

Seconds later there was a harsh roar. An angered guttural growl cutting through the snow followed by two shots from a rifle, piercing through the winter night, and a scream.

Then nothing.

"We can't leave him out there!" Lauren insisted.

"I'm not going to get him!" Dex shouted, trying to resist rubbing the deep gash in his bleeding forehead.

"You're an asshole, Dex," Shane said, moving towards the door.

"I know," was his response as he stood up and started towards the front door.

From the side Jodi reached out and grabbed Dex's hand. "Wait."

She pulled at him with surprising strength and looked up imploringly at him. Her once green eyes had shifted to a slightly sick-lier yellow.

He flashed on how she had looked when they had first met, and it was beautiful, for a second. And now she was someone else, and now they were here. In the middle of a snowstorm, fighting God knows what. He turned away from her jaundiced gaze and pulled his arm free.

"Okay, fine. We all go for the truck. Now." He ordered, moving towards the front door, knowing Adrian and whatever else was out there had gone in the opposite direction.

"I'm not going to make it," Jodi whimpered.

Dex knew she was right, even though he didn't want to admit it. It was too late. She was too far gone.

The others knew too.

"We have to leave her," Dex insisted. "And Adrian, he's not going to make it. You know that. We've gotta leave them both."

The decision floated between them all, solidifying like water freezing mid-air. A breath, a choice, a death...

"Damn it," Lauren declared. "We're not waiting. We're taking Jodi. We can make it to the truck. We must."

Adrian stood outside in the snow, the wind was picking up, the snow becoming a blinding flurry. He felt none of it. The cold didn't touch him, evaporating against his anger. Once again, the creature had gotten away. And now he had to deal with Jodi before she changed. Like Tamara had changed. Whatever the creature had infected her with would grow and transform within her. Like a parasite, until only the creature would be left. A hungry creature.

And then she would join the others.If you were bit, you were dead. That thing would be living inside you. He couldn't let it take Jodi too.

He didn't want Tamara to leave, but the thing took her anyway. Adrian managed to kill her... the thing that used to be her. He was left with a lifeless mound of flesh and fur, scales, and teeth. Nothing even resembling a human. He buried it under stones, in the lake. A grave he could visit every winter when the water froze solid.

He stood at the top of the hill, where he could see the side of the cabin, the light from the kitchen window playing amber on the night blue of the snow outside. He kept in the shadows and looked towards the frantic movements inside the cabin. Through the windows he could tell they were pacing about the rooms, trying to figure out what to do next. His thoughts settled, spinning soft like a mantra, a sentence that no longer meant anything. Spinning through his head until it becomes just a bitter blur of words. A soft, sharp-edged hum:

I hate you for taking her. I hate you for leaving me without her.

Adrian was so busy trying to ignore the voice in his head he didn't notice the others moving together towards the front door. As it opened, Lauren shouted a warning at Dex, while she and Shane followed with Jodi supported between them.

The shout alerted Adrian. His head snapped up and he started running towards the cabin. His feet catching on hidden obstacles in the snow, he stumbled and tumbled down the frozen slope. But it was too late for Dex.

Dex had walked out on to the front porch and into the cold night, but turned when he heard Lauren screaming. He saw the three of them inside, Shane pushing Lauren and Jodi towards the back door with his arms outstretched, as if he was a driver shielding them from a sudden stop.

Adrian was almost at the front porch, his shotgun pointing at the roof. He knew what was going to happen next.

Something flickered across the bricks of the chimney, like sparks from a flint, and a shadow slid over the Cypress shingles of the rooftop. Adrian shouted, and shot, but he wasn't fast enough. Like a buzzsaw, something shot towards Dex. From Adrian's vantage point it looked like something had passed right by Dex and into the cabin. It had gone right through him, splitting him in half with a razor serrated tail like appendage.

Screams of terror followed; shattering glass, and shots fired inside the structure.

"Shane! Lauren!" Adrian shouted, bursting into the cabin through the fractured doorway, shotgun pointing straight ahead.

"Bedroom!" It was Lauren.

He slammed his shoulder into the door and tripped over a body. It was Shane. There was blood and broken glass everywhere. His knuckles turned white as his hands clenched into fists, his finger-nails digging into skin. Lauren was in the corner of the room, her gun pointing at the door. Jodi lay still upon a pool of blood being soaked up by the blankets.

Adrian rushed over to Lauren, who collapsed in his arms.

"We need to go. If we don't leave, that thing will come back for us." He said, as he helped her back to her feet.

I hate you for taking her. I hate you for leaving me without her.

"Dex?" There was a whimper from the bed.

Adrian ran back to her side and sat next to her, "Dex is ... gone."

Jodi was still alive, barely. "I'm so hungry."

Adrian nodded, "I know."

He looked down at her, shivering. She reminded him of his wife. How she looked before she died. She's fading, but he could still feel her.

He held her hands in his and moved them up to his lips where he warmed them with a breath. He knew she'd never feel it.

"Adrian?" Lauren reached out to him. "Your wife... she was infected too, wasn't she."

Adrian nodded.

"You had to kill her... didn't you?" She knew the answer.

Another nod.

Jodi's eyes are closed. He pressed his lips against her forehead. It felt like marble, cold and smooth. It felt like the ice covering the lake.

"We have to make sure she doesn't survive, don't we." Lauren whispered softly.

"So, she doesn't come back."

He let go of Jodi's hands. They dropped like dead weights to her sides. She was colder than winter.

"She's gone." Adrian said, his breath leaving a soft fog in the air.

He knew it wasn't his wife. He knew they're both gone. He placed a hand on her chest, but she couldn't feel it anymore.

He lifted her up and carried her out into the snow. Lauren followed. He wanted to cry, but the tears were frozen inside, like her body was frozen outside. He knelt before her, in the snow, in the cold.

"I'm still so hungry." Jodi whispered; her voice barely discernible above the winds twisting around them. Her body almost translucent in the light.

Adrian paused; it was only the wind. Nothing more.

Jodi's death has given them their life back. The thing won't come back, not for another year. He touched the snow that was starting to cover her body like a hibernal blanket. A crystal duvet.

"I'm going to come back as well," Adrian promised. "Just wait until next winter comes around."

He looked out at the trees and stood up. He knew even though he wanted it to be a lie, it wasn't. No matter how hard he tried to stay away, he'd end up coming back. Lauren moved beside him and rested her hand on his shoulder.

"I'll come back with you," She vowed.

The two of them stood in front of the cabin and watched the sun rise and fight the last remnants of the storm as Jodi's body was covered softly by a blanket of fresh snow. Soon they would bury her, along with Shane and Dex, near his wife, in the lake.

Behind them, icicles slowly melted into blood-stained snow.

WARM

ANNE WOODS

Winifred Meyer didn't mean to die.

She had managed to sneak out of her parent's lavish Newport mansion a dozen or so times before, all without the tragedy that struck that autumn night. But as Winnie learned, all it took was a single moment to change the course of your life, or death forever. Some have learned that lesson after taking a wayward step and tumbling down the stairs, others by staying up for just one more cocktail when they should have been in bed. Winnie learned it after an early September freeze turned the puddles on the ground and on the window ledges into invisible discs of ice.

No, Winnie didn't mean to die. But the deaths that came after, those she meant in earnest.

On that brisk evening, Winnie crawled out of her second-story bedroom window, giggling and a little drunk on the champagne she had with dinner. She eased the window shut behind her, mindful of how dreadfully it could creak, and snuck quietly along the narrow shelf, ducking past the window that led to her mother's bedroom next to her own.

Winnie paused, turning back for just a moment to peek. Her

mother was inside, seated at her vanity and staring blankly into the mirror. The lights were low around her, flickering candles from her bedside table casting an orange glow to the room and creating long shadows from the edges of her mother's angular frame. Winnie watched as her mother reached up with both hands and pulled at the skin on her face, as if it would help the previous twenty years disappear from her features. Winnie moved along before she was spotted. She burned a little with shame for her mother but had none for herself at the private moment she had intruded upon. Winnie wasn't a child anymore, but she was still young enough to believe she was entitled to her parents' secrets.

Winnie's heart raced as she drew near the threshold of the ledge. The next stage required bravery, a moment when she would need to step out into the thin air and trust she could make it to the other side. The roof of the covered entryway sat several feet lower and a good foot away from the ledge she was standing upon, and she had to stretch with all her might to reach across the gap.

It thrilled her every time she did it. It was her favorite part of these adventures, the suspension of herself in the air before she landed on the roof below. She felt weightless, as if one day, she might simply sail off into the night sky forever.

After that, it was easy to get free. Winnie would simply scurry over to the drainpipe and shimmy down. She would quietly trot down the drive to meet the other rebellious sons and daughters of Newport society who had also snuck away. Somewhere in the dark up ahead, they were waiting. She knew they peered in from the giant iron gates that marked the entrance to the house, two stately lions sitting on either side keeping guard.

Winnie stepped off and her foot slipped on the thin veneer of ice she hadn't known was there. Instead of that delightful feeling of lightness in her stomach, that sensation of floating, she tumbled head over heels, flashes of the ground and the rising stone walls of the house flipping past her several times over and sending her head spinning. Winnie flailed about but only managed to twist herself partway around. She landed on her head with a crunch, disturbing the rocks of the gravel driveway below and bending her neck at an awkward angle.

Hard snow, closer to ice than to rain, began to pitter-patter down as she lay there. Winnie could only feel the faintest touch where it settled on her hair and face.

Drat, she thought, even as her mind thinned to the merest whisp.

It was frigid outside. Winnie's wet clothes quickly hardened against her body. Small drifts of pelleted snow filled the crooks of her armpits and the angles where her legs were bent away from one another. Most of the house had already gone to bed, the youths wandering away from the gates when she had not appeared.

It was hours before she was finally spotted by the night watchmen making his rounds. He found her, wheezing out gasps of fog, still lying where she fell. The last sounds she heard were the cascade of running footsteps and her mother's frantic screams. Winnie tried to hold on, to feel her mother reach out and touch her one last time, but she was too tired and too cold, and she slipped away into nothing.

Winnie awoke the next evening on her bedroom floor, tucked underneath her grand four-poster bed. She had never felt such a deep sense of cold before, not even after hours of ice skating on the small pond that sat behind the house, her cheeks rosy and numb where they peeked out from between layers of scarf and hat. After she came inside, her fingers would scream as she sat by the fire and warmed them again on a mug of hot cocoa. The rich fumes would rise and mix with the scent of woodsmoke that floated into the room. Her body would tingle in the heat, pins and needles of delicious sensation that made her feel alive again.

Now though, Winnie wasn't just numb in the very tips of her limbs. Her legs and arms were useless blocks of ice, her torso so chilled she left little crystalline patterns of ice where she lay. She ached for a fire, a blanket, anything to help suck the chill from inside her bones. She cried a little because of the unfairness of it all.

Her tears tinkled to the marble floor beneath her face in a glassy melody.

Winnie couldn't walk or lift her arms or even kick her feet. But through trial and error, she discovered she *could* pull herself along with only the movement of her chin. Though her body should have been too heavy to proceed in such a manner, she found it was so light she hardly noticed the strain of it at all. Indeed, she felt as she did when she stepped off the ledge, weightless and suspended in nothing, and she wanted to purr with joy.

Winnie pulled herself down the carpeted hall and up again, then went up and down the stairs for good measure, powered by no more than the bobbing of her head. Her useless arms and legs slid along the floor behind her. She was positively delighted, and having solved one problem, went off in search of whatever warmth she could find in the house. The fireplace in her own bedroom was dark and cold, but surely someone else had one burning bright. The wind howled through the trees, bringing with it the type of cold that froze the glass in the windows.

A light was on in her mother's room, the glow just visible around the edge of her cracked door. Winnie pulled herself inside. There was a little set of stairs at the end meant for her mother's terrier, Lady Jane, and Winnie used them to pull herself up and onto the end of the bed. She could feel her mother's warmth, the heat rolling off her like the crashing waves at the beach. Lady Jane growled from where she was nestled between her mistress' feet, but the dog fell silent when Winnie growled back.

Cold Winnie slithered closer. She pressed up against her mother's form, snoring and with one arm tossed above her head. Winnie tried to pull herself closer, to quietly nestle into the hollow space between her mother's ribcage and the mattress, but her chin slipped on the satin sheets and Lady Jane barked. Her mother rolled to the side groggily and opened her eyes to see Winnie staring back. Winnie smiled wide, the sound of cracking ice accompanying her grimace.

Her mother screamed and screamed, great shrieking noises that hardly left room for a breath in between. It sounded so much like the cries the night that she fell that Winnie began to scream too, though it came out breathless and airy, sounding like no more than a swollen door creaking in a faint breeze. Her mother's hair turned to icicles around her face in Winnie's cold breath. Winnie escaped and pulled herself down the hall to hide under the safety of her own bed. Though she could sense the warmth in her mother, when Winnie burrowed close, the woman turned as cold as ice.

How very curious, Winnie thought. Her mother had never looked that old to Winnie.

Winnie stretched out in the dark and tried to stay awake as she listened to frantic noises in the hall outside. People spoke in hushed whispers and footsteps pounded close, then receded. As the morning rays of dawn reached her room, Winnie grew tired and slipped away, just as she had done the night before, face down in the frigid gravel.

The family was gone when she awoke the next evening. Their things were hidden away under sheets, and Winnie wandered among them, the moonlight streaming in through the tall arched windows in the rooms where they had forgotten to close the drapes. She went to her father's bedroom and tugged at the edges of the sheets around his sofa with her teeth, pulling them down to the floor. She tried to wrap herself up in them, but they held no memory of warmth anymore. Just the faint scent of her father's hair and her mother's perfume, captured from mornings spent lounging together reading the paper.

Winnie waited for them night after night, but no one appeared. After a while, she forgot she ever had a family in the first place.

All she could think about was the cold, the shards of it stabbing at her whenever she awoke. She pulled herself up to the great ovens in the kitchen and then into the fireplace in the ballroom, but she could only pretend to feel heat still lingering in the ashes left behind.

The house settled around her, and Winnie lay in the dark for years and waited.

One night, she woke to find strangers had come inside. She heard their voices from under the bed and scooted herself out into the hall to peek from between the balusters of the second-floor railing. It was a group of young adults, dressed in clothing she didn't recognize and talking in too casual of a tone. They threw about words that she knew but used them in a manner that she didn't. Their chatter blurred together in Winnie's ears and her head ached from it. Winnie watched as they gathered in front of the bottom step of the grand staircase, lighting thick, stubby candles and sitting cross-legged in a circle on the ground.

"Ghosts of Grandview Manor, come out and make your presence known!" said a tall girl, a solemn look on her face. Someone else in the circle giggled and there was rapid shushing, stoney-faced youths looking grim in the pale light.

"Come out, we mean you no harm!" Winnie looked about the hall to the left and right of her and waited for ghosts to appear from the darkness. She rolled her head from side to side, craning it as far as she could make it turn, but a deep and unsettling click resonated from her neck with the movement and so she stopped. It felt as if the ends of a stick rubbed together deep inside her, and it made her even colder when she tried to remember why.

The group looked disappointed and exchanged low conversation, too quiet for Winnie to hear from the second floor. They stood and split up into twos and threes. Each cluster took a candle and wandered to a different part of the house. Winnie scooted back to her bedroom. She hid behind the door as the tall girl and another young lady climbed the stairs and stood in front of it. Winnie could just barely see them with her right eye, the rest of her hidden behind the post of her bed.

The light from their candle flickered across her vision. Winnie could see the tall one was flushed with excitement, but the other clutched the candle in two shaky hands, spilling wax upon the marble and glancing about fretfully. Winnie could smell the acrid scent of fear, sharp as copper in her nostrils, but tasting sweet across her tongue.

"Are you sure it's safe?" asked the timid girl.

"I'm sure. We'll just take a quick look around and then we'll head to Brian's." The tall one looked up and down the halls, staring into the portraits of the stoic men and women who hung on each side. "No one has been in here for decades, can you believe it? If I had a house like this, I'd never leave."

The sound of their voices faded as they shuffled to the room next door. Winnie could hear the squeak of drawers opening and closing. She could almost smell the dust filling the air, disturbed from the top of whatever objects they moved and touched with their sweaty, grubby hands. Downstairs she could hear laughter and something delicate breaking on a tile floor, thumping footsteps as one youth chased another through the house's corridors. Winnie felt as if they were digging their hands into the very center of her, dragging their fingers through her core and dirtying little bits that would never get clean again.

When the two girls stepped out of the room and stopped on the landing at the top of the stairs, Winnie rushed out at them. Her chin made a quiet *shush shush shush* noise on the carpet as she dragged herself forward out of the darkness and into the dim light of their candle. The sound echoed off the marble walls.

Both girls turned and shrieked at the sight of her. The tall one leaned back, covering her mouth with both hands. but the timid girl scrabbled away, tangling one ankle about another as she tried to run. She fell into the empty space where the staircase met the second floor and hung there for a moment, windmilling her arms before she tumbled down. The light from the candle blew out but Winnie could hear the girl rolling over and over in the dark. She smacked each tread with a wet thump, the noise muffled by the thick red carpet that waterfalled down the steps and spilled out into the grand room below. Winnie shivered and ached, as if she too had hung and fallen.

There were screams from all about the house. A moment of confusion, and the others fled as one pack, the tall girl dashing past the body of her friend at the bottom of the staircase without a glance back.

Winnie slunk down the stairs, curious. She inched herself close to where the girl lay in an impossible tangle of limbs. One wide eye rolled over to land on Winnie and there was a gurgle and a gasp, and then the girl was still.

Winnie hardly noticed the noise. She was too busy with more important things. For the first time, Winnie could feel *heat*, a small spark that exploded into a burst of flame in the moment of death. It left behind a sweet warmth like a vacated bed in a chilled room, and Winnie pressed herself against the girl and basked in it till they both grew cold.

Winnie wanted more.

Winnie waited and waited, but no one else came back after that night, except for the few who arrived shortly after to take the girl's body away. She was already safely hidden upstairs when the front door creaked open. Her vantage point allowed her to see the policeman and people in official uniforms zipping up a body in shiny black plastic. They struggled to fit the broken and twisted limbs inside.

The policemen cast nervous glances about the group. They shined the light from their handheld torches in a wide arc about them, as if to ward off encroaching danger. They came upstairs only once, to inspect the landing at the very top. Winnie concealed herself behind the edge of the bedroom door as they stood outside.

"Must have slipped." said one. The other nodded, and Winnie nodded too, her chin lifted high into the air, so it didn't grab the floor and inch her out of her hiding spot. One of the men shined a light into the bedrooms. Winnie considered rushing these two as she had the young girls. She could almost feel the full, satisfying heat that would leak out from inside them. But the men turned away and set off downstairs at a quick clip, as if they could sense her intentions.

Selfish. Winnie thought.

They left out the front doors and let them slam shut with an echo; the noise of a chain being pulled across the front rattled up the stairs with finality. Winnie circled and tucked herself into the blanket hidden under the bed, but even her little nest couldn't hold the remaining warmth in. The last little bit she had stolen from the girl seeped out of her body as she lay there. By the next night, she was frozen solid again.

She ventured downstairs to look about. Someone had been there in the daytime. The police tape was gone, and the carpet was scrubbed where a little blood from the girl's mouth had leaked out. It was the only clean spot on the dusty rug, the rest had faded and grown filthy with the passing of years. No one else came that night or any other, not for some time.

Winnie itched to feel the heat again. But now, she also itched for the quiet solitude she had known before. Some nights she could hear a girl crying downstairs. To Winnie, it sounded like the race of a winter squall through a cracked window, and it made her even colder if such a thing was possible.

One evening, Winnie awoke with moonlight reaching for her under her bed, the silver-blue light casting long shadows across the floor, hiding the dust and the little pawprints of the mice that gathered under her wardrobe. Slowly the sounds of hammers and saws coming from downstairs made themselves known.

Winnie pulled herself out into the hall. Bright lights were staged about the main room below. The glare was harsh, the white lights laying plain the dirtiest corners and how the long, velvet curtains were slowly rotting away from the bottom up. There were people down there doing something, but Winnie could see only flashes of their movements as they rushed from here to there.

Winnie moved down the hall and onto the back staircase. Her chin swished and then thumped along the ground as she moved from the marble floor to the wooden planks that marked the beginning of the servant's hallway. She slid down the staircase as it made tight spirals in its descent, the world rushing by until she finally emerged near the kitchen.

"You ever seen anything like this?" Winnie heard a man's voice coming from the butler's pantry nearby. She inched along until just the tops of her eyes appeared around the corner, her neck creaking in warning as she twisted herself around to get a look.

A squat man was surveying the cabinets full of delicate glassware and the safe in the corner where the best silver was kept. Another man with sunken eyes leaned against the counter in the back, idly rotating the knife sharpener mounted to the surface. He let go and ran a hand along the butcher block counter, his dry palms scratching loudly against the wood. Winnie bristled as he touched it.

How dare he, she thought. She was as disgusted as if he had run a hand up her leg at dinner.

"I worked on one of them big houses down the street," the man at the counter said. "They're all the same. Too big and too much money to keep up with." He wiped his palms on his denim pants and shook his head a little. "This place is falling apart. They should just tear it down."

"God, imagine the heating bills alone. What are they doing with this one?"

"Some tech guy bought it, wants to spend his summers here. Wants everything working as soon as possible, just like it would have before." The two exchanged a look, a mutual rolling of eyes that Winnie was frustrated at because she didn't *understand*. The men moved into the kitchen.

Winnie pulled herself across the tiled floor and down the hall to the ballroom, the sound of her movements covered up by some tool roaring to life, where she could hear some tool roaring to life. She wasn't thrilled at the idea of someone moving into her house. But in her cobweb mind, she remembered someone once telling her that any situation could be a good or bad, one, it just depended on your approach. Winnie had the distinct memory of a soft voice, of the smell of lavender and a pair of brown eyes, and someone called "Mother".

She inched her way along. Maybe the man who owned the house

would have a family. And maybe that family would throw a party. And maybe two hundred guests would arrive, their bodies pushed tight into all the spaces of the house, the warmth radiating off them as they laughed and drank cocktails together. The sound would be so loud it would drown out the noise of the cold wind finding its way in through the cracks.

Winnie would like that very much. Perhaps then, the warmth would stay, and she wouldn't feel cold anymore. She could crawl among the guests and soak in their heat, slithering between their ankles across the dance floor and burrowing into the hems of their gowns.

Winnie imagined one of them tripping on that same gown and snapping their pale little swan neck. Then she could drink in the hot fire as it left them. She smiled wide until the corners of her mouth hurt.

She reached the ballroom, and spotted the source of the noise, a screaming tool that was either causing the house pain or suffering some malady itself. If Winnie could have moved her frozen arms, she would have put her hands over her ears and blocked the wretched noise out.

Winnie crawled quickly toward it, determined to stop it and restore the quiet.

The fireplace was a grand marble behemoth that lay at the end of the room and could fit four people inside comfortably. There was a man in dusty coveralls standing just outside of it, his head and shoulders disappearing up inside. He had a tool in one hand that had a thick wire running out of it. She could see he was feeding it up the chimney and then pulling it out again, the tool shrieking every time he inserted it. He pulled it out and turned it off, to Winnie's relief.

The man stepped out of the fireplace and placed his tool aside and began retrieving logs from a pile stacked next to him. He set them carefully inside and added some sticks and some of the bark that had fallen off the stack. He pulled out a box of matches.

Winnie's eyes went wide as he struck the first one. It was what she had dreamed of for years, a burning fire to wrap herself in and chase away all the little frozen bits of her. The first match went out and the man cursed, and Winnie cursed as well. Then he lit another and shielded it with one hand, carefully lowering it to the pile of tinder below. Winnie's mouth watered in anticipation, the saliva freezing solid underneath her tongue.

Winnie watched the smallest bits catch first. They turned into bright orange embers that raced quickly from one bit of wood to the next. The man knelt and blew gently on the fire and the bigger pieces began to catch, the sticks and the snapped-off bits of lumber that made up the kindling he had gathered. Winnie held herself back, not wanting to interrupt the sacred process taking place before her. It was beautiful, *so* beautiful, more beautiful than anything she had known.

The big, dry logs exploded into flames with a loud crack. Then Winnie could hold herself back no more.

She scooted across the varnished wood floor of the ballroom, a path wiped through the dust by her dragging torso.. She cooed in excitement, the sound covered up by the delicious crackle of the fire. The man did not hear her. He stood with his arms crossed and appraised his work. He peeked up into the chimney and seemed satisfied that the smoke was being transported up and away, then turned his back on the fire.

Winnie was waiting at his feet, inches away. She twisted her head to look up at him, her neck releasing a single loud *click* that echoed in the mostly empty room.

The man's jaw dropped, and the color went out of his face, but Winnie didn't notice. She was already past him and squirming into the fire, burrowing into the pile of embers that had fallen off the log and landed on the grate below. She didn't notice as he threw a hand up and clutched his chest, falling to his knees and collapsing face-down onto the cool wooden floor.

Winnie rubbed up against the logs like a cat but was disappointed. She could feel only the barest hint of heat, so faint she thought it may have been just her imagination. She had hoped the icy parts of herself would melt, had imagined the heat would leave behind a delicious liquid that sloshed inside her limbs, but she was as frozen as ever. She turned this way and that, even as the fire died down around her.

Too soon, the logs had burned down to nothing. Someone came in and shouted, "Oh my god!" and startled her, but Winnie saw it was said in surprise at discovering the man's body and not her own presence. She was safely hidden deep within the ashes, trying her best to drink the last bits of heat emanating from them.

When they came and took away the man on a stretcher with a sheet over his face, Winnie regretted that she hadn't curled up next to him and taken his warmth instead.

What a waste, she said to the house, which responded with silence.

The next night, Winnie could hear something scuttling up on the roof. It dashed from one chimney to the next until it scrambled down the one that led into her bedroom, the noise of sharp claws grasping at brick. An upside-down head appeared, ashes covering everything except two wide eyes. Winnie saw it was the man from the night before. She shook her head at him and glared, and he disappeared again, racing up and away to somewhere else. Toenails clicked across the ceiling.

Squirrels in the attic, she thought. Such a shame. It wasn't unheard of, even in a grand old cottage like this.

For a while, the house looked cleaner and more restored each time she awoke, as if some sort of fairytale creature was arriving in the daytime and putting it all back together again just for her while she slept.

One evening, Winnie awoke and made her way downstairs, only to find a man crouched on some scaffolding way up high. She watched as he scraped swaths of gray mud up onto the ceiling and covered up what remained of the intricate fresco painted there. The plaster had started to crumble some time ago, but it left behind small patches where, if she rolled to her back, Winnie could still make out the scene of cherubs in a garden, eating fruit and drinking wine.

Winnie loved the ceiling and rushed to stop him.

When she tried to climb up and instead simply bumped the legs of the scaffold like an excited small dog, the man lost his balance, tumbling from his perch and flashing an open-mouthed grimace at her as he fell. He kept the look even after he landed when she curled up around him. This man's fire was less like an explosion and more like the sunset, a bright warmth that started strong but gradually faded with time and with the disappearance of his heartbeat. Winnie was pleased she hadn't wasted a moment of it.

After the accident, the work stopped completely, and the house fell quiet again. Dust began to accumulate in the dark corners. Winnie could hear the skittering of rodents and the whistle of the wind, and now she could hear the creaking of the house itself, old joints grown rusty with disuse. Occasionally she thought it didn't sound like the house at all, but like the low moan that comes when the last bit of breath abandons a man's chest.

The house fell into disrepair again, only this time, it rotted for real.

The soft things went first, the carpets and the drapes and the mattresses turning to little more than piles of wet mildew wherever they had lain before. Then the solid bits began to crumble as well. The walls of the grand ballroom buckled, and the roof caved in, the skylights shattering under the unexpected pressure from the collapsing house. Once the rain got inside, the whole structure started to melt towards the ground, a slow race to rejoin the soil underneath the foundation.

Winnie felt suffocated in rooms that were half the size they were before. She had grown cold again after the man from the scaffold was gone, the sloshy bits of her refreezing in the absence of any more heat. Her body became a solid thing that ached deep into each night. The bedroom disappeared in a maze of timbers and her own memory, so Winnie moved downstairs to hide in the library instead. The scent of the rotting books comforted her and reminded her of winter days gone by. She could almost imagine the feeling of the bright fireplace fighting back the cold snow and frost trying its best to creep in from outside.

On the last night Winnie awoke, she found the house had collapsed completely while she slept. The walls and the ceiling of the last standing room had fallen in upon her. She sought refuge, crawling through the minute spaces between the debris but not recognizing anything around her. The boards and the sharp chunks of stone tore at her as she passed, but she could not feel it in her deadened limbs and so she pressed deeper still toward the center of the house.

She met faces in the darkness once or twice, wide eyes that widened further when they spotted her, the owners scuttling off quickly for somewhere else to hide within the house's bones.

Winnie grew tired. Once she could go no farther, she stopped and curled around a bit of old timber, feeling very sorry for herself indeed. Her mind began to slip as the night ended.

I only wanted a bit of warmth, she thought. *Was that so much to ask?*

As if in reply, a tiny bit of light came through the gaps in the debris around her. At first, she thought it was the morning rays of the sun and she beamed. How proud she was, that she had held on so long. It had been years since she had seen a sunrise. It seemed the longer time went on, the shorter the nights grew outside the house, and the more tired and cold she grew within.

Winnie squinted. It was not golden rays of sunlight, not like she remembered them anyway. The glow danced and flickered orange and red instead. It was a flame, racing in from somewhere close, the dry old wooden beams that lay atop her head catching quickly and erupting into an inferno around her.

"It's lit!" cried a muffled voice from outside. She could hear men moving about and some sort of low rumbling, and then the edges of the house began to push in towards her. The movement collapsed even the smallest spaces to nothing, and soon she was trapped and had no room to drag herself free.

Winnie turned molten as the house was consumed in the fire around her. It thawed her to the tips of her ears and the bottoms of her feet, and every little bit of her in between. She tried to stand and dance as she had always imagined she would in this moment, throwing her arms above her head and spinning with life. But she could not. Though she was thawed completely, she couldn't move anything but her head on her broken neck. Her limbs were still immobile, but now she could feel how they screamed with pain in the heat. Winnie was filling with a warmth so intense she would slowly turn to ash from the inside out.

Winnie and the house burned together, at the whims of the ferocious heat about them. They cried and their voices sounded like the whistle of moisture in mildewed wood, chased out by the lick of flames. Little by little, their bodies came together in the glowing embers that grew beneath them, one bit indistinguishable from the next.

How curious, Winnie thought, just before the last of her melted away to nothing and she sailed off into the night sky forever. For an instant, the first time she could remember, Winnie missed the deep cold she had felt before.

SATURN
FREDERICK STREET

F rank spent his morning chopping wood for the stove. The day started with him leaning over his rusted cot and hacking phlegm into an ancient coffee can half filled with piss. He pulled on old, crusted socks and rose to his feet. Wrapped in a reeking quilt, he kicked through mounds of wet trash to the wood stove. He sawed open a can of beans with a broken boning knife, stepping over a faded photograph of a woman holding a child and paying it no mind. As his breakfast warmed on the stove, he looked at a Belgian Mauser .30-06 propped up behind the door and thought again about sticking it in his mouth. He didn't. He ate and went out in the cold to the chopping block.

He took off the glove covering his left hand, as he was accustomed to doing for better traction, and set to work. For the better part of an hour, he stood at the block. Raising the axe high above his head, allowing gravity to take it from him. His right hand slid down the handle to join his left, cleaving the wood in twain with a sharp THUNK that echoed through the clearing. All one fluid motion, again and again. It was in these mindless tasks that his thoughts were allowed to drift as if in a state of self-hypnosis, interrupted only when the wood would refuse to split clean and he'd lift the axe with it impaled on the wedge, an extra two or three sloppy impacts finally getting it to split. Even then, it required very little of his attention, and he continued to drift far back behind his eyes.

Chop. Chop.

He traversed through lazy fantasies. Being somewhere else as someone else, perhaps in another time, a different world than this. No structure, no form. He was long past examining the failures in his real life, how he'd abandoned his family and become a forgotten old hermit half-frozen and drinking himself to death in the snow. It was complete dissociation. This was the only resemblance of peace he could hope for.

Chop. Chop.

Today, the fantasies would not come. He thought of the dreams. Last night. The night before. However many nights before.

Chop. Chop.

He was in the old house. In the good times, as much as they could be. But an air of something wrong. The Child nowhere to be found. Curiously, for the man he was then, this did not concern him. Often, the dreams were of the old house. Sometimes dark out. He'd rise to the window in the stuttering walk of dreams and see lights in his field, trespassers of unknown origin and vague malicious intent. Seeking the Mauser but unable to find the cartridges, and they were coming, surely they were coming, coming for what was his.

Chop. Chop.

Other times, he dreamed that somewhere in the house, she was there. Which "she"? The answer was not always specific. Sometimes his mother. Sometimes the sister he lost when he had barely started to walk, and of whom he only had scant memories. Often the Woman. Mother of the Child. She was there. Somewhere in the house, unseen but felt. Looking for him.

Chop. Chop.

A woman possessed of no malicious temperament in life, but perhaps in death found her buried anger to be righteous and true, and intended to act upon it. She was seeking him. And he had to get out of that house. And only if he was very quiet...

Chop. Chop.

It was when he got close to the door, turning the knob ever so slowly to avoid any noise, just barely retracting the catch enough to push it open would she appear, bare feet suspended several inches off the ground in her white nightdress, long black hair over her face, pale lips sneering. Rushing to envelope him. Frank screaming himself awake.

Chop. Chop.

Out here, he'd had a sense of escape from the old nightmares. Recently, though, the dreams returned. Adapted to the new land-scape. She'd followed him here. He'd be standing at the door. Shaking. She'd be out there in the trees. Dress as bright as a cold winter moon in the darkness of the forest. Saying nothing but saying every-thing. Face shrouded in her hair black as death, except for her mouth. Those plump and pale lips that used to be his whole world, pulling back to reveal a wolf's fangs.

Chop. Ch-...

With a loud crack, the axe head split from the handle. It flew up and struck him in the shoulder with a dull impact, before lifelessly burying itself in the snow, leaving an ambivalent wedge-shaped hole in the harsh sea of white.

"Shit." Frank muttered.

He stood for several moments, staring dumbly at the broken axe handle. He resisted the adolescent urge to pitch it into the yard.

He could fish out the head, tap the broken wood out of the bracket, maybe fit the handle of the old maul from the shed into it, and make do. Otherwise, it would mean a trip back into town to get a replacement.

The town. With all those people. And he'd have to speak with one of them. The Sheriff's idiot boy, the one with that ridiculous hippy mop on his head at the hardware store, most likely. He'd have to deal with a dozen disgusted looks as he walked in. Walked, as the old pickup had breathed its dying breath long ago.

The last time the town saw him, he was at the Red Barn Tavern, ranting and frothing at the mouth at any one of those good-for-nothing little shits that looked at him cross-eyed. The night ended with him doing a one-nighter at the sheriff's office, released on his own recognizance with the warning that if he came back for anything other than the bare essentials, he'd be sent upstate on vagrancy or whatever bullshit charge Sheriff Townsend had to conjure up.

No.

No, he would make do. The wood would last a few weeks or more. He'd figure something out. There was time. Frank looked up and studied the sky. Tasted the air. Another storm was coming. He had enough fuel for the fires and provisions to sustain himself. This was a problem for later. He just needed to fish out the axe head and...

A loud metallic SNAP. Somewhere just beyond the tree line. Frank's heart leaped into his throat.

No other sound followed beyond the wind. Frank stood listening for a minute.

"Trap." he muttered to himself.

He turned and walked back to the cabin, stamping the snow off his boots in the entryway and feeling the scarce warmth almost immediately as he crossed to his cot in the back.

"Bobcat, maybe."

Frank knelt and reached for the old tin box under the cot, lifting the lid and removing the old model 10-38 special his father carried during his brief, unremarkable stint as a lawman. Though Frank never cleaned it, it remained in passable working order, despite a few errant rust spots at the end of the six-inch barrel created by a regular application of saliva. Frank gently pressed open the cylinder with his middle and third fingers to ensure it was loaded. Six brass cartridges, dulled with age and grime, sat in the cylinder. He pressed it shut, rotating it onto the stopper. He stood and headed back out into the cold.

Frank trekked across the clearing to the tree line in the iconic gait of a seasoned wintertime New Englander, high-kneed like a show-time Clydesdale horse. In his head, the 13 traps were mapped out with precision, a map so alien to others with its vague and, to any other party, indecipherable landmarks, inaugurated by nonsensical associations and memories.

Over here on the southwest edge was a Victor number 2 rig, right where the old oak used to be. This was where the Woman would read to the Child when they were here in the summer.

"Shut up." muttered Frank, as his boots crunched through the thin crust and the harsh wet beneath. Trudging his way through the snow and the brush, he entered the tree line to the spot and scanned the ground, picking up the deployed jaws of the trap almost immediately. It was empty.

No. No, not empty.

Half of a thick branch was clamped in its jaws. Frank stood dumbfounded for a few moments. He crouched into the snow suddenly, reacting as an unprepared child suddenly called on by a schoolteacher. He held the revolver out in front of him with one hand, swiping his other over his face in disbelief.

Footsteps in the snow. Human. Who? Who could be here? Frank got his breathing and bewilderment under control. He scanned the ground.

Frank spat. Wiping his mouth.

"Okay." he said to no one.

Frank stood and crept up to the wild brush of the tree line. He squatted, looking back at the cabin. Scanning the ground, the foot-steps different from his own were clear. They circled the natural perimeter of the clearing and drifted back toward the general direc-tion of the cabin. Frank was being hunted.

Crouched low, Frank slowly breached the tree line and made his way back to the cabin. As he approached, his intruder made no further effort to hide himself. He was standing in front of the massive woodpile. Frank closed in, raising the revolver and sighting it at the center of the man's back, clad in a navy-blue parka.

"Don't move!" Frank shouted, "Or I'll kill you."

Silence from the Man. There were several breathless moments, both of them standing still, an ominous winter tableau. Finally, the man spoke.

"You always kept enough wood. I'll give you that."

The Man raised his hands outward at waist level.

"You kept the house warm."

The Man turned and faced Frank.

"It wasn't nothing. But that's all you were ever really good for."

Frank kept the sights of the revolver at the center of the man's chest, taking a few steps forward.

"Who are you?" said Frank, "You the law?"

The Man chuckled.

"You haven't changed. I don't know if that should make me laugh or that should make me cry."

Frank moved closer. A few arms lengths from the Man. Frank raised the revolver to the Man's face. The Man looked him straight in the eyes.

"Maybe both," he said. The Man crouched down in the snow before the woodpile. He looked up and studied the sky as a particularly strong gust of wind battered them both. Frank's balance wavered against the gale.

"Storm's coming. Maybe we should head inside and talk."

Frank's arms went rigid at the suggestion of his personal space being violated. He took two steps forward, just out of arms reach of the Man.

"Bullshit. You ain't going nowhere, 'cept off my property or hell. Get those hands where I can see 'em."

The Man laughed. "You practice that?" The Man shook his head. "You've been waiting for a day like this. Ever since I could remember."

The Man spread his hands, fingers splayed so Frank could see they held nothing, a position of surrender. Of vulnerability.

Frank's finger tightened ever so slightly on the trigger.

"We should talk. There're some things I need to say to you, then I'll be gone. Forever."

Frank took another half-step forward. Closer than he dared.

"I ain't hearin' you say shit. Now you get your ass off this property, or you're goin' under it. Choice is yours."

The Man chuckled again. The merriment did not reach his eyes. He dug his gloved hand into the snow with mild disinterest. "Okay. Have it your way then."

The Man clenched his fist, tensing at the shoulder and then whipping his arm forward, spraying a fine mist of powder right into Frank's eyes. He sprang forward from his knees and kept low, driving his shoulder into Frank's waist. The two hung in the air for what seemed like an eternity, suspended forever in time, and then they collided with the ground.

The cold and the wet soaked into Frank's old coat. He was looking up at the darkening gray sky and thought that the fire needed to be fed, must be fed. He did not have time for this. The cabin would get cold, cold as death.

They were wrestling now, the Man's hands clasped on Frank's right arm, the arm that held the revolver. Frank jerked his finger and there was a sharp BANG, a bullet screamed toward that grey, grey sky. They rolled the Man screaming as Frank bit him on the face. The Man loosened a hand and jammed a thumb at Franks's eye socket, Frank screaming out and jerking his head away and they rolled again and Frank lost the gun somewhere in the snow.

The Man's hands were around Frank's throat, squeezing, squeezing, squeezing with deadly intent and he was muttering something like, *"I didn't want this, you made this happen,"* and squeezing harder, and Frank's hand was searching, searching for the gun, digging into the snow with his ungloved left hand and it was cold, so cold, his hand was going numb, but not so numb it couldn't feel something hard and metal. Not the gun, but something else, and he grasped it as best as he could, swinging it up hard and hitting the Man in the head.

The Man fell off to the side and into the cold as Frank coughed., desperate for breath. He crawled, crawled, crawled to the Man and he struck him in the head again, and again, and then a third time. The Man went limp, and Frank knelt there, hacking phlegm, sucking in great gouts of air as a pool of blood spread from the Man's head.

Frank looked down into his ungloved hand and saw the broken axe head there in his whitened fingers.

He sank back onto his haunches and crab walked back until he was pressed up against the gargantuan woodpile, like a new colossus in the forest of nowhere. The Man coughed. His body spasmed uncontrollably, and pink material seeped through the chasm in his skull. Frank's ungloved hand nudged something hard on the ground. It clunked against the wood, but he did not feel it. He looked down and saw the revolver. He gathered it in his gloved hand and stood, pointing it at the vulnerable form of the Man, bleeding, bleeding, and gasping.

As Frank squeezed the trigger, the Man uttered one word: "Dad."

The revolver bucked in Frank's hand. Three rounds vaguely impacted the Man's torso, the fourth a misfire and the fifth entered the Man's opened mouth, striking a tooth in its path, knocking it loose from his gums. It flew out and embedded itself into Frank's cheek, a pitiful and final act of revenge. Frank clapped his numb hand over it, cursing, unable to remove it, and then he tucked the hot barreled revolver into his armpit and picked the bone out of his face with his good hand, dropping it somewhere in the snow.

Frank's legs went out from under him, and he sank to his ass in the cold. Breathing hard, he looked up at the sky and away from the perforated body leaking out into the snow. It was darkening into a muted gray up above, and scant icy flakes were now beginning to fall and be whipped around ever frantic by the wind, cutting deeply into his exposed flesh. The storm was here. Each second that passed, it seemed to be growing more menacing.

"You're a liar." Frank muttered to himself, the storm, the wind, the dead hunk of meat before him. "You're a fuckin' liar. Don't think I don't know."

He sat for several long moments. He sat until the empty space above his left wrist entered his thoughts and a feeling of desperate urgency filled his bones.

"Sheriff sent you, didn't he? They wouldn't've sent just you, whoever you are." Frank said.

Frank willed himself to look at the Man. The Man lay stiff. Eyes bulging towards the sky. Frank shook his head.

"Waitin' somewhere. Waitin' for you to come back."

Frank wrestled himself to his feet, swiping at his pants.

"Tell 'em all about me. Ain't they!"

Frank kicked the Man in his ribs. The Man gave no reaction.

"Well, they ain't gonna come for you. Not 'til after this shit."

Frank limped with great effort around the corpse. He knelt down and got both hands, best as he could with feeling left only in one, and dug them underneath its shoulders, lifting it into a sitting position.He wrapped both arms around its waist and, grunting and struggling, hefted it to its feet, dragging it, heels digging into the snow. He got it around and drug it backward, ever so slowly towards the door of the cabin. He would keep it in there. Secret. Out of sight. Once the storm was over, he would stow it somewhere until spring came and the ground softened. Make a place for it no one would ever find.

Great effort it took, but he got the Corpse through the door, and dumped it in a heap at the southeast corner. The wind kicked up all the more fierce just as he shouldered the door back into the frame and, for good measure, shot the ancient and rusted bolt home. Alone again at last.

He averted his eyes from it, would not acknowledge its presence or the words it gave before its current state, and he fixed himself a dinner of beans once again. Satiated, he splayed out on the cot in his work clothes, and sleep came easily. There were no dreams.

There were no dreams until the second night of the Great Ice Storm of '98.

Freezing rain had been falling steadily and destroying the infrastructure of New England civilization for well over forty-eight hours, but Frank paid no mind.

Frank's left hand was coated in a thin sheen of ice. Completely numb and white. He alternated between holding it before the fire, closer than he would normally dare, and tucking it under his armpit, willing the blood back into it. A slight throbbing preceded an extreme and bone-deep pain. He cursed, chewed his lips, and kicked at the nightstand barrel with his boots as he writhed on the floor, and it left a dent, scattering his effects into the trash carpeting the surface.

And hours later, after the agony died down, he chose to ignore it, moving it or touching it very little; he held it before him like some fragile burden, a fading torch in the darkness he'd always been asking for in some way.

He remained apathetic towards his cold guest until he shut his eyes on that second night and the woman appeared once again, teeth flashing under her raven hair. Like a contract had been sealed and she approved of the result.

When he woke from the dream early that morning, that's when the Corpse started talking.

He was sat, hunched over on his cot, smoking, getting ready to stoke the woodstove, listening to the pounding, bitter, frozen rain on the roof when he heard the dry chuckle from the thing in the corner. He looked up and saw the corpses's eyes, green, like his own, staring wide-eyed at him from out of the shadow of the corner he'd been dumped in.

Frank gasped. He threw off the blanket and sank to the floor, throwing open the box which contained the thirty-eight.

The Corpse chuckled again.

"You tried that already," it rasped.

"What?!" Frank shouted, "What?!"

Frank fumbled at the pistol with the hand that hadn't started to blacken and form enormous and painful blisters, and heard the heart-sinking clatter as he dropped all the cartridges to the floor, rolling off in every direction.

Frank reached for the runaway ammunition in the half-light, but his fingers only served to chase them away. He glanced up at the corpse.

It stared back into his eyes.

"So. You heard from Mom?"

Frank ceased fumbling around on the floor and looked up at the corpse.

"You've dreamt about her, haven't you?"

Frank stood. He paused there several moments and then turned and went to the wood stove.

"Shut up." Frank said, no longer daring to look at the Corpse. "You're not real, so you just shut your mouth."

The flames inside the stove were dying down to embers again. He stooped down to the woodbox and began to fill the stove.

"Yeah," said the Corpse, "Yeah, you have."

Frank tapped the wood against the floor to free it of any leftover snowpack and he shoved it in, holding his blackening hand close to his chest. He looked at it and grunted. He stood and went to the kitchen table, covered in junk, and sifted through it until he came up with an old box of elastic compression bandages. He thumbed open the box and tore it out of the packaging with his teeth, and began to clumsily wrap the hand in it.

"Doesn't look good." said the Corpse, "Might lose it."

Frank finished the wrap and went back to tend to the stove. He stared into it with an almost academic intent.

"You'll be crippled for sure. If you don't die first."

Frank continued to stare into the flames.

"A pathetic old cripple lost out here in the woods. Or you die here. With me."

The Corpse laughed. An icy, rasping sound.

"Plenty of time to talk, then. More time than you and me ever had."

Frank stood. He cradled his frostbit hand and trudged over to his cot, laying down on it, wrapping himself in his blanket and facing the wall.

"More dreams?" Chuckled the Corpse, "Good. Get your rest. We have a lot to get through."

Frank squeezed his eyes shut as the wind rose outside and the freezing rain battered the roof of the cabin so hard that he thought the whole structure would collapse. But it held on. After what seemed like hours, with total silence from his companion, he slept.

Whether real or nightmare, he was aware of having opened his eyes at the sound of the howling wind shaking the structure he occupied. His doomed hand throbbed vaguely, and his toes were freezing.

He hauled the blankets tighter around himself and dared to open his eyes and gaze into the darkness. A vague shape, female, shrouded in darkness and only discernible from the fish-belly white of her skin, stood at the foot of the cot. He thrashed to his left to avert his eyes, which settled on the corner where the dead meat was deposited. No longer the full-grown man, but the child from the discarded photo. In the fading light of the stove, he could just barely see its face. It was slack-jawed. The eyes were open, fixed securely on him.

A whisper.

"See? See what you did? See what you are?"

Frank averted his eyes, which landed on the shape of the woman just as she pitched forward onto the cot, hair flying wild and teeth flashing. She wrapped her horrible form around him.

Frank woke with a start. He sat up on the cot, tucking the blankets around him, and stared at his hand. The light through the frosted-over window was dim, and he did not know if it was morning or evening. It did not matter anymore. He pulled his dead hand loose and forced himself to look at it. He held it before him like an ancient artifact worthy of study. The fingers were fat and swollen, charred like burned sausages, ripe and ready to explode. Incapable of movement. Frank could detect a smell but it was unclear whether it came from the rotting extremity or a sudden awareness of the filth he had chosen to dwell in.

The Corpse tittered. "Looks bad. No saving it now."

Frank turned the hand in the dying light, studied an engorged blister between his thumb and forefinger, and began to poke at it with his other hand.

"It's pretty typical of you, you know?" said the Corpse. "You'd live with something being wrong like that forever, given the chance. Dead limb, dead marriage. Even without the storm, if this happened? You'd try to fix it yourself. And if you couldn't? Fuck it, right? You'd just tell yourself you'd adapt. Wouldn't bother with anyone or anything that could actually help. Even if that help was offered. You're too proud. And proud of what?"

Frank did not look up but could sense his guest gesturing widely to his living space.

"Proud of this? This little world you've created for yourself? This little slice of paradise? Is this what you imagined for yourself?"

"Fuck you. Shut up." Frank muttered, feverishly picking at the large blister on his hand.

"Is this the life you imagined for yourself? Did you tell yourself this was just temporary? Until you got some things together? Did you think you could hack it out here? Because you half-remember some things your own father taught you to do? Tell me. Who do you think you really are? Is your perception of yourself so strong? Listen. Listen to the wind. Feel how cold it is in here. Feel how alone you are. How alienated. When you go to town, they all look at you with disgust. Pity, but disgust. And what do you tell yourself then?"

"I don't care about them. About anyone," Frank said, digging his fingernails harder into his hand.

The Corpse laughed.

"But you do. You care a lot about how others perceive you. Some kind of lone wolf, isn't that it? You have such an image of yourself. But you're just a child, really. A large child. Looking for a mother. That's all you ever were. It was she who had a job. She put food on the table. You? You were obsessed with your perceived self-sufficiency. A slave to no man!"

"She got a good enough job to cover the bills, and you told her you'd do your little trades and odd jobs and be home for the kid, isn't that it? But you were really thinking 'jackpot,' weren't you? Someone will take care of everything, and I can continue to be a fucking bum. A bum. You were a bum. And without her?"

Frank picked at the blister harder.

"Without her, you would've been here a lot sooner. Right where you belong. Alone. Dying in the cold."

Thick yellow pus seeped out of the blister.

"Fuck." hissed Frank. He stood and stumbled to the overflowing table in his blanket, digging and knocking junk over and onto the floor, seeking something to wipe off the wound.

The Corpse sneered audibly.

"I was surprised it took her that long to leave you. She most likely did it for me. Wait for me to get out of the house and then handle her business. Hard enough taking care of two other people on your own, and only one of them is a child. Maybe she thought that's when her life could really begin. Her second chance. Cut you off like, well..."

Frank could feel the Corpse gesturing at his hand.

"Like a dead limb. Which might not be a bad idea, by the way."

Frank found and old rag that looked clean enough and pressed it to the wound as he cradled his hand to his chest. He sat back on the cot, rocking back and forth and glaring at the frosted window, trying to focus on the wind and the patter of rain on the roof, think of anything other than the truth. He laid back on the cot, tucking his knees to his chest. Sleep came again and the icy wind howled.

Waking again, or not.

Frank sat up, and it was dark. Too dark. He sank off the cot and to the floor, dragging the blankets with him and shivering. Crawling through trash and empty bottles to the woodstove. He opened it, and not even a single dying ember was left. His frostbit hand was dark and gnarled and curled, and he held it against his chest as he shoved wood into the stove and crumpled discarded newspaper from the floor and shoved that in too, to use as kindling .He struck a match and lit the fire. Slowly, the flames grew, and he shut the lid, sat cross-legged in front of it. He looked up at the Corpse. The Corpse looked back.

"Did you love her? Or was she convenient?" the Corpse asked.

Several moments of silence.

"I don't know." Frank said.

"Was she really the monster you make her out to be?"

Frank shut his eyes, tilting his head to the floor.

"Look at her," said the Corpse. Frank looked up. At the corner, near the door, only barely visible in the pitiful light of the stove. She stood there, much as in his nightmares. She was still and pale. Hair hanging over her face, arms limply at her sides. His heart skipped wildly, and the room somehow seemed a little colder, but Frank didn't move. He had no urge to defend himself.

"No," Frank said. "I needed... I needed her to be that. I couldn't... I couldn't."

Slowly, she seemed to evaporate into the shadows and was no more.

Frank nodded his head at nothing.

With great effort, he made eye contact with the Corpse. The frozen rain had started again, harder than ever before. The cabin shuddered with the anticipation of almost certain destruction.

"Can you forgive me?" asked Frank, "For this? For all of it?"

The Corpse stared back into his eyes. Not in the sneering mockery that Frank had come accustomed to. There was the slightest hint of genuine pity there.

"I had probably only *heard* the storm was coming. Despite everything you were and everything you put us through, I probably just came here to check on you. Get you out of here. Put you up, maybe. So you didn't have to be alone. Maybe I still cared enough not to let you die out here."

Tears came to Frank's eyes, spilling out. Hot on his cheek. "Can you forgive me?"

The Corpse seemed to smirk, and seemed to wail, and seemed to scream half-shadowed in the flickering firelight that played illusions on its face. And then it spoke no more and was just a corpse. A dead human being and no reason to it at all.

Frank let both hands, dead and alive, drop to the floor and the hand that still felt, felt something amongst the trash next to him. The photograph, long discarded. He picked it up, and his eyes went blurry as he stared. And he screamed. And screamed, and screamed. The wind howled, and he screamed. Frank stood and slammed his blackened hand onto the surface of the stove, and as the dead flesh bubbled, he picked up the broken carbon steel boning knife and put it to his wrist, and he started sawing. And he screamed, and screamed, and screamed forevermore.

A week later, the storm passed.

Sheriff Townsend and his deputies slept very little over the last seven days. The Sheriff had saved Frank for last, being the furthest visit and most likely to be unpleasant. To add to the troubles, there was the matter of the man who had come up before the weather turned. The Sheriff figured him for family, slightly surprised that old Frank had anyone willing to talk with him. The Sheriff heard that the man had come up to try and to see Frank himself. Hearing nothing else left him with an uneasy feeling.

They'd parked their vehicles and edged up to the property, had the cabin in sight, and the Sheriff was just about to issue further caution to the young men with him, when one of them took a step, and the teeth of a Victor trap sank into the deputy's ankle with a SNAP. The deputy screamed out and pitched sideways into the snow, grasping at his leg.

The Sheriff knelt at the man's side as his other deputy stood dumbfounded. Before the Sheriff could articulate speech, an inhuman screech issued forth from the cabin. The Sheriff looked up.

A man stood at the door, holding... no... cradling an old-looking bolt-action rifle. The man's left arm was wrapped in some kind of stained linen or very old bandaging, and the spot where his hand was supposed to be was stained a reddish brown. He tucked his forearm under the barrel of the rifle. Still shrieking, he leveled it in their direction and fired.

The Sheriff, still kneeling by his trapped deputy, heard the round snap through the air and heard the other deputy let out a choking hiss. The man pitched backward into the snow, clasping at his throat as bright red arterial blood began to spray through his fingers.

"God dammit," growled the Sheriff as he pulled out his service revolver, still kneeling, and fired two shots toward the cabin. The shrieking man's rifle cracked again, and the Sheriff dove to his belly, aiming his revolver through the brush. He could barely make out the shrieking man but saw him struggle to work the bolt on his rifle with one hand. The Sheriff sighted in and fired once, twice, three times.

More shots issued from the cabin. One round impacted mere inches from the trapped deputy, and he wailed in fear. The Sheriff aligned the front sight nearly dead center on the shrieking man and squeezed the trigger. He heard the man grunt, a rush of air like he'd been punched in the stomach.

The man staggered back, colliding with the side of the cabin, but he did not fall. He stood there for several moments, holding the rifle loosely by his side. The Sheriff rose to one knee, sighted in again, and squeezed the trigger.

Click.

"Shit." muttered the Sheriff as he swung open the cylinder on his revolver and fumbled with his dump pouch for spare ammunition. As he reloaded, he glanced up at the shrieking man.

His head was turned. Something had caught his attention. All was strangely quiet in the brief reprieve of that chaos and the way that sounds were traveling on the air that morning, he was sure he could hear the man speaking to someone, though no one alive was ever found.

As the Sheriff swung the loaded cylinder shut on his revolver, the shrieking man turned and, across the distance, had seemed to be staring directly into his eyes. Then turned and took off running. Away from the Sheriff, away from the cabin, and into the woods beyond. In a futile effort, the Sheriff squeezed off three more shots after the man, but if he hit anything, he did not know.

The deputy Frank had shot expired an hour later, despite the Sheriff's best. A manhunt was called, dogs and all, but the tracks ran far into the woods before going haphazard and nonsensical. The trail went cold, and no trace of Frank was ever discovered.

It took less than the fifteen years the sheriff served for the rumors to spread. Sightings. Noises. Dead animals.

If you're near those woods in the night and the winter winds blow, you can sometimes hear an agonized scream upon them.

THE SQUALL
BRYAN HOLM

The seed of the storm was planted deep in the heart of the Rockies, and it grew exponentially as it barreled across the vast Dakota plains. By the time it hit Minnesota it was a monster, all swirling snow and subzero winds, one of the largest blizzards to pummel the Great Lakes.

It was a Wednesday, which meant church supper for Joey's family, a large dinner held in the basement of their church every week. The church had contemplated canceling the weekly gathering, but the forecast predicted the heaviest snow wouldn't arrive until after ten.

The family took two cars. Joey's parents would stay late for choir practice, and Joey's twin brothers, Brandon, and Matt would drive him home. Joey wouldn't get his driver's license for another six years, a lifetime away.

The storm had intensified while they were eating, coming in faster than expected. There were already several inches of snow on the ground when the boys left. The wind was howling, brutal and cold, the windchill already nearing zero degrees. Heavy snow whipped across their headlights as they left the steep parking lot.

Brandon took a right too fast, fishtailing in the snow, heading down a long winding hill away from home.

Joey's stomach sank. "Where are we going?"

Matt grinned from the passenger seat. "Just making a quick pit stop."

"Mom said we had to go straight home." Joey whined.

"It won't take long. You can keep a secret, can't you?" Brandon asked, eying Joey in the rear-view mirror.

Joey sat in silence. He could confirm that all the cliches one heard about twins were true. His brothers were of one mind, connected in a way that he never felt with either of them. When they were together, he was forever the third wheel, and not just because he was younger. Not that Matt and Brandon were cruel big brothers, at least not most of the time. They were generally good sports with Joey, and often took him with on adventures around town.

The blizzard guaranteed that Thursday would be a snow day. Joey's brothers were giddy about this prospect as they drove, planning to meet a group of girls to go sledding the next morning.

The car the twins shared, an '87 Honda hatchback, smelled faintly of cigarette smoke, and Joey wondered if his brothers had started smoking. He also wondered what his dad would do if he ever caught them smoking in his car. Joey looked out his window and watched a man slip on the ice, the wind blowing him over as he tried in vain to salt his sidewalk.

Joey couldn't take it anymore. "C'mon, what are we doing?"

"It's been on the radio all day. They're saying twenty-foot waves!" Brandon replied.

"What?"

"These might be the biggest waves of our lifetime. We have to check it out!"

"This might be the storm of our lifetime. It's gonna be epic!" Matt added.

"We're going to the harbor? Why not the overlook? We'll never make it back up the hill!"

Brandon tapped the dash. "You don't give Old Blue enough credit."

Brandon gunned the engine, and Matt burst out laughing as the ten-year-old car struggled through the snow. Joey could feel the frigid wind worming its way through the doors and windows, easily overpowering the half-broken heater.

Matt gave Brandon a light punch on the shoulder. "Don't want to tell your little brother the real reason we're going down there?"

Brandon's cheeks flushed, but he kept quiet.

"Fine," Matt turned back to Joey, "I'll give you one guess."

Joey noticed Brandon's camera on the seat next to him. "Mallory?"

"Ha!" Matt smacked the front seat. "The kid's a genius!"

Mallory was Brandon's current crush. A girl likely out of his league, but fate had paired them up for the final project in his black-and-white photography class. He hadn't stopped talking about her for a month.

"It's not about Mallory! Some good shots of a storm like this? Instant A-plus on our final."

"Well, we know you need all the A's you can get." Matt said.

"It'd be my first!" Brandon floored it, the small car shaking from the stress.

The city of Duluth was nestled into a steep hill, the bottom of which opened onto Lake Superior. The harbor ended at a long pier anchored by a towering lift bridge that could be raised up and down, allowing enormous ships to pass beneath it.

If they were going to the harbor, that meant they were going to the bridge, and the bridge terrified Joey. Twenty years ago, a woman had rushed onto the bridge just as it began its ascent, ready to welcome in a Russian freighter. The bridge operator never saw her, and when the bridge reached its apex, the poor woman jumped. Before hitting the water, she became entangled in the machinery of the moving bridge, and, according to the talk on the playground, her body was ripped in half.

One of Joey's classmates claimed his grandfather had been fishing in the harbor when it occurred. According to him, the woman's intestines were dangling from the bridge like a rope ladder, dipping all the way down to the churning waters below. That image seared itself into Joey's brain.

At night, when Joey couldn't sleep, he would imagine that horrendous scene, replaying it in his mind. Could her intestines really reach all the way down into the water? He had almost asked his brothers that very question on several occasions, but the fear of ridicule kept him from opening his mouth.

That and the fact that a few local fishermen had claimed to still catch glimpses of the woman over the years. A shadowy figure alone on dark, foggy nights, roaming the harbor, swaying on the bridge, pleading for help, attempting to shove her intestines back inside her gaping wounds. Joey's brothers didn't believe those stories at all. According to them, those fishermen were just a bunch of old drunks looking for some attention at the local watering hole.

They continued down the hill, sliding their way towards the harbor. There was a main street near the shoreline, checkered with red brick, lined with shops and restaurants. The city was in the midst of revamping the area, tearing down the old factories and ware-houses, making it more tourist friendly. That night it was a ghost town. Most businesses had closed early, and only a handful of cars were still on the street. Brandon parked, their car buckling in and out of the icy ruts.

The twins popped out of the car, Brandon grabbing his camera, and Joey reluctantly followed. He had never felt cold like that in his life. The wind was a wall of ice hammering at his cheeks, sucking his breath away. It felt like icicles stabbing his lungs.

Joey wanted to wait in the car, to plead with them not to go, but he knew better. They would call him a whiny little twerp, and he would have to hold back tears, which would only egg them on. Matt sensed his fear and squatted down, pulling Joey's hood over his winter hat, tightening the strings, tying them in a bow.

"Just hold my hand, buddy, okay? We'll be really quick." Joey pulled on his mittens, fingers already half-numb, and took Matt's hand.

The boys made their way down the deserted harbor streets, slipping in the snow, leaning into the lashing wind. Joey stared up at the lift bridge towering above them, its endless beams of crisscrossed steel shimmering in the dark. The top of the bridge was hidden behind a wall of snow, as if it rose so high into the night sky that it disappeared into the clouds. Joey tightened his grip on Matt's hand. Matt winked, giving him a squeeze back. It didn't help.

They reached the base of the bridge and Brandon took off in a sprint for the other side. As Joey tentatively stepped onto it, he could feel the metal vibrating beneath his sneakers. Even in the howling wind, he could hear the bridge as it creaked and moaned against the storm, its bolts and joints putting up a hell of a fight.

Winter had come with a vengeance that year, the first deep freeze hitting the state mid-October. The black water beneath them was already littered with large chunks of ice that slammed against the cement walls of the channel. Joey couldn't help thinking about the woman who jumped.

They made it to the other side safely and headed down the pier towards the lighthouse. The wind was even more ferocious, swirling around them, biting at any exposed skin. Joey's nose throbbed in alarm.

Joey didn't like the lake any more than he liked the bridge. Joey's uncle had given him a book on shipwrecks for his birthday, and it had been a terrible mistake. The book was chockfull of unsettling details that forever haunted Joey.

There had been hundreds of shipwrecks in the lake's history, claiming over ten-thousand lives. Even worse, the lake was so deep and cold that the corpses that drowned couldn't create enough gas to rise back to the surface. That meant they were still down there somewhere, just existing.

There was an overlook near his house, and Joey would often stop there on his bike and stare at the colossal lake below. The idea of being deep underwater, in the ice-cold darkness with all those dead bodies, made his stomach spin.

The boys stood at the railing surrounding the lighthouse, leaning into the storm as it raced ashore to meet them. Brandon grabbed Joey's other hand, and he and Matt lifted Joey off the ground, all of them screaming into the darkness, Joey's feet swaying in the wind. They screamed until they were hoarse, and then their screaming turned to laughter as they stared down Mother Nature in all her righteous fury.

The wind was a ferocious roar, a whistling shriek that hurt Joey's ears. Giant flakes of snow whipped against him, icy chunks that battered his raw cheeks. His nose ached from the bitter cold, a numbness spreading through his limbs. Joey couldn't help but smile.

Matt leaned into Brandon. "We should probably head back!"

"Another minute!" Brandon yelled, and he shrieked into the night again, a huge grin on his face. He let go of Joey's hand and grabbed the camera hanging around his neck. He struggled to take some photos, but he couldn't keep the snow off his lens, let alone focus on anything in the chaos of the storm.

As they stood there, the temperature plummeted even further, and the wind shifted direction. Instead of hitting the shore head-on, it battered them from the side as the eye of the storm moved closer.

Matt let go of Joey's hand. Alarmed, Joey turned around and found his brother staring at the pier behind them. Their only way back was now being pounded by an endless cycle of massive waves, completely engulfing the walkway to the bridge. Every surface touched by a wave was encased in ice.

"Shit!" Brandon followed their eyes, taking it in.

Joey was panicked. "What are we gonna do?"

Matt banged on the door of the lighthouse.

"It's just a light! Those aren't manned anymore!" Brandon yelled.

Matt yanked on the door anyway, but it was locked, and made of thick steel.

Brandon huddled with his brothers. "Listen! You guys wait here and try to stay dry! I'm gonna make a run for it!"

"You can't!" Joey pleaded. He was shaking, his jacket already soaked, his toes numb.

Matt piped in, "He's right. You'll never make it!"

Brandon smiled. "C'mon, give me a little credit here! Who won State last year?! I'll get some help from the coast guard office. Rope, or something! They'll know what to do!"

Brandon was a track and field star, more so than Matt, and it was something he always held over his brother. Matt squeezed Brandon's shoulder. "Be careful!" Brandon gave him a mocking salute and took off.

He stayed along the outer perimeter of the pier, as far away from the channel as he could get. He jogged a few feet, crouched down as a wave bombarded him, and then scrambled forward a few more steps. Even from a distance, Joey could see Brandon shaking from the bitter cold.

Over the lake, a howling rose from the heart of the storm. It sounded like a helicopter roaring overhead, ready to crash on top of them. Joey twisted back to look, and a massive gale hit them, knocking him and Matt down, their hands separating.

"Brandon! Watch out!" Matt screamed as he slid away from Joey.

Matt and Joey watched helplessly as a vicious wave barreled down the channel, breaking hard against the pier. It boomed like a cannon as it washed over Brandon, quickly receded, and took him with it.

The boys clambered on the ice to the edge of the pier, scanning the channel below. At first, only inky black water and chunks of jagged ice were visible. Then Brandon's body surfaced, as if pushed up, face down, limp, a ragdoll floating on the surface. The rip current pulled him out of the channel and into the swirling lake. Another wave crashed against the outgoing current, and he was sucked below. He didn't surface again.

Matt led Joey back to the lighthouse on their knees. Joey was shivering, tears freezing against his red cheeks. His lips were raw, cracked and bleeding from the cold.

Matt put his arm around Joey, pulling him close. They sat in silence, catching their breath, trying to warm each other up. The numbness in Joey's feet had been replaced by a burning pain that shot through his toes and up his legs, his muscles cramping against the rancorous cold.

Joey finally spoke. "What are we going to do?"

"I don't know!"

The temperature continued to drop. Their soaked jackets were stiff as boards. The waves were relentless, growing in height and hitting the pier, an endless onslaught of water and ice. Joey tucked his raw, blistering hands into his jacket sleeves. He had lost his mittens.

"My hands hurt!"

"I know, mine too. I think we're going to have to try and run!"

"What?"

"We're gonna get hypothermia, and frostbite, soon. We can't stay out here!"

Another wave broke over the pier, drenching them in ice water. Matt stood, pulling Joey up with him. "If we don't let go of each other, we have a better chance, okay? We'll be heavier than Brandon was!" Joey nodded, wondering if that was true.

They waited for a break, and took off in a semi-sprint, slipping on the glassy ice deepening beneath their feet. Matt yanked Joey along behind him. Joey's hand screamed in pain, but he held on as tight as he could. The vortex of wind, snow, water, and ice was disorientating. Joey was pretty sure that they had already made it farther than Brandon had. The lights of the bridge blinked in and out ahead of them, gradually brightening behind the wall of snow.

The horrifying howl boomed again, another titanic wave rolling down the channel. Matt pivoted towards the water, and at first Joey didn't understand why. There were sporadic steel ladders, rising from the channel and over the lip of the pier, welded half-circles bolted into the pavement.

"Grab on!" Matt screamed, heaving Joey towards the nearest ladder.

Joey dove down and wrapped his arms around the bottom rung. Matt tried to do the same, but the wave hit them before he could, launching enormous chunks of ice into the air. A jagged hunk struck Matt's forehead, slicing it open. He dropped to the ground, his face covered in blood, and the receding current pulled his flailing body towards the water.

"No!" Joey shrieked, reaching out for his brother.

Their fingers briefly touched as Matt slid by, and then he was gone, sucked over the wall into the churning channel below. Joey was paralyzed with terror. He lay there, battered by the continuous waves, his arms, locked around the rung, numb. He wasn't sure how much longer he could hold on.

"Joey." It was faint, and Joey wasn't sure he had actually heard it at first, but then it came again. "Joey!"

Joey peered over the wall. Matt was below him, blood filling his eyes as he struggled to make his way up the ladder. Half of his forehead was flapping in the wind, the torn skin exposing a portion of his skull. Joey reached down, trying to help him. Matt feebly made his way up to the last rung, grasping at Joey's hand.

The dreaded howl roared again, and Matt's eyes went wide. He tried to scramble up and over the edge, but his shoe kept slipping on the ice-coated rungs. His other foot was bare, the shoe and sock gone, the foot numb and useless, already turning black. The wave slammed into the wall, and Matt's face cracked against the rung in front of him, Joey saw the crack in the bone. He dropped into the water.

Joey collapsed onto the cement. The waves came less than a second apart after that, over and over. He knew he couldn't hold on much longer.

Joey squinted in the wind and ice, trying to determine if he was closer to the bridge or the lighthouse. He knew it was unlikely he would make it to either, but he had to try.

As Joey stared at the lighthouse, the storm briefly waned, and the lull in the snow revealed a shadowy figure at its base. The wind returned, the silhouette disappearing behind the snow. Maybe there was someone manning the lighthouse after all?

Joey counted to three and leapt to his feet, dashing back towards the lighthouse. As he staggered on the ice, everything around him slowed down, and the sounds of the storm faded away. As if a tunnel opened up within the storm itself, free of snow, free of the bone-chilling wind, the vicious water and ice.

At the end of the tunnel, the shadow appeared again, and Joey could see that it was a woman, with long dark hair swirling around her long, black dress. Joey fell straight into her outstretched arms. The woman embraced Joey, and the fury of the storm returned, the world once again a maelstrom of wind and ice.

"I'll protect you," The woman hissed, holding him tight.

It was barely a whisper, but Joey heard her, a deep reverberation amidst the chaos, as if she had cracked open his chest and whispered the soothing words directly into his pounding heart.

As she clutched him, her arms a vice grip, he knew she was not of this world. Deep within her was a darkness, a darkness that began to seep into him. Or was it the other way around? Was his light leaching into her?

There was movement inside her belly. Her stomach, where it was split in two, breathing, her intestines slithering beneath the frozen fabric. They emerged from her torso, snaking down her body, rising up from the hem of her dress.

The entrails wound around Joey's legs, twisting behind his back. Joey could feel a warmth emanating from them, a heat that consumed him from limb to limb, building a welcome fire in his chest. Despite all that was happening, Joey wasn't scared. He knew she was his protector, and that was all that mattered.

The howling screamed across the lake again, and a monstrous

wave crashed over the lighthouse, enveloping them, sucking them violently into the lake. They broke the surface of the water with a crack, and slowly sunk beneath the waves. They floated in the relative calm below the storm, drifting deeper and deeper, away from the shoreline, towards the cold, black heart of the ancient lake.

Darting shadows joined them, swirling around them, growing in number as they descended the murky depths. The shadows became braver, swimming closer, and Joey caught flashes of cavernous eye sockets and loose, grey flesh.

Every soul the lake had taken before his own was coursing through his body, eternities of pain, terror, and loss consuming him. He could feel his brothers as well. The sadness he felt for his parents overwhelmed him. Their loss would be profound. That thought soon left his mind, and it was the last time Joey would ever think of his parents again, as his tether to the world above was fully severed in that moment.

The woman lifted Joey's head, her eyes locking with his. She smiled, kissing him gently on his forehead, and let him go, her entrails releasing him. The cold attacked him immediately, seeping into every pore of his body, his veins aching rivers of ice. Joey sunk deeper and deeper, staring up at his savior until she was gone, disappearing into the black, roiling waves.

For a moment Joey was afraid, but then he felt all the others who were with him, and he knew he would never be alone again. Joey spun in the water effortlessly, and dove deeper and deeper towards the center of the lake.

A black chasm opened before him, its arctic depths welcoming him home.

COLD CUTS

MARZIA LA BARBERA

There was blood in the snow.

The droplets were scattered in a circle-like pattern, as if the creature they came from had stepped around in the snow at least twice before moving away. Vanishing, even, as there were no prints on the hard-packed snow crunching under Catalina's boots.

A bleeding bird flying away.

That was the only explanation the woman could find for it in her mind, and she bit the inside of her cheek as her eyes moved from the white canvas at her feet to the grey sky above her, looking for signs of injured birds. She found none, her brow furrowing beneath the thick woolen hat she wore while she leaned a little more heavily against her walking stick.

As she neared her fiftieth birthday, Catalina Dragan was starting to think that she was getting too old for that life that served her so well as a young woman running from her past. She was twenty-five years old when she moved to Red Creek, Kansas, the end of the line for her escape aboard a cheap Greyhound bus that took her as far as she could from the fancy, blinding lights of Las Vegas. In Red Creek, young Catalina found the resistance of a small-town community facing a foreign stranger, but she also found a job as a caregiver for an old woman who was more of a mother to her than her own mother ever was.

Miss Betty had never needed a caregiver, only somebody who would care for her and appreciate her for who she was deep inside, the person she kept hidden from her own community. Over the years, Catalina remembered how people would dare call her a freak, and how entertaining it was to hear Miss Betty chortle and say how perhaps the two of them ought to have a fool's tongue for supper every now and again.

Yes, she was a peculiar old lady, but in her, Catalina had found a kindred spirit, an independent woman who would not be crushed by society's demands – someone who could know the full extent of her suffering without seeing her any differently for it. The years with Betty had been the happiest she could remember ever since her childhood in Romania had ended abruptly with her departure for America when she was only thirteen.

What a dream had it all been, leaving poverty and hunger and violence behind to reach the Land of the Free – and what a nightmare had it become.

With Betty, though, she had been able to forget – if only for a while. She had the chance to learn something other than how to earn a living on her back. And if she had been unable to create a social standing or have any kind of credibility in her new town, she had at least inherited a house out on the prairie just outside Red Creek, and a few barn animals that provided what she needed to get by.

It was a simple living, a lonely one with Betty gone, and it wasn't easy, especially when the plains of Kansas became covered in snow and the strong winds blew across the land, seeping through the cracks in the wooden planks that made her cabin. Yet Catalina had had worse in her life, and she was thankful for the peace that she found in the solitude of the prairie: for the time she spent walking and riding outside the property when the weather was good – for the rifle that she had learned to shoot to hunt animals and drive away men she didn't like.

With a soft sigh, the woman returned her gaze to the frozen drops of blood on the snow. *A hare, maybe?* she wondered silently, suddenly wishing she had her shotgun with her to hunt the bleeding animal and catch herself an easy supper.

Was the snow really untouched? A more careful examination found hastily covered footprints in the snow, difficult to see at a first glance. Despite the bulky winter coat she wore, a shiver ran down her spine. Her blue eyes widened as she bent down to take a better look at what had looked at first like untouched snow.

Now she *really* wished she'd brought her rifle.

Who would take such care to hide their tracks in the snow? Unless they didn't want to be seen by her, considering her house was the only one within twenty miles from town? That old feeling of dread that she hadn't felt in a long time suddenly resurfaced as Catalina turned around. It was the feeling of living on borrowed time, of having to answer for her mistakes sooner or later, as if she had a meeting with fate that she was just trying to delay until the very last possible moment. She felt a thousand small eyes in the snow tracking her every step, and she swallowed hard, her throat dry and aching in the frozen, late afternoon breeze.

The lone maple tree in the distance, from which she extracted her syrup the way Betty had shown her, was a ghastly skeleton at the edge of her property, providing neither shelter to whoever was hiding and watching, nor comfort to her. For a moment, with a bitter and slightly hysterical laugh, Catalina thought that all that tree needed was a raven sitting on its low hanging branches, cawing eerily as ravens always did in scary stories.

"Nevermore," she muttered, finding some relief in making light of the ancestral fear that was blooming in her chest and stealing the air from her lungs more easily than the bitter cold wind that whipped tendrils of her red hair across her pale cheeks. "Fuckin' Poe never had butchers like those on his heels now, did he."

Shaking her head with a soft grunt, Catalina tightened her fingers around the ridged handle of the hunting knife at her waist and pulled it out of its sheath before she forced herself to push through, one foot in front of the other.

Whatever was waiting at her door, running away was not an option anymore.

She had run before; she had covered her tracks with stolen money and a new identity that she forged for herself. Now she was too old to keep on running and try to start over again, too old to be terrorized again by those who wanted her to pay for what she had done when she left Las Vegas with that stolen money in her bag and blood on her hands. All that was left for her to do now was walk up to her own cabin.

The cabin was just like he had heard it described in town.

The half-demented owner of the general store was only too willing to prattle on about that old house and the lonely woman who lived there, a stranger that – people felt – didn't belong to their community for more than just her geographical origin. The general consensus was that the woman was odd and bad news right from the start, and her ties to the community were thin at best, if any. All the better for him; nobody would miss her or go looking for her, if his plan didn't work out as it should.

He had been out there for a while, stalling, observing the grey trail of smoke that rose from an old tin chimney. Now the blond man grinned to himself, already savoring the warmth and coziness of a hearth and homemade meal, and maybe a good fuck to get the blood in his frozen body pumping again. His forearm throbbed where the old wound, hidden beneath layers of fabric, had reopened that morning. Blood seeped through the soiled gauze and the worn wool of the sweater he wore, but he didn't notice the few drops falling down his wrist, turning the white snow red at his feet as he sensed movement and looked at the snow-covered dirt road to see the woman come up to the house.

She had some kind of utility knife in her hand, the sight of which only made his grin widen, but he wouldn't pretend he wasn't impressed by the confidence she showed despite clearly expecting trouble.

Or by that shapely figure she hid under those bulky winter clothes.

Definitely gonna have me a good fuck 'fore I leave here, he thought, smacking his lips. Whether the woman was willing or not – that had never been the kind of thing to stop a man like Wayne Odom before.

The woman had come fully into view by the time Wayne stepped out of the shadow cast by the snow-covered tin roof of the barn, his hands up and empty palms facing her.

"Howdy," he called out in a jovial tone, hesitating no longer than a beat before he pulled down his scarf to uncover his face. "How do, ma'am. Sorry to drop in on you like that." She clearly wasn't at ease, so he smiled widely, letting his voice carry. "I think I got turned around on my way to the nearest town, what with the wind an' all."

As if beckoned by his southern drawl, the icy wind began to blow strongly again, sending snowflakes billowing around his and the woman's faces. She, however, didn't lower her knife.

"The closest town is twenty miles out that way, Red Creek," she threw back at him, her English betraying an accent that Wayne couldn't quite place. "What the hell were you doing out here, mister?"

"Odom. Wayne Odom."

He took a few steps forward, closer to the woman, fighting a smirk as she held her ground.

"Not what I was asking."

It was a relief to find that the intruder wasn't anyone she knew from her past, but Catalina still didn't exactly trust him at a first glance. It wasn't any blatantly obvious thing in his appearance that had such an off-putting effect on her, but she was cautious as she approached, her knife ready in her hand. The man – Odom, he said – was tall and good-looking even under layers of clothes, and that was probably the only reason why she didn't try to run him off her property right away.

God, it had been a while since she'd felt that spark of interest in anybody, as if her own skin were tingling in anticipation under his gaze. He looked damn near good enough to eat, and she had been lonely for so long... Sometimes she felt starved for companionship.

"I was just tryina be polite, is all," the man said in reply to her curt interruption, taking a few more steps forward.

By now Catalina could see his tan face and light blue eyes, the full lips that curved in a smile as he looked at her, his hands still up in surrender. She had never seen him, and he didn't sound like any of the people she was used to seeing in Red Creek or the neighboring counties.

"You're far from home, aren't you?" She asked shortly, raising her voice when the wind picked up again, cutting her face with its ice-cold breath. A lock of her long red hair slipped free from the confines of her woolen hat, twirling around her eyes, and she pushed it back brusquely with her free hand.

"Yes, ma'am."

Anything else he tried to say was swallowed by a stronger gust of wind, almost sweeping Catalina off her feet, and she growled her displeasure under her breath as she pushed forward with a lurch and grabbed the front of Odom's coat, pulling him up the whitened-out path to the front door of her cabin. The man offered no resistance when she pushed him inside, even though her knife was still on display and too close to his back for comfort.

Catalina drew in a long, soothing breath when the door finally closed behind them, blocking out the wind and the snow.

"It's a fucking blizzard out there," she grumbled, ripping the damp hat off her head, and throwing it on the back of a chair close to the stove.

"How long d'ya think it'll last?" Odom asked, making a not entirely credible show of being worried by the weather and what was shaping up to be like forced proximity with a stranger for an undetermined period of time.

"Could be gone tomorrow, could be three days of this shit," Catalina replied, giving him a warning look before she sheathed her knife again with deliberately slow movements. "You can't go back out in the blizzard," she added, every word leaving a bad taste in her mouth. She noticed the way Odom seemed to be fighting the urge to smile at her declaration and felt the sudden need to spit, at once disgusted by him and by her own reaction to his mere presence in her house.

"You may stay here." The words came out slowly, sticking to her tongue, to the roof of her mouth, unwilling to open the door to the chance of finding herself trapped with that stranger to whom she was inexplicably attracted and by whom she was repulsed so intensely at the same time.

"I am much obliged, ma'am." Odom's voice was polite but unctuous, a sharp contrast to the way his dark eyes followed her every movement as she unzipped and discarded the bulky wet coat that kept her warm outside, the thin sweatshirt she wore underneath doing little to shield her figure from his hungry gaze. "If there's anything I can do-"

"Yeah, you can take off those wet clothes. You're dripping all over my floor."

It was almost unbelievable that the blizzard should give him such easy access to the house and to the woman herself. Wayne tried hard not to look too obviously pleased with the unexpected turn of events, something that was harder to do by the second as the woman before him started to discard the thick outwear in the cozy heat of the cabin. There was something about this woman that intrigued him, something that would certainly prevent him from acting on impulse the way he usually did.

The woman was his prey, but he sensed in her the predator as well, and she proved it once again when she snapped at him, cutting off his admittedly greasy remarks with that sharp voice that had already sent a thrill through him before.

I wonder how she sounds when she screams, he thought not for the first time since laying eyes on her, his teeth digging into his lower lip as he automatically moved to obey her order of discarding his wet clothes. *She must look delicious with blood between those pretty legs of hers.* A powerful surge of lust went through him, a feral longing that made his teeth drown in saliva as his mouth watered in anticipation.

"I came up here from Louisiana," Wayne offered, willing himself to break the tension in his own body. The woman looked at him with a frown, gauging his intentions, probably bemused by the ease with which he shared that unrequited information. "You were asking before, weren't ya?" Wayne flashed her a smile, removing his coat and handing it to her.

At a first glance, there was only an old TV and a whole lot of books in that cabin, and while the woman seemed to be infamous in town, she didn't look like the type to go out often to socialize. There was no harm in telling her where he came from: he couldn't imagine news of his crimes reaching a small, forgotten town like Red Creek, Kansas, and the woman herself didn't give him the impression of somebody with a keen interest in national crime news.

There was a beat of silence as the woman hung his dripping coat on the back of a chair alongside her own, then she threw a log into the stove before she trained her green eyes on him again. The irises gleamed golden in the soft orange light that bathed the room.

"You sound like it," she said at last, a hint of a smile playing around her lips. She moved to an old-looking, beige lamp on a corner table and turned it on, unpinning her hair before she looked at him again. "I'm Catalina," she offered, a long overdue introduction, and Wayne thought that such an innocent-sounding name clashed with her looks, with the light in her eyes and that fiery hair unbound and loose on her shoulders.

"You go by Lina?" He asked, a faint smirk on his lips. He didn't miss the way her eyes flashed, and her mouth curled in a soundless snarl, nor did he miss the thrill that passed through him at her reaction.

Eliciting her irritation would be the best way to whet his appetite before the game he intended to play with her came to fruition.

"I go by Catalina."

Her reply was almost a growl, irritation showing plainly on her face as she pushed past him.

When she had first arrived in the United States, as a child that had been promised a bright future and was thrust into the horrifying world of prostitution instead, her captors' first act was to drill into her mind that the name Catalina wouldn't fly in America. *Lina* was their choice, an easy name with a sweet sound that would entice the men who took their pleasure fucking a fourteen-year-old whore. Thus, young Lina's virginity had been sold for a couple thousand dollars to a dirty old man that smelled like expensive aftershave and used her willowy teenage body as if she were a ragdoll in his hands, and that had been the beginning of the end for her. Ten years later, on a hot summer day, Lina died with a scalpel in her hand, in a pool of another man's blood, and Catalina was born again.

Now, even hearing that name made her sick, anger and fear creating an explosive mix within her, but she forced herself to keep her emotions in check when faced with that stranger. Especially when a more thorough look at Odom revealed blood trickling down his wrist and her mind flashed back to the drops in the snow.

With a realization that chilled her down to the bone, Catalina suddenly knew that he had been around the cabin longer than he claimed to have been, trying to hide his tracks, too, and she couldn't fathom one single reason why a man who was not ill-intentioned would do something like that. He'd watched her then, perhaps just to make sure she was all alone out there, maybe reporting directly to someone else who hired him to find her and kill her. Her throat closed up as panic rose inside her, but her voice was surprisingly steady when she pointed at his arm: "You're bleeding, man." She reached for a cloth quickly and threw it to him across the table. He caught it one-handed with ease.

Fuck.

That spoke of training beyond what any regular guy should be familiar with.

"Bathroom's the third door on the left," she added, swallowing that new wave of fear that threatened to choke her. "You can clean up. I'll fix something to eat."

And in the meantime, she'd think of an escape plan, just in case being trapped with him during the blizzard ended up being a fight for her life.

That damn woman was far too observant – too much for her, or his, own good. Fighting the urge to smack his hand against the wood of the doorframe, Wayne followed her directions to the bathroom, where he stripped off his shirt and threw it in the old-looking metal tub in the corner. Like every other room Wayne had the chance to see in that house, the bathroom seemed to be built for function rather than luxury and design. Yet the array of beauty products on the shelf above the basin told him that Catalina appreciated some of the finer things in life as well – things she certainly wasn't getting at the general store in Red Creek.

The realization, paired with the hint of fear he saw in her eyes right before she shooed him off to the bathroom, suddenly forced him to regret his openness. There was, after all, a chance that she'd seen any of those Internet articles about Wayne Odom, the so-called *Killer of the Bayou*. With his taste for torture and rape, and the long list of known victims attributed to him, he was already a legend in the right circles – something he couldn't help being proud of.

Testing his best charming smile in the mirror, Wayne used his uninjured hand to slick back his dark blond hair, white teeth shining in his reflection, as he allowed himself to reconsider his plans.

He could assault Catalina right away and make things easier for himself, in fact, finding pleasure in that supple body he couldn't wait to bite and cut until her skin was torn to shreds, an ivory canvas for his red art. His blood pumped faster, his smile becoming predatory as his dick began to harden and twitch in his pants.

"Fuck, I'mma rip that bitch in two when I get my hands on her," he muttered to himself, squeezing his cock through the fabric to relieve the pressure. It wasn't the right time, though; if he started to play hard so soon after the blizzard trapped them into that cabin, he would get tired of her, and it would be a long few days alone in there with her corpse. If he kept her alive, on the other hand, he would have someone to make and serve him meals, and earning her trust would make the ultimate betrayal of his assault even more delicious.

So, with his decision to bide his time, Wayne washed his injured arm carefully and bandaged it as best as he could before he returned to the small living room. Catalina was there, a platter of what looked like dried meat and cold cuts sitting on the table next to two mugs, and he flashed her that winning smile he rehearsed in the mirror as he noticed how her keen green eyes raked his figure, falling on the thin gauze he'd found in the bathroom to cover up his arm.

"Best I could do with your small first aid kit," he explained, his smile taking on an almost shy quality as his eyes met hers. "Thanks for letting me use it anyway."

"Mmhm," Catalina nodded noncommittally, pushing one of the mugs closer to him. "What happened to you?" She asked after a beat, before she brought her mug to her lips.

Wayne mimicked her motions, expecting coffee in the mug. It surprised him to find mulled wine instead, his gaze returning to her, and it took him a moment to register her question. "I was trying to fix my car and she won the fight," he lied breezily, a handsome, lopsided smile on his face. He wasn't about to say that his last victim had managed to disarm him and cut him with his own knife, nor that he had broken her neck right in two after that attack. Much better to elicit sympathy.

"Yeah, I didn't see a car around here."

Wayne nodded, grabbing a piece of meat off the tray with a flourish. "It broke down a few miles away from here. Had to walk the rest of the way." He took a bite of meat and hummed in appreciation. "I'll go find it again after the blizzard is gone... *what is* this thing I'm having, my God, it's delicious."

This time, he didn't imagine Catalina's smile, nor the hint of pride on her face as she took a piece of meat for herself.

"It's deer," she said simply. "I hunt it and prepare it myself."

Wayne sighed contentedly as he dropped down in one of the chairs around the table. "Man, I could eat this for days. It must be the spice – what is it that you use?"

Outside, the storm raged on while the night sky darkened further, the icy wind whistling as it crashed on the windows and walls of the cabin, but the two people inside the room hardly seemed to notice as they stared at one another, a light in Catalina's eyes to match the mischievous glint in Wayne's eyes.

"It's a secret recipe I learned as a young woman," she replied with a faint grin. "Nothing I can share with a stranger."

Wayne chuckled. "You're sharing your house with a stranger," he pointed out teasingly. "I thought we'd get a little cozier before this whole thing was over."

This time, Catalina laughed, though it sounded mirthless and mocking. "If that's what you're getting at, I'm sorry to kill your hopes, mister. That ain't gonna happen."

✳

She had more than her fair share of men in the years she worked for the Bratva in Vegas, and after that too, whenever the need to scratch an itch occurred to her. And for all that Wayne Odom looked like a viable candidate to warm her bed for a night or two, Catalina knew better than to get tangled up with a man who raised more red flags than she thought existed at all.

"Speaking of that," she said instead, after the laughter died out, "you're lucky I have a guestroom, so you won't have to sleep on the couch." Her eyes were trained on him as she drank her wine, observing his reaction carefully.

On his part, Wayne only nodded, popping a rolled prosciutto slice into his mouth. "It's more than I expected, to be honest." He chuckled again, another humorless sound. "I was plannin' on waiting out the storm in somebody's barn, with horse and cow shit to keep me warm. Your cabin looks like a five-star hotel right about now." He selected another piece of cured meat from the platter and whistled softly. "The food alone is worth it, and I'd never complain about the company of a beautiful woman."

Rolling her eyes, Catalina scoffed, pushing back her chair just far enough to hoist her feet up on the table. "No need to turn up the charm, John Wayne," she quipped, an eyebrow quirked up as she stared at him, unimpressed.

This time, the laughter coming from the man was genuine, his sharp white teeth gleaming and light blue eyes dark with interest as he trained his gaze back on her in that way that made her squirm imperceptibly.

"Wouldn't I like to be John Wayne," he mused softly, throwing back half the contents of his mug to wash down a few more bites of meat. The platter was already more than half empty, and Catalina had only had a few pieces here and there, hardly enough to fill her stomach.

"Oh, I know I would like it if you were John Wayne," she retorted with a smirk. "But since you're not him, I ain't interested." She caught a flash of irritation pass over his face, but it was gone in the blink of an eye. She watched him shrug instead as they lapsed into a silence that was charged with unspoken questions. She certainly anticipated the one that passed his lips after a few seconds, even though it caused her blood to freeze in her veins.

"So where do you really come from, Catalina?" He uttered her name as if he were savoring it on his tongue, in a way that made her shiver with both revulsion and pleasure, and she held his gaze as she tapped her fingers slowly on the hardwood table.

"Romania." She watched him closely for signs of recognition. She saw none, but the obvious interest in his blue eyes didn't sit well with her, so she decided to throw him a bone and see what he would do with it. "I came here over thirty years ago as a whore," she said, eyes void of any emotion that could give him leverage over her.

He wet his lips with the tip of his tongue and shifted in his chair, undoubtedly intrigued, but he didn't look like he might have had an inkling as to what she used to do for a living before she revealed it herself. That was a relief, truly, even as his lascivious looks made her skin crawl. "Got out of that a long time ago, mister," she added, lowering her feet back to the ground and leaning forward on the table, a determined look on her face. "You ain't getting any pussy tonight, no matter how much you're willing to pay for it."

The smile that appeared on Wayne's face after he chewed the last bite left on the platter was chilling, dark and dangerous, his upper body leaning forward for a beat before he stood up, glancing briefly in the direction of the guestroom Catalina had pointed at.

"Bold of you to assume I'm willing to pay for it at all," he murmured in an ominous tone, his eyes shining malevolently for a split second before the look on his face turned less predatory. "Sleep well, Catalina."

He left, and it was only too clear to Catalina that she wouldn't find any sleep at all that night – or for the foreseeable future, at least until she managed to get rid of that man. A shame, too, because if he'd been just a little less arrogant and creepy, she would have prob-ably liked to keep him around for a while. As it was, she retired for the night with her hunting knife under her pillow and her rifle within reach, but she made a point of not getting out of her locked bedroom, not even when she distinctly heard his footsteps just outside the door and the sound of him rummaging through her kitchen cabinets and pantry.

There were flurries of snow outside her window, the dark night sky looking white and grey beyond the fogged-up windowpane. She knew the weather well enough to know that if it kept at it, they would be stuck come the morning. The blizzard might be gone, but there was no way either she or Odom were leaving the cabin. She tried to envision the contents of the pantry, the food reserve she kept for times such as these, and she dozed off in the end with thoughts of her cold cuts and cured meats in her mind, of canned vegetables and hard cheese that would survive the winter and let her survive it just as well.

In the morning, however, when the first light revealed that her prediction had come true, Catalina ventured out of the room to find her pantry and fridge raided. Gone were most of the meat prepara-tions, a dirty knife and a few stale slices of bread sitting on the messy kitchen counter, and she jumped out of her skin as she felt the cool touch of a hand low on her back. She didn't hear Wayne approach, but God, she would have given anything to erase that smug, self-satisfied smile from his face.

"Good morning," the man greeted her casually, lowering that hand on her back to cop a feel of her ass through her pajama pants. "I had a bit of a snack last night. Hope you don't mind."

Catalina's eyes widened in horror as she realized that he did it on purpose, and she twirled around, furious, to glare at him. "You ate almost everything I had in the house. We're gonna fucking starve in here."

His smile was once again chilling, terrifying, as he grabbed her chin and leaned in to take a whiff from her neck, his sharp teeth grazing her skin. "I can still eat you, can't I." He goaded her, biting her neck in earnest before he released her roughly. "I'll catch us something else to eat, princess. Don't you worry about that, I'm a good hunter too."

Waiting to ruin that little whore wasn't going to work. Wayne had realized that during the night, when the restlessness had made him ravage her kitchen and pantry in search of something that would fill the hole in his soul. Nothing worked, however, not even her perfectly smoked meat – not when all he wanted was to sink his teeth into her thighs and taste her blood as he fucked her with the thick handle of that knife that she carried around everywhere she went. *Fuck*, that would be a sight to see, and then she would scream for him when he turned the knife upside down and fucked her with the blade, before he carved his name with the bloodied steel on the soft white skin of her stomach.

The thought was still sending him into a frenzy long after he raided her pantry, long after he took his heavy, hard cock in his palm and stroked himself until he came all over the soft leather-covered pillow on what looked like her favorite armchair. It was a poor substitute for the real thing, but by then Wayne knew that he would have the real thing soon enough, too.

Now, he only needed to make good on his promise to catch them something to eat, even if it was only one of the animals she kept in the barn.

The snow was piled up high outside the door, the patio completely hidden under a white blanket of snow, high enough that he had to slip out of the window in the living room after he dressed in his outwear, a knife at his waist. Hunting was a fool's task, admittedly, because no animals would be out in the cold after the blizzard, so he went straight to the barn, whistling a tune to himself. Within minutes he would have a cow's or a pig's warm blood on his fingers, just a little taste to whet his appetite, and Catalina's blood would soon follow, painting his aching cock as well as the rest of his body. "I'll put it in her mouth first," he muttered to himself, chuckling darkly. "That will finally shut her up for a while."

Yet, as he approached the pigs' corral and peered inside, already focused on selecting the fattest pig for slaughter, it was Wayne that was caught up short, a furrow in his brow as he caught a glimpse of what peeked just beneath the mud near the trough. Because *goddammit*, he would have recognized bones anywhere, but there was no place he was more surprised to find human bones than in the barn of a little hermit whore.

"What the fuck-"

He had just picked up one of the bones, looking it over in shock, when a shadow loomed large over him, the unmistakable silhouette of an axe raised high above his head.

"I'm sorry," he heard Catalina say, though she didn't look sorry at all as she smiled down at him: a terrifying smile that chilled him down to the bone. "You should have just left my fucking food alone."

There was blood in the snow.

Red rivers seeped into the icy surface as Catalina Dragan worked with a vast array of hunting tools to cut fillets and portions of meat that she would take great care to spice and cure and smoke, to be consumed in the seasons to come. Once she was finished, she would treat the skin to make a new pillow cover, perhaps, or another lamp.

Lifting one hand to wipe the sweat off her forehead, Catalina smiled to herself. It wasn't every day that she got fresh meat nearly delivered to her door, but that had been a particularly lucky hunting spree, and she was grateful for a chance to replenish her pantry and fridge after that hideous Wayne Odom had eaten everything she stored for the winter.

Slicing a thigh to set the lean meat in the snow-filled cooler, she started to hum a song in the quiet of the snow-covered prairie, finally at peace for the first time in two days. "I knew you would be useful somehow," she murmured to the corpse lying in the snow, carefully extracting the liver to set it aside. She would cook it that very night, maybe pair it with some of the canned green beans that had escaped Odom's ravenous hunger.

Ah, what a lovely meal that would be.

Catalina smiled again, laying the knife on the snow in order to stretch her tired arms over her head.

Now only a bit more work to take some of the belly fat that would make the salami and sausages even more delicious, then she would move on to the skin. "A thick skin," she remarked, stroking a finger down a muscular arm. "Could be useful to make something to wear, too." After all, in all the years she was with her as her caregiver and faithful disciple, Betty had taught her everything about how to prepare the skin as well as the meat, and what kind of garments would be more durable if treated properly and well preserved through the years. She wasn't just the finest cook: she had a keen eye for fashion, too.

First, though, she would take the tattoo. She had been wanting to lighten up the place with a new painting for a while, and that lovely bald eagle wrapped in the Stars and Stripes of the American flag that was tattooed in color on Wayne Odom's back would be the perfect design for a lovely painting she couldn't wait to display in her home.

"It's America," she told herself with a chuckle as she began the incision with a scalpel, and she smiled as she thought of the first man who'd been under her scalpel so many years ago, his blood pouring out of his throat while she lost herself in the throes of her very first real orgasm. She patted the dissected corpse beneath her and chuckled again. "Say, Wayne. Ain't you happy to be free?"

THE FINAL REPORT ON THE GERRARD PATROL
MATT DODGE

The final report on the Gerrard Patrol of 1915,
As compiled by Constable Smyth
- May 1st, 1915.
Fort Mackenzie, Yukon Territory

Sirs, the facts that can be determined regarding the fate of the Gerrard Patrol are few. I will endeavor to include them while providing all additional information we can ascertain regarding these tragic and unpleasant events.

The remains of Inspector Gerrard, including his personal logbook, were found wedged between two pieces of rock. This log is the only account of the mission, as fragmentary and nonsensical as it may be. I will include all relevant excerpts in this report.

The Gerrard Patrol consisted of Inspector William Gerrard, age 31, in command and Constables Arthur Robinson, age 27, and Stephane Leduc, age 26. Their purpose was to complete the regular patrol from Fort Mackenzie to Dawson City and then return with mail and additional supplies for the coming spring. The total distance in one direction is approximately 585 kilometers. Depending on weather conditions, previous patrols have completed this route in 10 to 21 days.

The Gerrard Patrol departed Fort Mackenzie on the morning of March 11th. Each patrol member was equipped with their own sled and a team of 6 dogs, and enough supplies to last between 14 to 21 days according to the store master at Fort McKenzie. Gerrard was reported to be confident that this was more than adequate, as the last major blizzard of the season was surely behind them.

Gerrard's log: *"March 11 -- 7:00 hours, -22 centigrade. We are prepared to embark on patrol. Robinson and Leduc are strong and able, despite inexperience. Dogs well-rested and fed, with fat to shed after the winter. Perhaps we may set a record upon arrival at D.C. Departing at first light, 8 o'clock."*

RCMP staff at Fort Mackenzie confirm their departure date and time. The patrol headed south-west, towards the Plume River whose course would lead them through the mountain range crossing before continuing to Dawson City. Guards report that the men appeared in a chipper mood, prepared to perform their duties. It was a sunny day, increasing the temperature and melting the top layer of snow and ice. Upon departure, the guards could see the patrol follow the trees toward the river until the tree line shifted and they disappeared from view.

Gerrard's log: *"March 11 -- 18:30, -25 centigrade. First day a success. Made good time, completed 12.5 kilometers before sundown. Made camp with Leduc while Robinson prepared food for us and dogs. Allowed one ration of whiskey each to toast our journey. Spirits are up; weather is on our side. I hope it does not get too warm too quickly. Intend to enjoy the last days of winter. The night came quickly but without alarm. Will depart at sunrise."*

From all available evidence, the first week of the patrol proceeded thusly without any issues. There is no indication of distress or unexpected challenges that can be found in the logs.

Gerrard's log: *"March 17 -- 17:45, -31 centigrade. Completed 12 kilometers. Made camp with little effort, despite brief dip in air temperature. Leduc's turn to prepare food. Tents remain strong. Dogs having no trouble with snow level. Temperature cold but not unheard of. Robinson not pleased, but the boy is from Ontario. I told him to try and enjoy the climate. There is a certainty to this season as the sun sets. It is cold and you will be too. Will depart at first light tomorrow."*

This excerpt shows that Gerrard and his team remain in good spirits one week into their journey. The lower temperature noted is likely the first indication of the cold front that would settle over the area in the next several days. The result of a low-pressure system that clung to the mountains, trapped by the preceding warmer temperatures that kept the moisture in the air. They could not know what lay in their path.

Gerrard's log: *"March 19 -- 18:00, -38 centigrade. Cold today. Much more than expected. Wind speed picking up. Steady, not in bursts. Tents are holding up. Dogs and team are persevering. Will make it through this night and the rest. Still on pace to cross the gap at Klondike ridge in four days. Hope any worse weather will wait for us to cross. The peaks will provide some protection. Will leave at dawn and gain time."*

. . .

It is unfortunately easy now to see that Gerrard's optimism was indeed blind, but in the moment, it was not without merit. He had eight years of experience in the territory and had survived worse storms during his service. This included the blizzard of 1909 which claimed the lives of four servicemen sent to install a telegraph wire.

Gerrard returned with the only other survivor, whose limbs had already suffered extensive frostbite. These injuries later turned septic, and he died in hospital without regaining consciousness.

Undoubtedly tragic, these events provided Gerrard with experience. His plan to cross at the gap in the ridge to beat the weather was ambitious, but not unreasonable given the information at hand.

Gerrard's log: "*March 22 -- 19:30. -41 centigrade. Eight kilometers. Snow has set in late in the day and the winds did not wait for us. Squalls affecting visibility and progress is slower than hoped. Robinson and Leduc are weary. First big storm for both. They don't know what it's really like here. How quickly it can turn. They must learn. Crossing should occur in two days. Top of my tent is growing heavy as I write, the night brings more storms.*

The blizzard was fully setting in. These were the perfect conditions for the storm to linger. It was serious, the patrol had supplies and experience on their side.

Gerrard's log: "*March 23 -- 13:00, -45 centigrade. Two kilometers. Visibility awful. Might as well be pitch black. Tried to push through but forced to make camp. Winds exhausted the dogs by midday. Hands still thawing. Tents erected together to provide support. Supplies spread for anchoring. No choice but to rest and try tomorrow.*"

. . .

The drop in temperatures was severe. Store masters from Fort Mackenzie reported that over the next three days an extra cord of wood was used for adequate heating. The patrol had only their winter service-issued clothes and tents, with a small oil stove for cooking.

Gerrard's log: "*March 24 -- 16:00, -41. No progress today. Visibility near zero. Cook stove producing barely enough heat to melt snow for water. Canned rations frozen solid. Chipped out small pieces. Can see the concern on Robinson and Leduc's faces. Gave them permission for a double whiskey ration and encouraged the singing of songs through our tents to lift spirits.*"

Records from the Fort indicate a minimum of 36 centimeters of snowfall during that day. Combined with the wind, any attempt at progress in the open was foolhardy at best. Gerrard's decision to remain at camp under such conditions adhered to regulations.

Gerrard's log: "*March 25 -- 17:30, -45. 2nd day of no progress. Snow not letting up. Impossible to stay on route, risk of getting lost is high. Cannot get stuck again. Had to run the dogs around camp to avoid tissue damage. They nipped and snapped. It is for their own good.*"

Records show that another 30 centimeters of snow fell that day. Gerrard's appraisal of the viciousness of the storm remains accurate. As far as can be ascertained, the patrol was still 15 kilometers from the crossing.

. . .

Gerrard's log: "*March 26 -- 19:00, -47. Ordered camp broken. Snow still falling but slight improvement in visibility. Cannot allow 3 days with no progress. Leads to poor effects on morale. Dogs were reluctant and had to be mushed hard to stay moving. Traveled approx. 5 kilometers. I'd hoped to sight Mt. Elgin but conditions remain unfavorable. The storm must abate soon.*"

It is known that the system was still feeding itself as the cold current remained pushed against the mountains. Conditions would not see dramatic improvement for the next week. Gerrard reports never making more than four kilometers progress in a single day. The effort to make these distances in such conditions would have expended tremendous energy from the sled team.

Gerrard's log: "*April 2 -- Night, -52. Progress slow. Wind relentless. Must be near pass. Must. Ordered rationing, meals reduced by ⅓. Robinson and Leduc growing weary. Told them this was nothing. Told them about the last storm. Not all, but enough. They are chattering in their tents anyway. The wind must break soon. Rumbles all night. We'll find a way.*"

The weather conditions make it improbable to fully ascertain the position of the patrol during this time. By our estimates, they continued to make progress along the eastern ridge of the mountains, but it seems that they moved beyond the trail that would have led to the pass. It is possible that extreme weather, perhaps even small avalanches, had significantly obscured the landscape.

Gerrard's log: "*April 5 -- Night, -50. Following mountains. The crossing must be near. Leduc, Robinson, and the dogs are unhappy. Rations reduced to half. Will attempt to hunt any animals we see. Dogs and stomachs growling. Fire weak, barely heats food. Another low sun. Won't these infernal mountains ever end?"*

At this point, it was likely clear to all patrol members that they were off course, if not lost altogether. We cannot know what Robinson and Leduc felt at this time. This was the first patrol for both, but given their territorial experience, they would have realized that they faced severe hardship if they were going to regain their position.

Gerrard's log: *"April 6 -- Night. -49. Hunting unsuccessful. Not a damned deer or hare in sight. Had to make do with the weakest dog. Must press on soon. Head is sore. Light always behind eyes. Leduc woke with a coughing fit this morning. Sometimes this is how it starts."*

It is unclear what Gerrard means. The effects of extreme hunger would have been felt, but a coughing fit is harder to place. The exacerbation of an existing illness is a possibility, as is a general weakening of the immune system. Leduc has been reported in good health before departing Fort Mackenzie. No signs of consumption, pneumonia, or glandular malfunction.

Gerrard's log: *"April 6 -- Night, cold. Unsuccessful hunt. Two more dogs gone. Robinson prepared food for us and team. They nip and yap and then eat. Sun will not abate even through storms. Very bright even when so low in the sky. Leduc coughing again. Hearing him not in his tent. Wet. Robinson angry, staring. Feeling it right now. Push on tomorrow."*

This is the date the commander at Fort Mackenzie noted he had not received confirmation of the patrol's arrival in Dawson City. They were officially reported late. A note was made of the severe weather conditions and instructions were relayed to the outpost guards to be prepared for any sign of the patrol. It was considered likely they would arrive in some distress.

Gerrard's log: *"April 7 -- Night, cold. Slow going. Dogs unhappy. Snow persists and blocks our view. So bright, wary of snow blindness. Keeping to the mountains. There will be a break. Leduc's cough is worse. Hearing it over the wind. Could barely light campfires. Hungry."*

With clear conditions, the mountains behind them would have allowed for a course readjustment. The remnants of the storm were still severe enough to disrupt their positioning. By continuing to press forward for the crossing, the patrol was moving further away.

Gerrard's log: *"April 8 -- Cold night. Pushed hard today. Mountains changing. Peaks lower. The pass must be near. Will push again tomorrow. Must have enough for dogs. If it is near, we can make do. Will wake up early and use this infernal light if we must."*

Without any longitude and latitude coordinates, we cannot know the exact location of the patrol. They may have been nearing a drop in elevation in the range where it meets with the Parris shelf that connects with flatlands.

Gerrard's log: *"April 9 -- Evening. Short break. No more rest. Crossing is close. Heating food chipping ice dragging the sled. Robinson is warming water to help Leduc's cough. The cold wind making it worse. Still here no dark no rest until we cross."*

. . .

At this point there is a half-page break in the log. When it resumes, there is no date or time, an abandonment of service protocol. The handwriting is much more frenetic and difficult to follow.

"no, no, no not the crossing it can't be there's only ice and water when the trail breaks a lake? How can it be this is the crossing this is the gap it's here it has to be not some half frozen lake we can't cross can't go they know by now they know they know how do I explain so they understand? why is it so bright always all the time where is the night how did we get here its so far too far to go what did we do?"

The only plausible explanation for this record is that they had found an inlet of Lake Agassiz. However, this positioning would place the patrol 400 kilometers from the crossing which does not corroborate the estimated distance traveled during the storm. Rations were deeply depleted, and the sled team was exhausted to the point of delirium. We are unsure how such a distance could have been traversed.

Gerrard's log: *"April 10120 -- cold. Camp has built. Leduc and Robinson extremely reluctant. No option. Only 4 cans of food remaining. Dogs reduced by half. Stringy. Fort will know we're missing. Tomorrow will attempt to break ice. Safe for fishing. Sun should help. Should do something. Thaw must come."*

Gerrard's dates become unreliable. On the 12th of April, the service headquarters in Dawson City reported to Fort Mackenzie that the patrol had failed to arrive in the expected time frame. The news was considered alarming but not yet catastrophic due to lack of information. The storm had depleted us and, I must confess, we were not eager to venture out.

The decision was to wait two days to see if the patrol could find their way. We would begin prep for a search after the two days. Leaving sooner would put additional lives at risk. I stand by this decision and will testify as such before the commission.

Gerrard's log: *"April 13 -- Sun. Fortified camp by the shore. Think it is the shore. The ice changes. Chipping away at a hole for fishing. Any attempt near the open water risks a plunge. Slow going. Leduc will not cease his cough. Robinson sleeps now, resisting wakeup call and fire maintenance. Fish with what? Leather straps and bent nail? Hard to judge ice from glare. Tent always bright. Told men we must establish a better camp. Someone should find us. Must notice we're gone. Must not let it happen."*

As patrol leader, Gerrard still seems aware that any search party would take days, if not weeks, to locate them. Establishing a fortified location could aid search efforts, as would building a steady fire for both cooking and smoke signaling.

Gerrard's log: *"April 14 -- Sun. Two dogs disappeared in the night. Must have slipped their harnesses. Leduc should have secured them, cough be damned. Threatened him with court-martial. He laughed, exacerbating the cough. Robinson still resisting orders."*

Standard protocol would dictate the felling of nearby trees to create reinforced structures around the tents, improving their resistance to the elements. There should be an attempt to establish a more sustainable food source through hunting, fishing, or foraging. Aside than attempts to chip through the ice, the log indicates no specific action taken to create a more fortified camp.

Gerrard's log: *"April 16̵5 -- sun. Dogs almost done. Any fewer will make travel impossible, no chance of finding the pass. Leduc grows quiet at last. Hopefully in reflection upon his failures. Broke small hole in the ice, straps, and hook set. No bites yet. Small but it could do. Will check in the morning. When is morning? No difference."*

It appears that psychological panic and physical delirium were taking a severe toll at this stage. An officer of Gerrard's experience should have realized that to try to return the distance back to cross would mean certain death. The thought itself must be attributed to the stress of the situation and the effects of malnourishment, and not a problem in his training.

Gerrard's log: *"18. Cold. Night not returning. No hits on the line. A small bird landed on the warm stove over the fire. Tried to hit it with a rock. Grazed it. Broke a wing. It flopped and squeaked when it tried to fly away. Hit it again. Shared the small carcass with Robinson. Leduc could not be roused from tent. Beak was very tough."*

The patrol is displaying a serious failure to follow proper service procedure. Certain allowances must be made given their state of mind, but correct survival protocols should supersede these feelings with proper training.

Gerrard log: *"19. Cold. Bright. Coughing stopped. Dog whines quieter.*

Trying to sleep. Tent bright. Eyes bright. No fish. No bite. Glare. Must make it this time. Be strong even as it fades. Sleep and eat and leave."

The brightness mentioned repeatedly in the log is difficult to account for. Fort McKenzie records show normal sunrise and sunset times for this time of year. It must be posited that Gerrard may have been suffering from some sort of snow blindness. Every patrol member had a pair of tinted goggles in their pack to protect against this. Even if all three pairs of goggles had been lost, Gerrard would know to craft a pair of bone blockers from the femur of a sled dog or after a successful hunt to minimize the sun.

Gerrard's log: *"20. Bright. Made fire high today. Still not enough to cook all at once. Small pieces, bit by bit. Took all day. Hungry. Hard to wait so long. Smoke travelling far. Smell everywhere. Bears will not come they stay away. Can't block it. Eat now."*

As part of the search for the patrol, we spoke to members from the Athabaskan village north of the mountain ride, with hunting lands extending far. Three hunters at the village, given a general time frame, spoke of an unexpected appearance of black smoke two weeks previously. The hunters had been returning from an overland trip to set the spring trap lines after the storm and crossed on the far side of Lake Agassiz on the thick part of the ice. They noticed a column of smoke originating from the side of the lake exposed to the elements. It was impossible to cross given the ice conditions. They had a rifle with a telescopic lens and used to trace the smoke to its origins.

They report spotting the faint outline of a rudimentary camp. It consisted of one tent, a fire pit, and a scattering of other supplies. They could make out a small rail over the fire with pieces of game set in place for cooking, likely deer or moose given the proportions. To them, it was a peculiar place to dress a carcass given that the scent was liable to attract newly awoken bears.

There was a brief discussion of traveling to the camp, a diversion that would have delayed their return to the village by another day. Their sled dogs reacted strongly, barking, and whining, and making every effort to leave. The scent from the fire had begun to reach them, and they noticed its foulness.

Mindful of their responsibilities at home, the group pushed on and returned to the village three days later. This is the last sighting known of the patrol, as it matches the area where they would have traveled, and the descriptions found in Gerrard's log.

However, their sighting does not line up exactly with the record. They report a dilapidated camp, not something our officers would allow to happen. The hunters were adamant that they did not see signs of multiple people, and the cooking fire itself was the only sign of inhabitation. Perhaps the members of the patrol were attempting another hunt. We can only hypothesize.

Gerrard's log: "*Better. Stronger. No sleep. Enough. Time to rest today. Eyes sore. We can leave if everyone is strong. Leave & go home & be warm. Rest. Save strength for the walk across mountains.*"

The patrol must have known they were so far off course that a rescue from a well-supplied team was their only viable option. There are no indications that a specific need or issues drove them forward, only a matter of failing to adhere to protocol.

Gerrard's log: "*Strong. Bright. Fire burns in. Maybe cause of the food. Rations were poisoning us. Needed more. Maybe it knew. Snow is resting. Rest too. Nice to be warm. Want to sleep. Rest. Eat. Warm. Leave. Now or never. Mountains coming tomorrow.*"

. . .

Despite an apparent improved food supply, the conditions experienced were still taking a serious toll on the patrol. Perhaps a deficit of vitamins had induced scurvy, or some of the canned rations had proved defective and spoiled. Both had been known to cause adverse physical effects and contribute to further mental degradation.

Gerrard's log: *"Leaving today. Away from the sun from the light back to night. Will find the pass. Will get back. Eat. Rest. Be warm again. Eat. Taking provisions and extra clothing. Long walk. Dogs would be nice. Gone gone they are gone gone gone."*

The lake shore was still frozen when our rescue team located the camp after seven days of searching. Wind had knocked over the tents and extinguished the fire pit. What remained was charcoal mixed with charred bones. They stood out even with snow that slowly blew over the shallow earthen barrier. The elements had shredded the tents to pieces, leaving scraps to flutter in the wind. The degradation was to the extent that it was difficult to determine exactly how many tents there had been.

We found only a few items of note. These include a suspender clasp from a standard service uniform, along with a belt that had gotten too close to the fire and blistered from the heat. Perhaps this had been an attempt to dry damp clothes.

Our sled dogs grew agitated as we approached and remained aggravated during our search. They nipped and clawed at one another and pulled the sleds back and forth until they were brought to heel. They only grew calm after departure.

A long depression in the snow indicated a potential path away from the camp. Snowmelt made it impossible to tell exactly who had left the camp or the state in which they traveled. We decided to follow the path despite the lateness in the day in the slim possibility that we would locate any of the patrol members alive. We were determined to take some hope from the fact that no definitive remains were initially found at the camp. The depression led toward where the mountain ridge emerged from the lowlands surrounding the frozen lake. The sun trailed as we mushed ahead.

Gerrard's log: "*Mountains are tall. Shadows. Away from the light. Taking a break. Rest now. Then get high get up there. Keep going. Hungry again. Meat not keeping. Getting warmer. Fingers hot. Placed hands in snow before writing and it melted can you believe? Going now keep going.*"

We cannot understand the exact nature of this journey. Dates or times were no longer recorded in the log. It took us two hours to reach the first incline of the mountain ridge, and that was with a supplied sled team. We decided to push forward. The sun was nearing the horizon, but we could not have lived with ourselves without knowing if any were still alive.

Gerrard's log: "*High. Bright. Hot. First fingers, now everywhere. Get away. It's coming. Keep going. Hungry. Need. Eat. Go. See. Go.*"

The dogs grew almost hysterical as we drew close to the mountain. We disembarked from the sleds and left them tied to a sturdy tree as we approached on foot. After thirty minutes of climbing, we located Gerrard's body on a rocky outcropping a short way up the mountain.

His body was a pale figure against a gray rock. In a sitting position, his body was naked except for one boot on his left foot, with tatters of his uniform scattered around him. This is a sign of hypothermia, where sufferers often feel a burst of heat before their bodies fail. It made it easier to see his mangled state, as though a Kodiak bear had mauled and partially consumed him.

Blood surrounded the remains, forming small pools on the ground that had frozen over. The flesh and bones on the chest were open, revealing the empty internal cavity. The hands were clasped in two fists on his lap, the fingers were bloody. We saw glimpses of white bone poking through the tips. So horrific was the initial sight that I must confess it took a moment to realize that his eyes were gone. Staring through black holes into his skull, I felt great shock before my stomach retched and I had to divert my sight.

Animals have been known to scavenge the softer organs from prey, but we were not prepared to see the results in person. Once slightly settled, we examined the body for signs of teeth and claw marks. None were found on the face or torso that would indicate a predator feeding. It was during this closer examination that I located the logbook.

Below is the final log in Gerrard's book. The handwriting appears different, clumsier, with the letters jagged like a carving. The pages themselves were dotted with blood and smeared across by a hand passing over them while still wet.

Gerrard's log:

"OUT STILL THERE HOW STILL SEEING BRIGHT SO BRIGHT EVEN NOW OUT HOW"

When close to the body, I noticed his hands were clasped around something. In desperate need of an explanation, I made the decision to try to open them. It was very difficult, as the bones and tendons of the hands had grown very rigid in the cold post-mortem. I managed to turn the hands over to face upwards and found myself looking into a pair of eyes grasped firmly in white, black and red fingertips.

I could not even retch again.

We made a final search of the area for any signs or clues. Failing to locate any, the decision was made to cover the body in small rocks as a makeshift burial. Returning the body to Gerrard's kin in such a state would only be cruel. We must think of something kind to tell them.

We made camp for the night on the other side of the mountain, blocking the worst of the elements. Feeling the darkness grow and cover the grave provided some strange comfort. At least we could not see it, though we knew it remained as the hours passed under the stars.

We returned to the suspected patrol camp the next day and thoroughly searched the area. Nothing was found to indicate the fate of Robinson and Leduc, and there were no additional trails large enough to have been made by a person. Given what is known, we must accept that they perished as well. Perhaps we can return to try and find their remains after the thaw.

Mindful of our own supplies, we decided to begin the return journey to Fort McKenzie. Our journey was otherwise uneventful, though mostly silent. Our return took only five days as the weather was favorable and we made sure not to waste our supplies.

There is nothing further to add to this report. The loss of the patrol is a tragedy, one that happens too often in the north. We must mourn their passing and try to prevent a similar occurrence.

On a personal note, I fear that this case may be one of the lingering moments of my career. The remaining questions are perplexing and the answers few and blood-soaked. Its effects are strange indeed. Even now, finishing this report late in the night after our return, I feel bleariness come over myself and my senses. Almost as though I find myself under a midnight sun, bright in the sky.

-Constable Smyth.

ABOUT THE CONTRIBUTORS

Anne Woods

Anne Woods is the author of various short stories published by Creepy Podcast, as part of the Horror Over Handlebars anthology, and in 7th Circle Pyrite, with others forthcoming. When not writing horror, she can be found reading horror, watching horror, or walking her beloved mutts and listening to podcasts about horror (or DnD).

Bryan Holm

Bryan Holm grew up in Minnesota and lives in St. Louis Park with his wife and dog. He is a photographer by day who spends his nights writing and consuming all things horror. His short fiction has been published in anthologies by Sinister Smile Press, Eerie River Publishing, HellBound Books, and Strange Wilds Press. He was featured on the Bloodlist as a Fresh Blood Selects for his screenwriting. His debut novella, *Satanic Static,* was published by Anuci Press. www.bryanholm.com

David Rider

David Rider grew up roaming the alleyways of Calumet City, Illinois. Like most Gen X kids, he lived an unsupervised, feral existence. This included consuming horror movies and Stephen King novels at too young an age. His stories have appeared in anthologies from Sinister Smile Press and Grendel Press. He has published three novels: *We Are Van Helsing* Books One and Two and *Anca's Undead Playlist.* He lives with his wife, kids, and dogs, and he needs coffee to transform into a functional adult. Visit his website at www.davidrid-erauthor.com.

E.J. Bramble

E.J. Bramble is an author of horror with a degree in psychology who enjoys writing weird things. Her work has been published in anthologies and magazines such as *Crawling* and *Seaside Gothic*, and often incorporates aspects of body horror and a sense of unease. She lives in England, and, while working towards that elusive novel, enjoys running, cooking, and being by the sea.

Frederick Street

Frederick was born and raised in Maine but now resides in Southern California. When not learning to cook new things or exploring his love of archery and the outdoors, he writes stories inspired by his rural upbringing, his career in close-protection security, and his fascination with the fire that drives the human heart, for good or for ill."

G.M. Garner

Growing up amidst the violent anxieties of Northern Ireland's "Troubles," G.M. Garner quickly found escape in the fictional world of the macabre. Fantastically reclusive, he currently resides in Nottingham, England, with his wife, dogs, and a lasting infatuation with all things monstrous and grim.

Jay T. Dane

Jay T. Dane is a Canadian author who started her writing journey at a young age. With one self-published horror novel from her high school years, she continues to create stories filled with all things scary and psychologically twisted. A lifelong lover of art and creativity, Jay spends much of her time drawing or painting, and enjoys studying art history. She resides in Ontario, Canada, with her family, her extra slobbery dog, and her partner, who've always encouraged and supported her in her storytelling endeavours.

L.W. Young

L.W. Young graduated from the University of Kent with a BA Honors degree in English literature and creative writing. He has experience with writing for theatre, film and YouTube, and is a passionate advocate of mindfulness and raising awareness of mental health issues. His favourite authors and influences include an eclectic bag: ranging from Stephen King to Cormac McCarthy to Ray Chandler to David Mitchell to Kazuyo Ishiguro to Margaret Atwood and Colson Whitehead. However, if you ask him, he will probably tell you his favourite books are the Point Horror novels he read in his High School library as a teenager.

Marcel Feldmar

Marcel Feldmar grew up in Canada, and then left.

He spent some time in Denver and Seattle but ended up living in Los Angeles, where his words get caught in traffic.

He has been a regular contributor to The Big Takeover Magazine since the mid 90's and has also been working on some spoken word / music collaborations, which can be found under the name *Blue Discordant Way* on Bandcamp. Feldmar has contributed poetry to the Curious Nothing, 7th-Circle Pyrite, Rabbit's Foot, Low Life Press, and Pulp. Feldmar's full-length novel, *Awkward on the Rocks,* is coming soon from Dead Sky Publishing. His work can also be found online on Reddit's nosleep forum, as the six-part serial "I Have To Get Rid Of This Guitar I Found" co-written with musician Kirk Hammett.

Marzia La Barbera

Marzia La Barbera is an Italian fiction writer and academic researcher. She writes science fiction and horror with a little bit of romance and a whole lot of blood, and enjoys delving into the mysteries of the human monster. Her short stories have appeared in magazines and anthologies in Italy. When she's not writing, she's definitely paying too much attention to pop culture phenomena and putting together eclectic, vaguely anarchist reading lists.

She is currently based in Palermo, Italy, with her two dogs and misfit family.

Matt Dodge

Matt Dodge is a Canadian writer of short stories, comics and a novel. His work has been featured in Shotgun Honey, JMWW, Grim & Gilded, Underwood Press, Cold Creek Review, and the Tales From The Cloakroom Vol. 1 anthology from Cloakroom Comics.

Neil Williamson

Neil Williamson lives in the often inhumanly frigid city of Glasgow, Scotland. His most recent book is the urban folk horror novella, Charlie Says (Black Shuck Books), and he has been a finalist for British Science Fiction Association, British Fantasy and World Fantasy awards. Find out more at neilwilliamson.blog

William Jensen

William Jensen is the author of *Cities of Men*. His short fiction has appeared in *North Dakota Quarterly*, *The Texas Review*, *Mystery Tribune*, and elsewhere. In 2022, he edited the anthology *Road Kill: Texas Horror by Texas Writers, Vol. 7*. He resides in Central Texas with his wife and daughters. Discover more at www.williamjensenwrites.com